THE BEST OF SAKI

by the same author

THE SHORT STORIES OF SAKI

THE NOVELS AND PLAYS OF SAKI

THE BEST OF
SAKI
(H. H. MUNRO)

Selected and with an Introduction by

GRAHAM GREENE

New York : THE VIKING PRESS : Publishers

VIKING COMPASS EDITION
Issued in 1961 by The Viking Press, Inc.
625 Madison Avenue, New York, N.Y. 10022

SBN 670-00088-4
Library of Congress catalog card number: 78-101367

Printed in the U.S.A. by the Murray Printing Company

Ninth printing March 1972

CONTENTS

CONTENTS

BEASTS AND SUPER-BEASTS
(1914)

THE TOYS OF PEACE
(1923) (1919)

INTRODUCTION

by

GRAHAM GREENE

THERE are certain writers, as different as Dickens from Kipling, who never shake off the burden of their childhood. The abandonment to the blacking factory in Dickens's case and in Kipling's to the cruel Aunt Rosa living in the sandy suburban road were never forgotten. All later experience seems to have been related to those months or years of unhappiness. Life which turns its cruel side to most of us at an age when we have begun to learn the arts of self-protection took these two writers by surprise during the defencelessness of early childhood. How differently they reacted. Dickens learnt sympathy, Kipling cruelty—Dickens developed a style so easy and natural that it seems capable of including the whole human race in its understanding: Kipling designed a machine, the cogwheels perfectly fashioned, for exclusion. The characters sometimes seem to rattle down a conveyor-belt like matchboxes.

There are great similarities in the early life of Kipling and Saki, and Saki's reaction to misery was nearer Kipling's than Dickens's. Kipling was born in India, H. H. Munro (I would like to drop that rather meaningless mask of the pen-name) in Burma. Family life for such children is always broken—the miseries recorded by Kipling and Munro must be experienced by many mute inglorious children born to the civil servant or the colonial officer in the East: the

arrival of the cab at the strange relative's house, the un-
packing of the boxes, the unfamiliar improvised nursery,
the terrible departure of the parents, a four-years' absence
from affection that in child-time can be as long as a generation (at four one is a small child, at eight a boy). Kipling
described the horror of that time in *Baa, Baa Black Sheep*
—a story in spite of its sentimentality almost unbearable
to read: Aunt Rosa's prayers, the beatings, the card with
the word LIAR pinned upon the back, the growing and
neglected blindness, until at last came the moment of
rebellion.

> " 'If you make me do that,' said Black Sheep very
> quietly, 'I shall burn this house down and perhaps I
> will kill you. I don't know whether I *can* kill you—you
> are so bony, but I will try.'
> "No punishment followed this blasphemy, though
> Black Sheep held himself ready to work his way to
> Auntie Rosa's withered throat and grip there till he was
> beaten off."

In that last sentence we can hear something very like
the tones of Munro's voice as we hear them in one of his
finest stories, *Sredni Vashtar*. Neither his Aunt Augusta
nor his Aunt Charlotte with whom he was left near Barnstaple after his mother's death, while his father served in
Burma, had the fiendish cruelty of Auntie Rosa, but
Augusta ("a woman," Munro's sister wrote, "of ungovern-
able temper, of fierce likes and dislikes, imperious, a moral
coward, possessing no brains worth speaking of, and a
primitive disposition") was quite capable of making a
child's life miserable. Munro was not himself beaten,
Augusta preferred his younger brother for that exercise,
but we can measure the hatred he felt for her in his story
of the small boy Conradin who prayed so successfully for

vengeance to his tame ferret. " 'Whoever will break it to
the poor child? I couldn't for the life of me!' exclaimed a
shrill voice, and while they debated the matter among
themselves Conradin made himself another piece of toast."
Unhappiness wonderfully aids the memory, and the best
stories of Munro are all of childhood, its humour and its
anarchy as well as its cruelty and unhappiness.

For Munro reacted to those years rather differently
from Kipling. He, too, developed a style like a machine
in self-protection, but what sparks this machine gave off.
He did not protect himself like Kipling with manliness,
knowingness, imaginary adventures of soldiers and Empire
builders (though a certain nostalgia for such a life can be
read into *The Unbearable Bassington*): he protected himself with epigrams as closely set as currants in an old-
fashioned Dundee cake. As a young man trying to make
a career with his father's help in the Burma Police, he
wrote to his sister in 1893 complaining that she had made
no effort to see *A Woman of No Importance*. Reginald
and Clovis are children of Wilde: the epigrams, the ab-
surdities fly unremittingly back and forth, they dazzle and
delight, but we are aware of a harsher, less kindly mind
behind them than Wilde's. Clovis and Reginald are not
creatures of fairy-tale, they belong nearer to the visible
world than Ernest Maltravers. While Ernest floats airily
like a Rubens' cupid among the over-blue clouds, Clovis
and Reginald belong to the Park, the tea-parties of
Kensington and evenings at Covent Garden—they even
sometimes date, like the suffragettes. They cannot quite
disguise, in spite of the glint and the sparkle, the loneliness
of the Barnstaple years—they are quick to hurt before
they can be hurt first, and the witty and devastating asides
cut like Aunt Augusta's cane. How often these stories are

stories of practical jokes. The victims with their weird names are sufficiently foolish to awaken no sympathy— they are the middle-aged, the people with power; it is right that they should suffer a temporary humiliation because the world is always on their side in the long run. Munro, like a chivalrous highwayman, only robs the rich: behind all these stories is an exacting sense of justice. In this they are to be distinguished from Kipling's stories in the same genre—*The Village That Voted The Earth Was Flat* and others where the joke is carried too far. With Kipling revenge rather than justice seems to be the motive (Aunt Rosa had established herself in the mind of her victim and corrupted it).

Perhaps I have gone a little too far in emphasising the cruelty of Munro's work, for there are times when it seems to remind us only of the sunniness of the Edwardian scene, young men in boaters, the box at the Opera, long lazy afternoons in the Park, tea out of the thinnest porcelain with cucumber sandwiches, the easy irresponsible prattle.

> "Never be a pioneer. It's the Early Christian that gets the fattest lion."
> "There's Marion Mulciber, who *would* think she could play Bridge just as she would think she could ride down a hill on a bicycle; on that occasion she went to a hospital, now she's gone into a Sisterhood—lost all she had, you know, and gave the rest to Heaven."
> "Her frocks are built in Paris, but she wears them with a strong English accent."
> "It requires a great deal of moral courage to leave in a marked manner in the middle of the second Act when your carriage is not ordered till twelve."

Sad to think that this sunniness and this prattle could not go on for ever, but the worst and cruellest practical joke was left to the end. Munro's witty, cynical hero, Comus Bassington, died incongruously of fever in a West African village, and in the early morning of November 13th, 1916, in a shallow crater near Beaumont-Hamel, Munro was heard to shout "Put out that bloody cigarette." They were the last unpredictable words of Clovis and Reginald.

GRAHAM GREENE.

REGINALD AT THE THEATRE

"AFTER all," said the Duchess vaguely, "there are certain things you can't get away from. Right and wrong, good conduct and moral rectitude, have certain well-defined limits."

"So, for the matter of that," replied Reginald, "has the Russian Empire. The trouble is that the limits are not always in the same place."

Reginald and the Duchess regarded each other with mutual distrust, tempered by a scientific interest. Reginald considered that the Duchess had much to learn; in particular, not to hurry out of the Carlton as though afraid of losing one's last 'bus. A woman, he said, who is careless of disappearances is capable of leaving town before Goodwood, and dying at the wrong moment of an unfashionable disease.

The Duchess thought that Reginald did not exceed the ethical standard which circumstances demanded.

"Of course," she resumed combatively, "it's the prevailing fashion to believe in perpetual change and mutability, and all that sort of thing, and to say we are all merely an improved form of primeval ape—of course you subscribe to that doctrine?"

"I think it decidedly premature; in most people I know the process is far from complete."

"And equally of course you are quite irreligious?"

"Oh, by no means. The fashion just now is a Roman Catholic frame of mind with an Agnostic conscience: you get the mediæval picturesqueness of the one with the modern conveniences of the other."

The Duchess suppressed a sniff. She was one of those people who regard the Church of England with patronizing affection, as if it were something that had grown up in their kitchen garden.

"But there are other things," she continued, "which I suppose are to a certain extent sacred even to you. Patriotism, for instance, and Empire, and Imperial responsibility, and blood-is-thicker-than-water, and all that sort of thing."

Reginald waited for a couple of minutes before replying,

1

Paolo + Francesca
5. thero

while the Lord of Rimini temporarily monopolized the acoustic possibilities of the theatre.

"That is the worst of a tragedy," he observed, "one can't always hear oneself talk. Of course I accept the Imperial idea and the responsibility. After all, I would just as soon think in Continents as anywhere else. And some day, when the season is over, and we have the time, you shall explain to me the exact blood-brotherhood and all that sort of thing that exists between a French Canadian and a mild Hindoo and a Yorkshireman, for instance."

"Oh, well, 'dominion over palm and pine,' you know," quoted the Duchess hopefully; "of course we mustn't forget that we're all part of the great Anglo-Saxon Empire."

"Which for its part is rapidly becoming a suburb of Jerusalem. A very pleasant suburb, I admit, and quite a charming Jerusalem. But still a suburb."

"Really, to be told one's living in a suburb when one is conscious of spreading the benefits of civilization all over the world! Philanthropy—I suppose you will say *that* is a comfortable delusion; and yet even you must admit that whenever want or misery or starvation is known to exist, however distant or difficult of access, we instantly organize relief on the most generous scale, and distribute it, if need be, to the uttermost ends of the earth."

The Duchess paused, with a sense of ultimate triumph. She had made the same observation at a drawing-room meeting, and it had been extremely well received.

"I wonder," said Reginald, "if you have ever walked down the Embankment on a winter night?"

"Gracious, no, child! Why do you ask?"

"I didn't; I only wondered. And even your philanthropy, practised in a world where everything is based on competition, must have a debit as well as a credit account. The young ravens cry for food."

"And are fed."

"Exactly. Which presupposes that something else is fed upon."

"Oh, you're simply exasperating. You've been reading Nietzsche till you haven't got any sense of moral proportion left. May I ask if you are governed by *any* laws of conduct whatever?"

"There are certain fixed rules that one observes for one's own comfort. For instance, never be flippantly rude to any inoffensive, grey-bearded stranger that you may meet in pine forests or hotel smoking-rooms on the Continent. It always turns out to be the King of Sweden."

"The restraint must be dreadfully irksome to you. When I was younger, boys of your age used to be nice and innocent."

"Now we are only nice. One must specialize in these days. Which reminds me of the man I read of in some sacred book who was given a choice of what he most desired. And because he didn't ask for titles and honours and dignities, but only for immense wealth, these other things came to him also."

"I am sure you didn't read about him in any sacred book."

"Yes; I fancy you will find him in Debrett."

REGINALD ON HOUSE-PARTIES

THE drawback is, one never really *knows* one's hosts and hostesses. One gets to know their fox-terriers and their chrysanthemums, and whether the story about the go-cart can be turned loose in the drawing-room, or must be told privately to each member of the party, for fear of shocking public opinion; but one's host and hostess are a sort of human hinterland that one never has the time to explore.

There was a fellow I stayed with once in Warwickshire who farmed his own land, but was otherwise quite steady. Should never have suspected him of having a soul, yet not very long afterwards he eloped with a lion-tamer's widow and set up as a golf-instructor somewhere on the Persian Gulf; dreadfully immoral, of course, because he was only an indifferent player, but still, it showed imagination. His wife was really to be pitied, because he had been the only person in the house who understood how to manage the cook's temper, and now she has to put "D.V." on her dinner invitations. Still, that's better than a domestic scandal; a woman who leaves her cook never wholly recovers her position in Society.

I suppose the same thing holds good with the hosts; they seldom have more than a superficial acquaintance with their guests, and so often just when they do get to know you a bit better, they leave off knowing you altogether. There was *rather* a breath of winter in the air when I left those Dorsetshire people. You see, they had asked me down to shoot, and I'm not particularly immense at that sort of thing. There's such a deadly sameness about partridges; when you've missed one, you've missed the lot—at least, that's been my experience. And they tried to rag me in the smoking-room about not being able to hit a bird at five yards, a sort of bovine ragging that suggested cows buzzing round a gadfly and thinking they were teasing it. So I got up the next morning at early dawn—I know it was dawn, because there were lark-noises in the sky, and the grass looked as if it had been left out all night—and hunted up the most conspicuous thing in the bird line that I could find, and measured the distance, as nearly as it would let me, and shot away all I knew. They said afterwards that it was a tame bird; that's simply *silly*, because it was awfully wild at the first few shots. Afterwards it quieted down a bit, and when its legs had stopped waving farewells to the landscape I got a gardener-boy to drag it into the hall, where everybody must see it on their way to the breakfast-room. I breakfasted upstairs myself. I gathered afterwards that the meal was tinged with a very unchristian spirit. I suppose it's unlucky to bring peacock's feathers into a house; anyway, there was a blue-pencilly look in my hostess's eye when I took my departure.

Some hostesses, of course, will forgive anything, even unto pavonicide (is there such a word?), as long as one is nice-looking and sufficiently unusual to counterbalance some of the others; and there *are* others—the girl, for instance, who reads Meredith, and appears at meals with unnatural punctuality in a frock that's made at home and repented at leisure. She eventually finds her way to India and gets married, and comes home to admire the Royal Academy, and to imagine that an indifferent prawn curry is for ever an effective substitute for all that we have been taught to believe is luncheon. It's then that she is really dangerous; but at her worst she is never quite so bad as the woman who fires *Exchange and Mart* questions at you without the least provocation. Imagine the other day, just when I was doing my best to understand half the things I was saying, being asked by one of those seekers after country home truths how many fowls she could keep in a run ten feet by six, or whatever it was! I told her whole crowds, as long as she kept the door shut, and the idea didn't seem to have struck her before; at least, she brooded over it for the rest of dinner.

Of course, as I say, one never really *knows* one's ground, and one may make mistakes occasionally. But then one's mistakes sometimes turn out assets in the long-run: if we had never bungled away our American colonies we might never have had the boy from the States to teach us how to wear our hair and cut our clothes, and we must get our ideas from somewhere, I suppose. Even the Hooligan was probably invented in China centuries before we thought of him. England must wake up, as the Duke of Devonshire said the other day, wasn't it? Oh, well, it was some one else. Not that I ever indulge in despair about the Future; there always have been men who have gone about despairing of the Future, and when the Future arrives it says nice, superior things about their having acted according to their lights. It is dreadful to think that other people's grandchildren may one day rise up and call one amiable.

There are moments when one sympathizes with Herod.

REGINALD'S DRAMA

REGINALD closed his eyes with the elaborate weariness of one who has rather nice eyelashes and thinks it useless to conceal the fact.

"One of these days," he said. "I shall write a really great drama. No one will understand the drift of it, but everyone will go back to their homes with a vague feeling of dissatisfaction with their lives and surroundings. Then they will put up new wall-papers and forget."

"But how about those that have oak panelling all over the house?" said the Other.

"They can always put down new stair-carpets," pursued Reginald, "and, anyhow, I'm not responsible for the audience having a happy ending. The play would be quite sufficient strain on one's energies. I should get a bishop to say it was

immoral and beautiful—no dramatist has thought of that
before, and everyone would come to condemn the bishop, and
they would stay on out of sheer nervousness. After all, it re-
quires a great deal of moral courage to leave in a marked
manner in the middle of the second act, when your carriage
isn't ordered till twelve. And it would commence with wolves
worrying something on a lonely waste—you wouldn't see them,
of course; but you would hear them snarling and scrunching,
and I should arrange to have a wolfy fragrance suggested
across the footlights. It would look so well on the pro-
grammes, 'Wolves in the first act, by Jamrach.' And old Lady
Whortleberry, who never misses a first night, would scream.
She's always been nervous since she lost her first husband.
He died quite abruptly while watching a county cricket match;
two and a half inches of rain had fallen for seven runs, and
it was supposed that the excitement killed him. Anyhow, it
gave her quite a shock; it was the first husband she'd lost, you
know, and now she always screams if anything thrilling
happens too soon after dinner. And after the audience had
heard the Whortleberry scream the thing would be fairly
launched."

"And the plot?"

"The plot," said Reginald, "would be one of those little
everyday tragedies that one sees going on all round one. In
my mind's eye there is the case of the Mudge-Jervises, which
in an unpretentious way has quite an Enoch Arden intensity
underlying it. They'd only been married some eighteen months
or so, and circumstances had prevented their seeing much of
each other. With him there was always a foursome or something that had to be played and replayed in different parts of
the country, and she went in for slumming quite as seriously
as if it was a sport. With her, I suppose, it was. She belonged
to the Guild of the Poor Dear Souls, and they hold the record
for having nearly reformed a washerwoman. No one has ever
really reformed a washerwoman, and that is why the competition is so keen. You can rescue charwomen by fifties with a
little tea and personal magnetism, but with washerwomen it's
different; wages are too high. This particular laundress, who
came from Bermondsey or some such place, was really rather
a hopeful venture, and they thought at last that she might be
safely put in the window as a specimen of successful work.

So they had her paraded at a drawing-room 'At Home' at Agatha Camelford's; it was sheer bad luck that some liqueur chocolates had been turned loose by mistake among the re-freshments—really liqueur chocolates, with very little choco-late. And of course the old soul found them out, and cornered the entire stock. It was like finding a whelk-stall in a desert, as she afterwards partially expressed herself. When the liqueurs began to take effect, she started to give them imitations of farmyard animals as they know them in Bermondsey. She began with a dancing bear, and you know Agatha doesn't approve of dancing, except at Buckingham Palace under proper supervision. And then she got up on the piano and gave them an organ monkey; I gather she went in for realism rather than a Maeterlinckian treatment of the subject. Finally, she fell into the piano and said she was a parrot in a cage, and for an impromptu performance I believe she was very word-perfect; no one had heard anything like it, except Baroness Boobelstein who has attended sittings of the Austrian Reichsrath. Agatha is trying the Rest-cure at Buxton."

"But the tragedy?"

"Oh, the Mudge-Jervises. Well, they were getting along quite happily, and their married life was one continuous ex-change of picture-postcards; and then one day they were thrown together on some neutral ground where foursomes and washerwomen overlapped, and discovered that they were hopelessly divided on the Fiscal Question. They have thought it best to separate, and she is to have the custody of the Per-sian kittens for nine months in the year—they go back to him for the winter, when she is abroad. There you have the material for a tragedy drawn straight from life—and the piece could be called 'The Price They Paid for Empire.' And of course one would have to work in studies of the struggle of hereditary tendency against environment and all that sort of thing. The woman's father could have been an Envoy to some of the smaller German Courts; that's where she'd get her pas-sion for visiting the poor, in spite of the most careful up-bringing. *C'est le premier pa qui compte,* as the cuckoo said when it swallowed its foster-parent. That, I think, is quite clever."

"And the wolves?"

"Oh, the wolves would be a sort of elusive undercurrent in

the background that would never be satisfactorily explained.
After all, life teems with things that have no earthly reason.
And whenever the characters could think of nothing brilliant
to say about marriage or the War Office, they could open a
window and listen to the howling of the wolves. But that
would be very seldom."

THE RETICENCE OF LADY ANNE

EGBERT came into the large, dimly lit drawing-room with the
air of a man who is not certain whether he is entering a dove-
cote or a bomb factory, and is prepared for either even-
tuality. The little domestic quarrel over the luncheon-table
had not been fought to a definite finish, and the question was
how far Lady Anne was in a mood to renew or forgo hos-
tilities. Her pose in the arm-chair by the tea-table was rather
elaborately rigid; in the gloom of a December afternoon
Egbert's pince-nez did not materially help him to discern the
expression of her face.

By way of breaking whatever ice might be floating on the
surface he made a remark about a dim religious light. He or
Lady Anne were accustomed to make that remark between
4.30 and 6 on winter and late autumn evenings; it was a part
of their married life. There was no recognized rejoinder to it,
and Lady Anne made none.

Don Tarquinio lay astretch on the Persian rug, basking in
the firelight with superb indifference to the possible ill-humour
of Lady Anne. His pedigree was as flawlessly Persian as the
rug, and his ruff was coming into the glory of its second winter. The page-boy, who had Renaissance tendencies, had
christened him Don Tarquinio. Left to themselves, Egbert and
Lady Anne would unfailingly have called him Fluff, but they
were not obstinate.

Egbert poured himself out some tea. As the silence gave no
sign of breaking on Lady Anne's initiative, he braced himself
for another Yermak effort.

"My remark at lunch had a purely academic application,"
he announced; "you seem to put an unnecessarily personal
significance into it."

Lady Anne maintained her defensive barrier of silence. The bullfinch lazily filled in the interval with an air from *Iphigénie en Tauride*. Egbert recognized it immediately, because it was the only air the bullfinch whistled, and he had come to them with the reputation for whistling it. Both Egbert and Lady Anne would have preferred something from *The Yeoman of the Guard,* which was their favourite opera. In matters artistic they had a similarity of taste. They leaned towards the honest and explicit in art, a picture, for instance, that told its own story, with generous assistance from its title. A riderless warhorse with harness in obvious disarray, staggering into a courtyard full of pale swooning women, and marginally noted "Bad News," suggested to their minds a distinct interpretation of some military catastrophe. They could see what it was meant to convey, and explain it to friends of duller intelligence.

The silence continued. As a rule Lady Anne's displeasure became articulate and markedly voluble after four minutes of introductory muteness. Egbert seized the milk-jug and poured some of its contents into Don Tarquinio's saucer; as the saucer was already full to the brim an unsightly overflow was the result. Don Tarquinio looked on with a surprised interest that evanesced into elaborate unconsciousness when he was appealed to by Egbert to come and drink up some of the spilt matter. Don Tarquinio was prepared to play many rôles in life, but a vacuum carpet-cleaner was not one of them.

"Don't you think we're being rather foolish?" said Egbert cheerfully.

If Lady Anne thought so she didn't say so.

"I daresay the fault has been partly on my side," continued Egbert, with evaporating cheerfulness. "After all, I'm only human, you know. You seem to forget that I'm only human."

He insisted on the point, as if there had been unfounded suggestions that he was built on Satyr lines, with goat continuations where the human left off.

The bullfinch recommenced its air from *Iphigénie en Tauride*. Egbert began to feel depressed. Lady Anne was not drinking her tea. Perhaps she was feeling unwell. But when Lady Anne felt unwell she was not wont to be reticent on the subject. "No one knows what I suffer from indigestion" was one of her favourite statements; but the lack of knowledge can only have been caused by defective listening; the amount of information available on the subject would have supplied material for a monograph.

Evidently Lady Anne was not feeling unwell.

Egbert began to think he was being unreasonably dealt with; naturally he began to make concessions.

"I daresay," he observed, taking as central a position on the hearth-rug as Don Tarquinio could be persuaded to concede him, "I may have been to blame. I am willing, if I can thereby restore things to a happier standpoint, to undertake to lead a better life."

He wondered vaguely how it would be possible. Temptations came to him, in middle age, tentatively and without insistence, like a neglected butcher-boy who asks for a Christmas box in February for no more hopeful reason than that he didn't get one in December. He had no more idea of succumbing to them than he had of purchasing the fish-knives and fur boas that ladies are impelled to sacrifice through the medium of advertisement columns during twelve months of the year. Still, there was something impressive in this unasked-for renunciation of possibly latent enormities.

Lady Anne showed no sign of being impressed.

Egbert looked at her nervously through his glasses. To get the worst of an argument with her was no new experience. To get the worst of a monologue was a humiliating novelty.

"I shall go and dress for dinner," he announced in a voice into which he intended some shade of sternness to creep.

At the door a final access of weakness impelled him to make a further appeal.

"Aren't we being very silly?"

"A fool," was Don Tarquinio's mental comment as the door closed on Egbert's retreat. Then he lifted his velvet fore-paws in the air and leapt lightly on to a bookshelf immediately under the bullfinch's cage. It was the first time he had seemed to notice the bird's existence, but he was carrying out a long-formed theory of action with the precision of mature deliberation. The bullfinch, who had fancied himself something of a despot, depressed himself of a sudden into a third of his normal displacement; then he fell to a helpless wing-beating and shrill cheeping. He had cost twenty-seven shillings without the cage, but Lady Anne made no sign of interfering. She had been dead for two hours.

GABRIEL-ERNEST

"THERE is a wild beast in your woods," said the artist Cunningham, as he was being driven to the station. It was the only remark he had made during the drive, but as Van Cheele had talked incessantly his companion's silence had not been noticeable.

"A stray fox or two and some resident weasels. Nothing more formidable," said Van Cheele. The artist said nothing.

"What did you mean about a wild beast?" said Van Cheele later, when they were on the platform.

"Nothing. My imagination. Here is the train," said Cunningham.

That afternoon Van Cheele went for one of his frequent rambles through his woodland property. He had a stuffed bittern in his study, and knew the names of quite a number of wild flowers, so his aunt had possibly some justification in describing him as a great naturalist. At any rate, he was a great walker. It was his custom to take mental notes of everything he saw during his walks, not so much for the purpose of assisting contemporary science as to provide topics for conversation afterwards. When the bluebells began to show themselves in flower he made a point of informing every one of the fact; the season of the year might have warned his hearers of the likelihood of such an occurrence, but at least they felt that he was being absolutely frank with them.

What Van Cheele saw on this particular afternoon was, however, something far removed from his ordinary range of experience. On a shelf of smooth stone overhanging a deep pool in the hollow of an oak coppice a boy of about sixteen lay asprawl, drying his wet brown limbs luxuriously in the sun. His wet hair, parted by a recent dive, lay close to his head, and his light-brown eyes, so light that there was an almost tigerish gleam in them, were turned towards Van Cheele with a certain lazy watchfulness. It was an unexpected apparition, and Van Cheele found himself engaged in the novel process of thinking before he spoke. Where on earth could this wild-looking boy hail from? The miller's wife had lost a child some two months ago, supposed to have been swept away by the mill-race, but that had been a mere baby, not a half-grown lad.

"What are you doing there?" he demanded.

"Obviously, sunning myself," replied the boy.

"Where do you live?"

"Here, in these woods."

"You can't live in the woods," said Van Cheele.

"They are very nice woods," said the boy, with a touch of patronage in his voice.

"But where do you sleep at night?"

"I don't sleep at night; that's my busiest time."

Van Cheele began to have an irritated feeling that he was grappling with a problem that was eluding him.

"What do you feed on?" he asked.

"Flesh," said the boy, and he pronounced the word with slow relish, as though he were tasting it.

"Flesh! What flesh?"

"Since it interests you, rabbits, wild-fowl, hares, poultry, lambs in their season, children when I can get any; they're usually too well locked in at night, when I do most of my hunting. It's quite two months since I tasted child-flesh."

Ignoring the chaffing nature of the last remark, Van Cheele tried to draw the boy on the subject of possible poaching operations.

"You're talking rather through your hat when you speak of feeding on hares." (Considering the nature of the boy's toilet, the simile was hardly an apt one.) "Our hillside hares aren't easily caught."

"At night I hunt on four feet," was the somewhat cryptic response.

"I suppose you mean that you hunt with a dog?" hazarded Van Cheele.

The boy rolled slowly over on to his back, and laughed a weird low laugh, that was pleasantly like a chuckle and disagreeably like a snarl.

"I don't fancy any dog would be very anxious for my company, especially at night."

Van Cheele began to feel that there was something positively uncanny about the strange-eyed, strange-tongued youngster.

"I can't have you staying in these woods," he declared authoritatively.

"I fancy you'd rather have me here than in your house," said the boy.

The prospect of this wild, nude animal in Van Cheele's primly ordered house was certainly an alarming one.

"If you don't go, I shall have to make you," said Van Cheele.

The boy turned like a flash, plunged into the pool, and in a moment had flung his wet and glistening body half-way up the bank where Van Cheele was standing. In an otter the movement would not have been remarkable; in a boy Van Cheele found it sufficiently startling. His foot slipped as he made an involuntary backward movement, and he found himself almost prostrate on the slippery weed-grown bank, with those tigerish yellow eyes not very far from his own. Almost instinctively he half-raised his hand to his throat. The boy laughed again, a laugh in which the snarl had nearly driven out the chuckle, and then, with another of his astonishing lightning movements, plunged out of view into a yielding tangle of weed and fern.

"What an extraordinary wild animal!" said Van Cheele as he picked himself up. And then he recalled Cunningham's remark, "There is a wild beast in your woods."

Walking slowly homeward, Van Cheele began to turn over in his mind various local occurrences which might be traceable to the existence of this astonishing young savage.

Something had been thinning the game in the woods lately, poultry had been missing from the farms, hares were growing unaccountably scarcer, and complaints had reached him of lambs being carried off bodily from the hills. Was it possible that this wild boy was really hunting the countryside in company with some clever poacher dog? He had spoken of hunting "four-footed" by night, but then, again, he had hinted strangely at no dog caring to come near him, "especially at night." It was certainly puzzling. And then, as Van Cheele ran his mind over the various depredations that had been committed during the last month or two, he came suddenly to a dead stop, alike in his walk and his speculations. The child missing from the mill two months ago—the accepted theory was that it had tumbled into the mill-race and been swept away; but the mother had always declared she had heard a shriek on the hill side of the house, in the opposite direction from the water. It was unthinkable, of course, but he wished that the boy had not made that uncanny remark about child-flesh eaten two months ago. Such dreadful things should not be said even in fun.

Van Cheele, contrary to his usual wont, did not feel disposed to be communicative about his discovery in the wood. His position as a parish councillor and justice of the peace seemed somehow compromised by the fact that he was harbouring a personality of such doubtful repute on his property; there was even a possibility that a heavy bill of damages for raided lambs and poultry might be laid at his door. At dinner that night he was quite unusually silent.

"Where's your voice gone to?" said his aunt. "One would think you had seen a wolf."

Van Cheele, who was not familiar with the old saying, thought the remark rather foolish; if he *had* seen a wolf on his property his tongue would have been extraordinarily busy with the subject.

At breakfast next morning Van Cheele was conscious that his feeling of uneasiness regarding yesterday's episode had not wholly disappeared, and he resolved to go by train to the neighbouring cathedral town, hunt up Cunningham, and learn from him what he had really seen that had prompted the remark about a wild beast in the woods. With this resolution taken, his usual cheerfulness partially returned, and he hummed a bright little melody as he sauntered to the morning-room for his customary cigarette. As he entered the room the melody made way abruptly for a pious invocation. Gracefully asprawl on the ottoman, in an attitude of almost exaggerated repose, was the boy of the woods. He was drier than when Van Cheele had last seen him, but no other alteration was noticeable in his toilet.

"How dare you come here?" asked Van Cheele furiously.

"You told me I was not to stay in the woods," said the boy calmly.

"But not to come here. Supposing my aunt should see you!"

And with a view to minimizing that catastrophe Van Cheele hastily obscured as much of his unwelcome guest as possible under the folds of a *Morning Post*. At that moment his aunt entered the room.

"This is a poor boy who has lost his way—and lost his memory. He doesn't know who he is or where he comes from," explained Van Cheele desperately, glancing apprehensively at the waif's face to see whether he was going to add inconvenient candour to his other savage propensities.

Miss Van Cheele was enormously interested.

"Perhaps his underlinen is marked," she suggested.

"He seems to have lost most of that, too," said Van Cheele, making frantic little grabs at the *Morning Post* to keep it in its place.

A naked, homeless child appealed to Miss Van Cheele as warmly as a stray kitten or derelict puppy would have done.

"We must do all we can for him," she decided, and in a very short time a messenger, dispatched to the rectory, where a page-boy was kept, had returned with a suit of pantry clothes, and the necessary accessories of shirt, shoes, collar, etc. Clothed, clean and groomed, the boy lost none of his uncanniness in Van Cheele's eyes, but his aunt found him sweet.

"We must call him something till we know who he really is," she said. "Gabriel-Ernest, I think; those are nice suitable names."

Van Cheele agreed, but he privately doubted whether they were being grafted on to a nice suitable child. His misgivings were not diminished by the fact that his staid and elderly spaniel had bolted out of the house at the first incoming of the boy, and now obstinately remained shivering and yapping at the farther end of the orchard, while the canary, usually as vocally industrious as Van Cheele himself, had put itself on an allowance of frightened cheeps. More than ever he was resolved to consult Cunningham without loss of time.

As he drove off to the station his aunt was arranging that Gabriel-Ernest should help her to entertain the infant members of her Sunday-school class at tea that afternoon.

Cunningham was not at first disposed to be communicative.

"My mother died of some brain trouble," he explained, "so you will understand why I am averse to dwelling on anything

of an impossibly fantastic nature that I may see or think that
I have seen."

"But what *did* you see?" persisted Van Cheele.

"What I thought I saw was something so extraordinary
that no really sane man could dignify it with the credit of
having actually happened. I was standing, the last evening I
was with you, half-hidden in the hedgegrowth by the orchard
gate, watching the dying glow of the sunset. Suddenly I became aware of a naked boy, a bather from some neighbouring pool, I took him to be, who was standing out on the bare
hillside also watching the sunset. His pose was so suggestive
of some wild faun of Pagan myth that I instantly wanted to
engage him as a model, and in another moment I think I
should have hailed him. But just then the sun dipped out of
view, and all the orange and pink slid out of the landscape,
leaving it cold and grey. And at the same moment an astound-
ing thing happened—the boy vanished too!"

"What! Vanished away into nothing?" asked Van Cheele
excitedly.

"No; that is the dreadful part of it," answered the artist;
"on the open hillside where the boy had been standing a
second ago, stood a large wolf, blackish in colour, with gleaming fangs and cruel, yellow eyes. You may think——"

But Van Cheele did not stop for anything as futile as
thought. Already he was tearing at top speed towards the
station. He dismissed the idea of a telegram. "Gabriel-Ernest
is a werewolf" was a hopelessly inadequate effort at conveying
the situation, and his aunt would think it was a code message
to which he had omitted to give her the key. His one hope was
that he might reach home before sundown. The cab which
he chartered at the other end of the railway journey bore him
with what seemed exasperating slowness along the country
roads, which were pink and mauve with the flush of the sinking sun. His aunt was putting away some unfinished jams and
cake when he arrived.

"Where is Gabriel-Ernest?" he almost screamed.

"He is taking the little Toop child home," said his aunt.
"It was getting so late, I thought it wasn't safe to let it go
back alone. What a lovely sunset, isn't it?"

But Van Cheele, although not oblivious of the glow in the
western sky, did not stay to discuss its beauties. At a speed for

which he was scarcely geared he raced along the narrow lane that led to the home of the Toops. On one side ran the swift current of the mill-stream, on the other rose the stretch of bare hillside. A dwindling rim of red sun showed still on the skyline, and the next turning must bring him in view of the ill-assorted couple he was pursuing. Then the colour went suddenly out of things, and a grey light settled itself with a quick shiver over the landscape. Van Cheele heard a shrill wail of fear, and stopped running.

Nothing was ever seen again of the Toops child or Gabriel-Ernest, but the latter's discarded garments were found lying in the road, so it was assumed that the child had fallen into the water, and that the boy had stripped and jumped in, in a vain endeavour to save it. Van Cheele and some workmen who were near by at the time testified to having heard a child scream loudly just near the spot where the clothes were found. Mrs. Toop, who had eleven other children, was decently resigned to her bereavement, but Miss Van Cheele sincerely mourned her lost foundling. It was on her initiative that a memorial brass was put up in the parish church to "Gabriel-Ernest, an unknown boy, who bravely sacrificed his life for another."

Van Cheele gave way to his aunt in most things, but he flatly refused to subscribe to the Gabriel-Ernest memorial.

CROSS-CURRENTS

VANESSA PENNINGTON had a husband who was poor, with few extenuating circumstances, and an admirer who, though comfortably rich, was cumbered with a sense of honour. His wealth made him welcome in Vanessa's eyes, but his code of what was right impelled him to go away and forget her, or at the most to think of her in the intervals of doing a great many other things. And although Alaric Clyde loved Vanessa, and thought he should always go on loving her, he gradually and unconsciously allowed himself to be wooed and won by a more alluring mistress; he fancied that his continued shunning of the haunts of men was a self-imposed exile, but his heart was caught in the spell of the Wilderness, and the

Wilderness was kind and beautiful to him. When one is young and strong and unfettered, the wild earth can be very kind and very beautiful. Witness the legion of men who were once young and unfettered and now eat out their souls in dustbins, because, having erstwhile known and loved the Wilderness, they broke from her thrall and turned aside into beaten paths.

In the high waste places of the world Clyde roamed and hunted and dreamed, death-dealing and gracious as some god of Hellas, moving with his horses and servants and four-footed camp followers from one dwelling ground to another, a welcome guest among wild primitive village folk and nomads, a friend and slayer of the fleet, shy beasts around him. By the shores of misty upland lakes he shot the wild fowl that had winged their way to him across half the old world; beyond Bokhara he watched the wild Aryan horsemen at their gambols; watched, too, in some dim-lit tea-house one of those beautiful uncouth dances that one can never wholly forget; or, making a wide cast down to the valley of the Tigris, swam and rolled in its snow-cooled racing waters. Vanessa, meanwhile, in a Bayswater back street, was making out the weekly laundry list, attending bargain sales, and, in her more adventurous moments, trying new ways of cooking whiting. Occasionally she went to bridge parties, where, if the play was not illuminating, at least one learned a great deal about the private life of some of the Royal and Imperial Houses. Vanessa, in a way, was glad that Clyde had done the proper thing. She had a strong natural bias towards respectability, though she would have preferred to have been respectable in smarter surroundings, where her example would have done more good. To be beyond reproach was one thing, but it would have been nicer to have been nearer to the Park.

And then of a sudden her regard for respectability and Clyde's sense of what was right were thrown on the scrap-heap of unnecessary things. They had been useful and highly important in their time, but the death of Vanessa's husband made them of no immediate moment.

The news of the altered condition of things followed Clyde with leisurely persistence from one place of call to another, and at last ran him to a standstill somewhere in the Orenburg Steppe. He would have found it exceedingly difficult to analyse his feelings on receipt of the tidings. The Fates had unexpectedly (and perhaps just a little officiously) removed an obstacle from his path. He supposed he was overjoyed, but he missed the feeling of elation which he had experienced some four months ago when he had bagged a snow-leopard with a lucky shot after a day's fruitless stalking. Of course he would go back and ask Vanessa to marry him, but he was determined on enforcing a condition: on no account would he desert his newer love. Vanessa would have to agree to come out into the Wilderness with him.

The lady hailed the return of her lover with even more relief than had been occasioned by his departure. The death of John Pennington had left his widow in circumstances which were more straitened than ever, and the Park had receded even from her notepaper, where it had long been retained as a courtesy title on the principle that addresses are given to us to conceal our whereabouts. Certainly she was more independent now than heretofore, but independence, which means so much to many women, was of little account to Vanessa, who came under the heading of the mere female. She made little ado about accepting Cyde's condition, and announced herself ready to follow him to the end of the world; as the world was round she nourished a complacent idea that in the ordinary course of things one would find oneself in the neighbourhood of Hyde Park Corner sooner or later no matter how far afield one wandered.

East of Budapest her complacency began to filter away, and when she saw her husband treating the Black Sea with a familiarity which she had never been able to assume towards the English Channel, misgivings began to crowd in upon her. Adventures which would have presented an amusing and enticing aspect to a better-bred woman aroused in Vanessa only the twin sensations of fright and discomfort. Flies bit her, and she was persuaded that it was only sheer boredom that prevented camels from doing the same. Clyde did his best, and a very good best it was, to infuse something of the banquet into their prolonged desert picnics, but even snow-cooled Heidsieck lost its flavour when you were convinced that the dusky cupbearer who served it with such reverent elegance was only waiting a convenient opportunity to cut your throat. It was useless for Clyde to give Yussuf a character for devotion such as is rarely found in any Western servant. Vanessa was well enough educated to know that all dusky-skinned people take human life as unconcernedly as Bayswater folk take singing lessons.

And with a growing irritation and querulousness on her part came a further disenchantment, born of the inability of husband and wife to find a common ground of interest. The habits and migrations of the sand grouse, the folklore and customs of Tartars and Turkomans, the points of a Cossack pony—these were matters which evoked only a bored indifference in Vanessa. On the other hand, Clyde was not thrilled on being informed that the Queen of Spain detested mauve, or that a certain Royal duchess, for whose tastes he was never likely to be called on to cater, nursed a violent but perfectly respectable passion for beef olives.

Vanessa began to arrive at the conclusion that a husband who added a roving disposition to a settled income was a mixed blessing. It was one thing to go to the end of the world; it was quite another thing to make oneself at home there. Even respectability seemed to lose some of its virtue when one practised it in a tent.

Bored and disillusioned with the drift of her new life, Vanessa was undisguisedly glad when distraction offered itself in the person of Mr. Dobrinton, a chance acquaintance whom they had first run against in the primitive hostelry of a benighted Caucasian town. Dobrinton was elaborately British, in deference perhaps to the memory of his mother, who was said to have derived part of her origin from an English governess who had come to Lemberg a long way back in the last century. If you had called him Dobrinski when off his guard he would probably have responded readily enough; holding, no doubt, that the end crowns all, he had taken a slight liberty with the family patronymic. To look at, Mr. Dobrinton was not a very attractive specimen of masculine humanity, but in Vanessa's eyes he was a link with that civilization which Clyde seemed so ready to ignore and forgo. He could sing "Yip-I-Addy" and spoke of several duchesses as if he knew them—in his more inspired moments almost as if they knew him. He even pointed out blemishes in the cuisine or cellar departments of some of the more august London restaurants, a species of Higher Criticism which was listened to by Vanessa in awe-stricken admiration And, above all, he sympathized, at first discreetly, afterwards with more latitude, with her fretful discontent at Clyde's nomadic instincts. Business connected with oil-wells had brought Dobrinton to the neighbourhood of Baku; the pleasure of appealing to an appreciative female audience induced him to deflect his return journey so as to coincide a good deal with his new acquaintances' line of march. And while Clyde trafficked with Persian horse-dealers or hunted the wild grey pigs in their lairs and added to his notes on Central Asian game-fowl, Dobrinton and the lady discussed the ethics of desert respectability from points of view that showed a daily tendency to converge. And one evening Clyde dined alone, reading between the courses a long letter from Vanessa, justifying her action in flitting to more civilized lands with a more congenial companion.

It was distinctly evil luck for Vanessa, who really was thoroughly respectable at heart, that she and her lover should run into the hands of Kurdish brigands on the first day of their flight. To be mewed up in a squalid Kurdish village in close companionship with a man who was only your husband by adoption, and to have the attention of all Europe drawn to your plight, was about the least respectable thing that could happen. And there were international complications, which made things worse. "English lady and her husband, of foreign nationality, held by Kurdish brigands who demand ransom" had been the report of the nearest Consul. Although Dobrinton was British at heart, the other portions of him belonged to the Habsburgs, and though the Habsburgs took no great pride or pleasure in this particular unit of their wide and varied possessions, and would gladly have exchanged him for some interesting bird or mammal for the Schoenbrunn Park, the code of international dignity demanded that they should display a decent solicitude for his restoration. And while the Foreign Offices of the two countries were taking the usual steps to secure the release of their respective subjects a further horrible complication ensued: Clyde, following on the track of the fugitives, not with any special desire to overtake them, but with a dim feeling that it was expected of him, fell into the hands of the same community of brigands. Diplomacy, while anxious to do its best for a lady in misfortune, showed signs of becoming restive at this expansion of its task; as a frivolous young gentleman in Downing Street remarked,

"Any husband of Mrs. Dobrinton's we shall be glad to extricate, but let us know how many there are of them." For
a woman who valued respectability Vanessa really had no
luck.

Meanwhile the situation of the captives was not free from
embarrassment. When Clyde explained to the Kurdish head-
men the nature of his relationship with the runaway couple
they were gravely sympathetic, but vetoed any idea of sum-
mary vengeance, since the Habsburgs would be sure to insist
on the delivery of Dobrinton alive, and in a reasonably un-
damaged condition. They did not object to Clyde administer-
ing a beating to his rival for half an hour every Monday and
Thursday, but Dobrinton turned such a sickly green when he
heard of this arrangement that the chief was obliged to with-
draw the concession.

And so, in the cramped quarters of a mountain hut, the ill-
assorted trio watched the insufferable hours crawl slowly by.
Dobrinton was too frightened to be conversational, Vanessa
was too mortified to open her lips, and Clyde was moodily
silent. The little Lemberg *négociant* plucked up heart once
to give a quavering rendering of "Yip-I-Addy," but when he
reached the statement "home was never like this" Vanessa
tearfully begged him to stop. And silence fastened itself with
growing insistence on the three captives who were so tragically
herded together; thrice a day they drew near to one another to
swallow the meal that had been prepared for them, like desert
beasts meeting in mute suspended hostility at the drinking-
pool, and then drew back to resume the vigil of waiting.

Clyde was less carefully watched than the others. "Jealousy
will keep him to the woman's side," thought his Kurdish captors. They did not know that his wilder, truer love was calling
to him with a hundred voices from beyond the village bounds.
And one evening, finding that he was not getting the attention to which he was entitled, Clyde slipped away down the
mountain side and resumed his study of Central Asian game-
fowl. The remaining captives were guarded henceforth with
greater rigour, but Dobrinton at any rate scarcely regretted
Clyde's departure.

The long arm, or perhaps one might better say the long
purse, of diplomacy at last effected the release of the prisoners,
but the Habsburgs were never to enjoy the guerdon of their

outlay. On the quay of the little Black Sea port, where the rescued pair came once more into contact with civilization, Dobrinton was bitten by a dog which was assumed to be mad, though it may only have been indiscriminating. The victim did not wait for symptoms of rabies to declare themselves, but died forthwith of fright, and Vanessa made the homeward journey alone, conscious somehow of a sense of slightly restored respectability. Clyde, in the intervals of correcting the proofs of his book on the game-fowl of Central Asia, found time to press a divorce suit through the Courts, and as soon as possible hied him away to the congenial solitudes of the Gobi Desert to collect material for a work on the fauna of that region. Vanessa, by virtue perhaps of her earlier intimacy with the cooking rites of the whiting, obtained a place on the kitchen staff of a West End Club. It was not brilliant, but at least it was within two minutes of the Park.

THE MOUSE

THEODORIC VOLER had been brought up, from infancy to the confines of middle age, by a fond mother whose chief solicitude had been to keep him screened from what she called the coarser realities of life. When she died she left Theodoric alone in a world that was as real as ever, and a good deal coarser than he considered it had any need to be. To a man of his temperament and upbringing even a simple railway journey was crammed with petty annoyances and minor discords, and as he settled himself down in a second-class compartment one September morning he was conscious of ruffled feelings and general mental discomposure. He had been staying at a country vicarage, the inmates of which had been certainly neither brutal nor bacchanalian, but their supervision of the domestic establishment had been of that lax order which invites disaster. The pony carriage that was to take him to the station had never been properly ordered, and when the moment for his departure drew near, the handyman who should have produced the required article was nowhere to be found. In this emergency Theodoric, to his mute but very intense disgust, found himself obliged to collaborate with the vicar's daughter in the task of harnessing the pony, which necessitated groping about in an ill-lighted outhouse called a stable, and smelling very like one—except in patches where it smelt of mice. Without being actually afraid of mice, Theodoric classed them among the coarser incidents of life, and considered that Providence, with a little exercise of moral courage, might long ago have recognized that they were not indispensable, and have withdrawn them from circulation. As the train glided out of the station Theodoric's nervous imagination accused himself of exhaling a weak odour of stable-yard, and possibly of displaying a mouldy straw or two on his usually well-brushed garments. Fortunately the only other occupant of the compartment, a lady of about the same age as himself, seemed inclined for slumber rather than scrutiny; the train was not due to stop till the terminus was reached, in about an hour's time, and the carriage was of the old-fashioned sort, that held no communication with a corridor, therefore no further travelling companions were likely to intrude on Theodoric's semi-privacy. And yet the train had scarcely attained its normal speed before he became reluctantly but vividly aware that he was not alone with the slumbering lady; he was not even alone in his own clothes. A warm, creeping movement over his flesh betrayed the unwelcome and highly resented presence, unseen but poignant, of a strayed mouse, that had evidently dashed into its present retreat during the episode of the pony harnessing. Furtive stamps and shakes and wildly directed pinches failed to dislodge the intruder, whose motto, indeed, seemed to be Excelsior; and the lawful occupant of the clothes lay back against the cushions and endeavoured rapidly to evolve some means for putting an end to the dual ownership. It was unthinkable that he should continue for the space of a whole hour in the horrible position of a Rowton House for vagrant mice (already his imagination had at least doubled the numbers of the alien invasion). On the other hand, nothing less drastic than partial disrobing would ease him of his tormentor, and to undress in the presence of a lady, even for so laudable a purpose, was an idea that made his eartips tingle in a blush of abject shame. He had never been able to bring himself even to the mild exposure of open-work socks in the presence of the fair sex. And yet—the lady in this case was to all appearances soundly and securely asleep; the mouse, on the other hand, seemed to be trying to crowd a Wanderjahr into a few strenuous minutes. If there is any truth in the theory of transmigration, this particular mouse must certainly have been in a former state a member of the Alpine Club. Sometimes in its eagerness it lost its footing and slipped for half an inch or so; and then, in fright, or more probably temper, it bit. Theodoric was goaded into the most audacious undertaking of his life. Crimsoning to the hue of a beetroot and keeping an agonized watch on his slumbering fellow-traveller, he swiftly and noiselessly secured the ends of his railway-rug to the racks on either side of the carriage, so that a substantial curtain hung athwart the compartment. In the narrow dressing-room that he had thus improvised he proceeded with violent haste to extricate himself partially and the mouse entirely from the surrounding casings of tweed and half-wool. As the unravelled mouse gave a wild leap to the floor, the rug, slipping its fastening at either end, also came down with a heart-curdling flop, and almost simultaneously the awakened sleeper opened her eyes. With a movement almost quicker than the mouse's, Theodoric pounced on the rug, and hauled its ample folds chin-high over his dismantled person as he collapsed into the further corner of the carriage. The blood raced and beat in the veins of his neck and forehead, while he waited dumbly for the communication-cord to be pulled. The lady, however, contented herself with a silent stare at her strangely muffled companion. How much had she seen, Theodoric queried to himself, and in any case what on earth must she think of his present posture?

"I think I have caught a chill," he ventured desperately.

"Really, I'm sorry," she replied. "I was just going to ask you if you would open this window."

"I fancy it's malaria," he added, his teeth chattering slightly, as much from fright as from a desire to support his theory.

"I've got some brandy in my hold-all, if you'll kindly reach it down for me," said his companion.

"Not for worlds—I mean, I never take anything for it," he assured her earnestly.

"I suppose you caught it in the Tropics?"

Theodoric, whose acquaintance with the Tropics was limited

to an annual present of a chest of tea from an uncle in Ceylon, felt that even the malaria was slipping from him. Would it be possible, he wondered, to disclose the real state of affairs to her in small instalments?

"Are you afraid of mice?" he ventured, growing, if possible, more scarlet in the face.

"Not unless they come in quantities, like those that ate up Bishop Hatto. Why do you ask?"

"I had one crawling inside my clothes just now," said Theodoric in a voice that hardly seemed his own. "It was a most awkward situation."

"It must have been, if you wear your clothes at all tight," she observed; "but mice have strange ideas of comfort."

"I had to get rid of it while you were asleep," he continued; then, with a gulp, he added, "it was getting rid of it that brought me to—to this."

"Surely leaving off one small mouse wouldn't bring on a chill," she exclaimed, with a levity that Theodoric accounted abominable.

Evidently she had detected something of his predicament, and was enjoying his confusion. All the blood in his body seemed to have mobilized in one concentrated blush, and an agony of abasement, worse than a myriad mice, crept up and down over his soul. And then, as reflection began to assert itself, sheer terror took the place of humiliation. With every minute that passed the train was rushing nearer to the crowded and bustling terminus where dozens of prying eyes would be exchanged for the one paralysing pair that watched him from the further corner of the carriage. There was one slender despairing chance, which the next few minutes must decide. His fellow-traveller might relapse into a blessed slumber. But as the minutes throbbed by that chance ebbed away. The furtive glance which Theodoric stole at her from time to time disclosed only an unwinking wakefulness.

"I think we must be getting near now," she presently observed.

Theodoric had already noted with growing terror the recurring stacks of small, ugly dwellings that heralded the journey's end. The words acted as a signal. Like a hunted beast breaking cover and dashing madly towards some other haven of momentary safety he threw aside his rug, and struggled frantically into his dishevelled garments. He was conscious of dull suburban stations racing past the window, of a choking, hammering sensation in his throat and heart, and of an icy silence in that corner towards which he dared not look. Then as he sank back in his seat, clothed and almost delirious, the train slowed down to a final crawl, and the woman spoke.

"Would you be so kind," she asked, "as to get me a porter to put me into a cab? It's a shame to trouble you when you're feeling unwell, but being blind makes one so helpless at a railway station."

ESMÉ

T C of C (1911)

"ALL hunting stories are the same," said Clovis; "just as all Turf stories are the same, and all——"

"My hunting story isn't a bit like any you've ever heard," said the Baroness. "It happened quite a while ago, when I was about twenty-three. I wasn't living apart from my husband then; you see, neither of us could afford to make the other a separate allowance. In spite of everything that proverbs may say, poverty keeps together more homes than it breaks up. But we always hunted with different packs. All this has nothing to do with the story."

"We haven't arrived at the meet yet. I suppose there was a meet," said Clovis.

"Of course there was a meet," said the Baroness; "all the usual crowd were there, especially Constance Broddle. Constance is one of those strapping florid girls that go as well with autumn scenery or Christmas decorations in church. 'I feel a presentiment that something dreadful is going to happen,' she said to me; 'am I looking pale?'

"She was looking about as pale as a beetroot that has suddenly heard bad news.

"'You're looking nicer than usual,' I said, 'but that's so easy for you.' Before she had got the right bearings of this remark we had settled down to business; hounds had found a fox lying out in some gorse-bushes."

"I knew it," said Clovis; "in every fox-hunting story that I've ever heard there's been a fox and some gorse-bushes."

"Constance and I were well mounted," continued the Baroness serenely, "and we had no difficulty in keeping ourselves in the first flight, though it was a fairly stiff run. Towards the finish, however, we must have held rather too independent a line, for we lost the hounds, and found ourselves plodding aimlessly along miles away from anywhere. It was fairly exasperating, and my temper was beginning to let itself go by inches, when on pushing our way through an accommodating hedge we were gladdened by the sight of hounds in full cry in a hollow just beneath us.

" 'There they go,' cried Constance, and then added in a gasp, 'In Heaven's name, what are they hunting?'

"It was certainly no mortal fox. It stood more than twice as high, had a short, ugly head, and an enormous thick neck.

" 'It's a hyæna,' I cried; 'it must have escaped from Lord Pabham's Park.'

"At that moment the hunted beast turned and faced its pursuers, and the hounds (there were only about six couple of them) stood round in a half-circle and looked foolish. Evidently they had broken away from the rest of the pack on the trail of this alien scent, and were not quite sure how to treat their quarry now they had got him.

"The hyæna hailed our approach with unmistakable relief and demonstrations of friendliness. It had probably been accustomed to uniform kindness from humans, while its first experience of a pack of hounds had left a bad impression. The hounds looked more than ever embarrassed as their quarry paraded its sudden intimacy with us, and the faint toot of a horn in the distance was seized on as a welcome signal for unobtrusive departure. Constance and I and the hyæna were left alone in the gathering twilight.

" 'What are we to do?' asked Constance.

" 'What a person you are for questions,' I said.

" 'Well, we can't stay here all night with a hyæna,' she retorted.

" 'I don't know what your ideas of comfort are,' I said; 'but I shouldn't think of staying here all night even without a hyæna. My home may be an unhappy one, but at least it has

hot and cold water laid on, and domestic service, and other
conveniences which we shouldn't find here. We had better
make for that ridge of trees to the right; I imagine the
Crowley road is just beyond.'

"We trotted off slowly along a faintly marked cart-track,
with the beast following cheerfully at our heels.

" 'What on earth are we to do with the hyæna?' came the
inevitable question.

" 'What does one generally do with hyænas?' I asked
crossly.

" 'I've never had anything to do with one before,' said
Constance.

" 'Well, neither have I. If we even knew its sex we might
give it a name. Perhaps we might call it Esmé. That would
do in either case.'

"There was still sufficient daylight for us to distinguish
wayside objects, and our listless spirits gave an upward perk
as we came upon a small half-naked gipsy brat picking blackberries from a low-growing bush. The sudden apparition of
two horsewomen and a hyæna set it off crying, and in any
case we should scarcely have gleaned any useful geographical
information from that source; but there was a probability that
we might strike a gipsy encampment somewhere along our
route. We rode on hopefully but uneventfully for another
mile or so.

" 'I wonder what that child was doing there,' said Constance
presently.

" 'Picking blackberries. Obviously.'

" 'I don't like the way it cried,' pursued Constance; 'somehow its wail keeps ringing in my ears.'

"I did not chide Constance for her morbid fancies; as a
matter of fact the same sensation, of being pursued by a persistent fretful wail, had been forcing itself on my rather over-
tired nerves. For company's sake I hullooed to Esmé, who had
lagged somewhat behind. With a few springy bounds he drew
up level, and then shot past us.

"The wailing accompaniment was explained. The gipsy
child was firmly, and I expect painfully, held in his jaws.

" 'Merciful Heaven!' screamed Constance, 'what on earth
shall we do? What are we to do?'

"I am perfectly certain that at the Last Judgment Con-

stance will ask more questions than any of the examining
Seraphs.

" 'Can't we do something?' she persisted tearfully, as Esmé
cantered easily along in front of our tired horses.

"Personally I was doing everything that occurred to me at
the moment. I stormed and scolded and coaxed in English
and French and gamekeeper language; I made absurd, in-
effectual cuts in the air with my thongless hunting-crop; I
hurled my sandwich case at the brute; in fact, I really don't
know what more I could have done. And still we lumbered on
through the deepening dusk, with that dark uncouth shape
lumbering ahead of us, and a drone of lugubrious music floating in our ears. Suddenly Esmé bounded aside into some thick
bushes, where we could not follow; the wail rose to a shriek
and then stopped altogether. This part of the story I always
hurry over, because it is really rather horrible. When the beast
joined us again, after an absence of a few minutes, there was
an air of patient understanding about him, as though he knew
that he had done something of which we disapproved, but
which he felt to be thoroughly justifiable.

" 'How can you let that ravening beast trot by your side?'
asked Constance. She was looking more than ever like an
albino beetroot.

" 'In the first place, I can't prevent it,' I said; 'and in the
second place, whatever else he may be, I doubt if he's ravening at the present moment.'

"Constance shuddered. 'Do you think the poor little thing
suffered much?' came another of her futile questions.

" 'The indications were all that way,' I said; 'on the other
hand, of course, it may have been crying from sheer temper.
Children sometimes do.'

"It was nearly pitch-dark when we emerged suddenly into
the high road. A flash of lights and the whir of a motor went
past us at the same moment at uncomfortably close quarters.
A thud and a sharp screeching yell followed a second later.
The car drew up, and when I had ridden back to the spot I
found a young man bending over a dark motionless mass
lying by the roadside.

" 'You have killed my Esmé,' I exclaimed bitterly.

" 'I'm so awfully sorry,' said the young man, 'I keep dogs
myself, so I know what you must feel about it. I'll do any-

thing I can in reparation.'

" 'Please bury him at once,' I said: 'that much I think I may ask of you.'

" 'Bring the spade, William,' he called to the chauffeur. Evidently hasty roadside interments were contingencies that had been provided against.

"The digging of a sufficiently large grave took some little time. 'I say, what a magnificent fellow,' said the motorist as the corpse was rolled over into the trench. 'I'm afraid he must have been rather a valuable animal.'

" 'He took second in the puppy class at Birmingham last year,' I said resolutely.

"Constance snorted loudly.

" 'Don't cry, dear,' I said brokenly; 'it was all over in a moment. He couldn't have suffered much.'

" 'Look here,' said the young fellow desperately, 'you simply must let me do something by way of reparation.'

"I refused sweetly, but as he persisted I let him have my address.

"Of course, we kept our own counsel as to the earlier episodes of the evening. Lord Pabham never advertised the loss of his hyæna; when a strictly fruit-eating animal strayed from his park a year or two previously he was called upon to give compensation in eleven cases of sheep-worrying and practically to re-stock his neighbours' poultry-yards, and an escaped hyæna would have mounted up to something on the scale of a Government grant. The gipsies were equally unobtrusive over their missing offspring; I don't suppose in large encampments they really know to a child or two how many they've got."

The Baroness paused reflectively, and then continued:

"There was a sequel to the adventure, though. I got through the post a charming little diamond brooch, with the name Esmé set in a sprig of rosemary. Incidentally, too, I lost the friendship of Constance Broddle. You see, when I sold the brooch I quite properly refused to give her any share of the proceeds. I pointed out that the Esmé part of the affair was my own invention, and the hyæna part of it belonged to Lord Pabham, if it really was his hyæna, of which, of course, I've no proof."

THE MATCH-MAKER

THE grill-room clock struck eleven with the respectful unob-
trusiveness of one whose mission in life is to be ignored.
When the flight of time should really have rendered abstinence
and migration imperative, the lighting apparatus would signal
the fact in the usual way.

Six minutes later Clovis approached the supper-table, in the
blessed expectancy of one who has dined sketchily and long
ago.

"I'm starving," he announced, making an effort to sit down
gracefully and read the menu at the same time.

"So I gathered," said his host, "from the fact that you were
nearly punctual. I ought to have told you that I'm a Food
Reformer. I've ordered two bowls of bread-and-milk and some
health biscuits. I hope you don't mind."

Clovis pretended afterwards that he didn't go white above
the collar-line for the fraction of a second.

"All the same," he said, "you ought not to joke about such
things. There really are such people. I've known people who've
met them. To think of all the adorable things there are to
eat in the world, and then to go through life munching saw-
dust and being proud of it."

"They're like the Flagellants of the Middle Ages, who went
about mortifying themselves."

"They had some excuse," said Clovis. "They did it to save
their immortal souls, didn't they? You needn't tell me that a
man who doesn't love oysters and asparagus and good wines
has got a soul, or a stomach either. He's simply got the instinct for being unhappy highly developed."

Clovis relapsed for a few golden moments into tender in-
timacies with a succession of rapidly disappearing oysters.

"I think oysters are more beautiful than any religion," he
resumed presently. "They not only forgive our unkindness to
them; they justify it, they incite us to go on being perfectly
horrid to them. Once they arrive at the supper-table they seem
to enter thoroughly into the spirit of the thing. There's
nothing in Christianity or Buddhism that quite matches the

sympathetic unselfishness of an oyster. Do you like my new waistcoat? I'm wearing it for the first time to-night."

"It looks like a great many others you've had lately, only worse. New dinner waistcoats are becoming a habit with you."

"They say one always pays for the excesses of one's youth; mercifully that isn't true about one's clothes. My mother is thinking of getting married."

"Again!"

"It's the first time."

"Of course, you ought to know. I was under the impression that she'd been married once or twice at least."

"Three times, to be mathematically exact. I meant that it was the first time she'd thought about getting married; the other times she did it without thinking. As a matter of fact, it's really I who am doing the thinking for her in this case. You see, it's quite two years since her last husband died."

"You evidently think that brevity is the soul of widowhood."

"Well, it struck me that she was getting moped, and beginning to settle down, which wouldn't suit her a bit. The first symptom that I noticed was when she began to complain that we were living beyond our income. All decent people live beyond their incomes nowadays, and those who aren't respectable live beyond other people's. A few gifted individuals manage to do both."

"It's hardly so much a gift as an industry."

"The crisis came," returned Clovis, "when she suddenly started the theory that late hours were bad for one, and wanted me to be in by one o'clock every night. Imagine that sort of thing for me, who was eighteen on my last birthday."

"On your last two birthdays, to be mathematically exact."

"Oh, well, that's not my fault. I'm not going to arrive at nineteen as long as my mother remains at thirty-seven. One must have some regard for appearances."

"Perhaps your mother would age a little in the process of settling down."

"That's the last thing she'd think of. Feminine reformations always start in on the failings of other people. That's why I was so keen on the husband idea."

"Did you go as far as to select the gentleman, or did you

merely throw out a general idea, and trust to the force of suggestion?"

"If one wants a thing done in a hurry, one must see to it oneself. I found a military Johnny hanging round on a loose end at the club, and took him home to lunch once or twice. He'd spent most of his life on the Indian frontier, building roads, and relieving famines and minimizing earthquakes, and all that sort of thing that one does do on frontiers. He could talk sense to a peevish cobra in fifteen native languages, and probably knew what to do if you found a rogue elephant on your croquet-lawn; but he was shy and diffident with women. I told my mother privately that he was an absolute woman-hater; so, of course, she laid herself out to flirt all she knew, which isn't a little."

"And was the gentleman responsive?"

"I hear he told some one at the club that he was looking out for a Colonial job, with plenty of hard work, for a young friend of his, so I gather that he has some idea of marrying into the family."

"You seem destined to be the victim of the reformation, after all."

Clovis wiped the trace of Turkish coffee and the beginnings of a smile from his lips, and slowly lowered his dexter eyelid. Which, being interpreted, probably meant, "I *don't* think!"

TOBERMORY

IT was a chill, rain-washed afternoon of a late August day, that indefinite season when partridges are still in security or cold storage, and there is nothing to hunt—unless one is bounded on the north by the Bristol Channel, in which case one may lawfully gallop after fat red stags. Lady Blemley's house-party was not bounded on the north by the Bristol Channel, hence there was a full gathering of her guests round the tea-table on this particular afternoon. And, in spite of the blankness of the season and the triteness of the occasion, there was no trace in the company of that fatigued restlessness which means a dread of the pianola and a subdued hankering for auction bridge. The undisguised open-mouthed attention of the entire party was fixed on the homely negative personality of Mr. Cornelius Appin. Of all her guests, he was the one who had come to Lady Blemley with the vaguest reputation. Some one had said he was "clever," and he had got his invitation in the moderate expectation, on the part of his hostess, that some portion at least of his cleverness would be contributed to the general entertainment. Until tea-time that day she had been unable to discover in what direction, if any, his cleverness lay. He was neither a wit nor a croquet champion, a hypnotic force nor a begetter of amateur theatricals. Neither did his exterior suggest the sort of man in whom women are willing to pardon a generous measure of mental deficiency. He had sudsided into mere Mr. Appin, and the Cornelius seemed a piece of transparent baptismal bluff. And now he was claiming to have launched on the world a discovery beside which the invention of gunpowder, of the printing-press, and of steam locomotion were inconsiderable trifles. Science had made bewildering strides in many directions during recent decades, but this thing seemed to belong to the domain of miracle rather than to scientific achievement.

"And do you really ask us to believe," Sir Wilfrid was saying, "that you have discovered a means for instructing animals in the art of human speech, and that dear old Tobermory has proved your first successful pupil?"

"It is a problem at which I have worked for the last seventeen years," said Mr. Appin, "but only during the last eight or nine months have I been rewarded with glimmerings of success. Of course I have experimented with thousands of animals, but latterly only with cats, those wonderful creatures which have assimilated themselves so marvellously with our civilization while retaining all their highly developed feral instincts. Here and there among cats one comes across an outstanding superior intellect, just as one does among the ruck of human beings, and when I made the acquaintance of Tobermory a week ago I saw at once that I was in contact with a 'Beyond-cat' of extraordinary intelligence. I had gone far along the road to success in recent experiments; with Tobermory, as you call him, I have reached the goal."

Mr. Appin concluded his remarkable statement in a voice which he strove to divest of a triumphant inflection. No one said "Rats," though Clovis's lips moved in a monosyllabic contortion, which probably invoked those rodents of disbelief.

"And do you mean to say," asked Miss Resker, after a slight pause, "that you have taught Tobermory to say and understand easy sentences of one syllable?"

"My dear Miss Resker," said the wonder-worker patiently, "one teaches little children and savages and backward adults in that piecemeal fashion; when one has once solved the problem of making a beginning with an animal of highly developed intelligence one has no need for those halting methods. Tobermory can speak our language with perfect correctness."

This time Clovis very distinctly said, "Beyond-rats!" Sir Wilfrid was more polite, but equally sceptical.

"Hadn't we better have the cat in and judge for ourselves?" suggested Lady Blemley.

Sir Wilfrid went in search of the animal, and the company settled themselves down to the languid expectation of witnessing some more or less adroit drawing-room ventriloquism.

In a minute Sir Wilfrid was back in the room, his face white beneath its tan and his eyes dilated with excitement.

"By Gad, it's true!"

His agitation was unmistakably genuine, and his hearers started forward in a thrill of awakened interest.

Collapsing into an armchair he continued breathlessly: "I found him dozing in the smoking-room, and called out to him to come for his tea. He blinked at me in his usual way, and I said, 'Come on, Toby; don't keep us waiting'; and, by Gad! he drawled out in a most horribly natural voice that he'd come when he dashed well pleased! I nearly jumped out of my skin!"

Appin had preached to absolutely incredulous hearers; Sir Wilfrid's statement carried instant conviction. A Babel-like chorus of startled exclamation arose, amid which the scientist sat mutely enjoying the first-fruit of his stupendous discovery.

In the midst of the clamour Tobermory entered the room and made his way with velvet tread and studied unconcern across to the group seated round the tea-table.

A sudden hush of awkwardness and constraint fell on the company. Somehow there seemed an element of embarrassment in addressing on equal terms a domestic cat of acknowledged mental ability.

"Will you have some milk, Tobermory?" asked Lady Blemley in a rather strained voice.

"I don't mind if I do," was the response, couched in a tone of even indifference. A shiver of suppressed excitement went through the listeners, and Lady Blemley might be excused for pouring out the saucerful of milk rather unsteadily.

"I'm afraid I've spilt a good deal of it," she said apologetically.

"After all, it's not my Axminster," was Tobermory's rejoinder.

Another silence fell on the group, and then Miss Resker, in her best district-visitor manner, asked if the human language had been difficult to learn. Tobermory looked squarely at her for a moment and then fixed his gaze serenely on the middle distance. It was obvious that boring questions lay outside his scheme of life.

"What do you think of human intelligence?" asked Mavis Pellington lamely.

"Of whose intelligence in particular?" asked Tobermory coldly.

"Oh, well, mine for instance," said Mavis, with a feeble laugh.

"You put me in an embarrassing position," said Tobermory, whose tone and attitude certainly did not suggest a shred of embarrassment. "When your inclusion in this house-party was suggested Sir Wilfrid protested that you were the most brainless woman of his acquaintance, and that there was a wide distinction between hospitality and the care of the feeble-minded. Lady Blemley replied that your lack of brain-power was the precise quality which had earned you your invitation, as you were the only person she could think of who might be idiotic enough to buy their old car. You know, the one they call 'The Envy of Sisyphus,' because it goes quite nicely up-hill if you push it."

Lady Blemley's protestations would have had greater effect if she had not casually suggested to Mavis only that morning that the car in question would be just the thing for her down at her Devonshire home.

Major Barfield plunged in heavily to effect a diversion.

"How about your carryings-on with the tortoise-shell puss up at the stables, eh?"

The moment he had said it every one realized the blunder.

"One does not usually discuss these matters in public," said Tobermory frigidly. "From a slight observation of your ways since you've been in this house I should imagine you'd find it inconvenient if I were to shift the conversation on to your own little affairs."

The panic which ensued was not confined to the Major.

"Would you like to go and see if cook has got your dinner ready?" suggested Lady Blemley hurriedly, affecting to ignore the fact that it wanted at least two hours to Tobermory's dinner-time.

"Thanks," said Tobermory, "not quite so soon after my tea. I don't want to die of indigestion."

"Cats have nine lives, you know," said Sir Wilfrid heartily.

"Possibly," answered Tobermory; "but only one liver."

"Adelaide!" said Mrs. Cornett, "do you mean to encourage that cat to go out and gossip about us in the servants' hall?"

The panic had indeed become general. A narrow ornamental balustrade ran in front of most of the bedroom windows at the Towers, and it was recalled with dismay that this had formed a favourite promenade for Tobermory at all hours, whence he could watch the pigeons—and heaven knew what else besides. If he intended to become reminiscent in his present outspoken strain, the effect would be something more than disconcerting. Mrs. Cornett, who spent much time at her toilet table, and whose complexion was reputed to be of a nomadic though punctual disposition, looked as ill at ease as the Major. Miss Scrawen, who wrote fiercely sensuous poetry and led a blameless life, merely displayed irritation; if you are methodical and virtuous in private you don't necessarily want every one to know it. Bertie van Tahn, who was so depraved at seventeen that he had long ago given up trying to be any worse, turned a dull shade of gardenia white, but he did not commit the error of dashing out of the room like Odo Finsberry, a young gentleman who was understood to be reading for the Church and who was possibly disturbed at the thought of scandals he might hear concerning other people. Clovis had the presence of mind to maintain a composed exterior; privately he was calculating how long it would take to procure a box of fancy mice through the agency of the *Exchange and Mart* as a species of hush-money.

Even in a delicate situation like the present, Agnes Resker could not endure to remain too long in the background.

"Why did I ever come down here?" she asked dramatically.

Tobermory immediately accepted the opening.

"Judging by what you said to Mrs. Cornett on the croquet-lawn yesterday, you were out for food. You described the Blemleys as the dullest people to stay with that you knew, but said they were clever enough to employ a first-rate cook; otherwise they'd find it difficult to get any one to come down a second time."

"There's not a word of truth in it! I appeal to Mrs. Cornett——" exclaimed the discomfited Agnes.

"Mrs. Cornett repeated your remark afterwards to Bertie van Tahn," continued Tobermory, "and said, 'That woman is a regular Hunger Marcher; she'd go anywhere for four square meals a day,' and Bertie van Tahn said——"

At this point the chronicle mercifully ceased. Tobermory had caught a glimpse of the big yellow Tom from the Rectory working his way through the shrubbery towards the stable wing. In a flash he had vanished through the open French window.

With the disappearance of his too brilliant pupil Cornelius Appin found himself beset by a hurricane of bitter upbraiding, anxious inquiry, and frightened entreaty. The responsibility for the situation lay with him, and he must prevent matters from becoming worse. Could Tobermory impart his dangerous gift to other cats? was the first question he had to answer. It was possible, he replied, that he might have initiated his intimate friend the stable puss into his new accomplishment, but it was unlikely that his teaching could have taken a wider range as yet.

"Then," said Mrs. Cornett, "Tobermory may be a valuable cat and a great pet; but I'm sure you'll agree, Adelaide, that both he and the stable cat must be done away with without delay."

"You don't suppose I've enjoyed the last quarter of an hour, do you?" said Lady Blemley bitterly. "My husband and I are very fond of Tobermory—at least, we were before this horrible accomplishment was infused into him; but now, of course, the only thing is to have him destroyed as soon as possible."

"We can put some strychnine in the scraps he always gets at dinner-time," said Sir Wilfrid, "and I will go and drown the stable cat myself. The coachman will be very sore at losing his pet, but I'll say a very catching form of mange has broken out in both cats and we're afraid of it spreading to the kennels."

"But my great discovery!" expostulated Mr. Appin; "after all my years of research and experiment——"

"You can go and experiment on the short-horns at the farm, who are under proper control," said Mrs. Cornett, "or the elephants at the Zoological Gardens. They're said to be highly intelligent, and they have this recommendation, that they don't come creeping about our bedrooms and under chairs, and so forth."

An archangel ecstatically proclaiming the Millennium, and then finding that it clashed unpardonably with Henley and would have to be indefinitely postponed, could hardly have felt more crestfallen than Cornelius Appin at the reception of his wonderful achievement. Public opinion, however, was against him—in fact, had the general voice been consulted on the subject it is probable that a strong minority vote would have been in favour of including him in the strychnine diet.

Defective train arrangements and a nervous desire to see matters brought to a finish prevented an immediate dispersal of the party, but dinner that evening was not a social success. Sir Wilfrid had had rather a trying time with the stable cat and subsequently with the coachman. Agnes Resker ostentatiously limited her repast to a morsel of dry toast, which she bit as though it were a personal enemy; while Mavis Pellington maintained a vindictive silence throughout the meal. Lady Blemley kept up a flow of what she hoped was conversation, but her attention was fixed on the doorway. A plateful of carefully dosed fish scraps was in readiness on the sideboard, but sweets and savoury and dessert went their way, and no Tobermory appeared either in the dining-room or kitchen.

The sepulchral dinner was cheerful compared with the subsequent vigil in the smoking-room. Eating and drinking had at least supplied a distraction and cloak to the prevailing embarrassment. Bridge was out of the question in the general tension of nerves and tempers, and after Odo Finsberry had given a lugubrious rendering of "Mélisande in the Wood" to a frigid audience, music was tacitly avoided. At eleven the servants went to bed, announcing that the small window in the pantry had been left open as usual for Tobermory's private use. The guests read steadily through the current batch of magazines, and fell back gradually on the "Badminton Library" and bound volumes of *Punch*. Lady Blemley made periodic visits to the pantry, returning each time with an expression of listless depression which forestalled questioning.

At two o'clock Clovis broke the dominating silence.

"He won't turn up to-night. He's probably in the local newspaper office at the present moment, dictating the first instalment of his reminiscences. Lady What's-her-name's book won't be in it. It will be the event of the day."

Having made this contribution to the general cheerfulness, Clovis went to bed. At long intervals the various members of the house-party followed his example.

The servants taking round the early tea made a uniform announcement in reply to a uniform question. Tobermory had not returned.

Breakfast was, if anything, a more unpleasant function than dinner had been, but before its conclusion the situation was relieved. Tobermory's corpse was brought in from the shrubbery, where a gardener had just discovered it. From the bites on his throat and the yellow fur which coated his claws it was evident that he had fallen in unequal combat with the big Tom from the Rectory.

By midday most of the guests had quitted the Towers, and after lunch Lady Blemley had sufficiently recovered her spirits to write an extremely nasty letter to the Rectory about the loss of her valuable pet.

Tobermory had been Appin's one successful pupil, and he was destined to have no successor. A few weeks later an elephant in the Dresden Zoological Garden, which had shown no previous signs of irritability, broke loose and killed an Englishman who had apparently been teasing it. The victim's name was variously reported in the papers as Oppin and Eppelin, but his front name was faithfully rendered Cornelius.

"If he was trying German irregular verbs on the poor beast," said Clovis, "he deserved all he got."

THE BACKGROUND

"THAT woman's art-jargon tires me," said Clovis to his journalist friend. "She's so fond of talking of certain pictures as 'growing on one,' as though they were a sort of fungus."

"That reminds me," said the journalist, "of the story of Henri Deplis. Have I ever told it you?"

Clovis shook his head.

"Henri Deplis was by birth a native of the Grand Duchy of Luxemburg. On maturer reflection he became a commercial traveller. His business activities frequently took him beyond the limits of the Grand Duchy, and he was stopping in a small town of Northern Italy when news reached him from home that a legacy from a distant and deceased relative had fallen to his share.

"It was not a large legacy, even from the modest standpoint of Henri Deplis, but it impelled him towards some seemingly harmless extravagances. In particular it led him to patronize local art as represented by the tattoo-needles of Signor Andreas Pincini. Signor Pincini was, perhaps, the most brilliant master of tattoo craft that Italy had ever known, but his circumstances were decidedly impoverished, and for the sum of six hundred francs he gladly undertook to cover his client's back, from the collar-bone down to the waist-line, with a glowing representation of the Fall of Icarus. The design, when finally developed, was a slight disappointment to Monsieur Deplis, who had suspected Icarus of being a fortress taken by Wallenstein in the Thirty Years' War, but he was more than satisfied with the execution of the work, which was acclaimed by all who had the privilege of seeing it as Pincini's masterpiece.

"It was his greatest effort, and his last. Without even waiting to be paid, the illustrious craftsman departed this life, and was buried under an ornate tombstone, whose winged cherubs would have afforded singularly little scope for the exercise of his favourite art. There remained, however, the widow Pincini, to whom the six hundred francs were due. And thereupon arose the great crisis in the life of Henri Deplis, traveller of commerce. The legacy, under the stress of numerous little calls on its substance, had dwindled to very insignificant proportions, and when a pressing wine bill and sundry other current accounts had been paid, there remained little more than 430 francs to offer to the widow. The lady was properly indignant, not wholly, as she volubly explained, on account of the suggested writing-off of 170 francs, but also at the attempt to depreciate the value of her late husband's acknowledged masterpiece. In a week's time Deplis was obliged to reduce his offer to 405 francs, which circumstance fanned the widow's indignation into a fury. She cancelled the sale of the work of art, and a few days later Deplis learned with a sense of consternation that she had presented it to the municipality of Bergamo, which had gratefully accepted it. He left the neighbourhood as unobtrusively as possible, and was genuinely relieved when his business commands took him to Rome, where he hoped his identity and that of the famous picture might be lost sight of.

"But he bore on his back the burden of the dead man's genius. On presenting himself one day in the steaming corridor of a vapour bath, he was at once hustled back into his clothes by the proprietor, who was a North Italian, and who emphatically refused to allow the celebrated Fall of Icarus to be publicly on view without the permission of the municipality of Bergamo. Public interest and official vigilance increased as the matter became more widely known, and Deplis was unable to take a simple dip in the sea or river on the hottest afternoon unless clothed up to the collar-bone in a substantial bathing garment. Later on the authorities of Bergamo conceived the idea that salt water might be injurious to the masterpiece, and a perpetual injunction was obtained which debarred the muchly harassed commercial traveller from sea bathing under any circumstances. Altogether, he was fervently thankful when his firm of employers found him a new range of activities in the neighbourhood of Bordeaux. His thankfulness, however, ceased abruptly at the Franco-Italian frontier. An imposing array of official force barred his departure, and he was sternly reminded of the stringent law which forbids the exportation of Italian works of art.

"A diplomatic parley ensued between the Luxemburgian and Italian Governments, and at one time the European situation became overcast with the possibilities of trouble. But the Italian Government stood firm; it declined to concern itself in the least with the fortunes or even the existence of Henri Deplis, commercial traveller, but was immovable in its decision that the Fall of Icarus (by the late Pincini, Andreas) at present the property of the municipality of Bergamo, should not leave the country.

"The excitement died down in time, but the unfortunate Deplis, who was of a constitutionally retiring disposition, found himself a few months later once more the storm-centre of a furious controversy. A certain German art expert, who had obtained from the municipality of Bergamo permission to inspect the famous masterpiece, declared it to be a spurious Pincini, probably the work of some pupil whom he had employed in his declining years. The evidence of Deplis on the subject was obviously worthless, as he had been under the influence of the customary narcotics during the long process of pricking in the design. The editor of an Italian art journal refuted the contentions of the German expert and undertook to prove that his private life did not conform to any modern standard of decency. The whole of Italy and Germany were drawn into the dispute, and the rest of Europe was soon involved in the quarrel. There were stormy scenes in the Spanish Parliament, and the University of Copenhagen bestowed a gold medal on the German expert (afterwards sending a commission to examine his proofs on the spot), while two Polish schoolboys in Paris committed suicide to show what *they* thought of the matter.

"Meanwhile, the unhappy human background fared no better than before, and it was not surprising that he drifted into the ranks of Italian anarchists. Four times at least he was escorted to the frontier as a dangerous and undesirable foreigner, but he was always brought back as the Fall of Icarus (attributed to Pincini, Andreas, early Twentieth Century). And then one day, at an anarchist congress at Genoa, a fellow-worker, in the heat of debate, broke a phial full of corrosive liquid over his back. The red shirt that he was wearing mitigated the effects, but the Icarus was ruined beyond recognition. His assailant was severely reprimanded for assaulting a fellow-anarchist and received seven years' imprisonment for defacing a national art treasure. As soon as he was able to leave the hospital Henri Deplis was put across the frontier as an undesirable alien.

"In the quieter streets of Paris, especially in the neighbourhood of the Ministry of Fine Arts, you may sometimes meet a depressed, anxious-looking man, who, if you pass him the time of day, will answer you with a slight Luxemburgian accent. He nurses the illusion that he is one of the lost arms of the Venus de Milo, and hopes that the French Government may be persuaded to buy him. On all other subjects I believe he is tolerably sane."

THE UNREST-CURE

ON the rack in the railway carriage immediately opposite Clovis was a solidly wrought travelling bag, with a carefully written label, on which was inscribed, "J. P. Huddle, The Warren, Tilfield, near Slowborough." Immediately below the rack sat the human embodiment of the label, a solid, sedate individual, sedately dressed, sedately conversational. Even without his conversation (which was addressed to a friend seated by his side, and touched chiefly on such topics as the backwardness of Roman hyacinths and the prevalence of measles at the Rectory), one could have gauged fairly accurately the temperament and mental outlook of the travelling bag's owner. But he seemed unwilling to leave anything to the imagination of a casual observer, and his talk grew presently personal and introspective.

"I don't know how it is," he told his friend, "I'm not much over forty, but I seem to have settled down into a deep groove of elderly middle-age. My sister shows the same tendency. We like everything to be exactly in its accustomed place; we like things to happen exactly at their appointed times; we like everything to be usual, orderly, punctual, methodical, to a hair's breadth, to a minute. It distresses and upsets us if it is not so. For instance, to take a very trifling matter, a thrush has built its nest year after year in the catkin-tree on the lawn; this year, for no obvious reason, it is building in the ivy on the garden wall. We have said very little about it, but I think we both feel that the change is unnecessary, and just a little irritating."

"Perhaps," said the friend, "it is a different thrush."

"We have suspected that," said J. P. Huddle, "and I think it gives us even more cause for annoyance. We don't feel that we want a change of thrush at our time of life; and yet, as I have said, we have scarcely reached an age when these things should make themselves seriously felt."

"What you want," said the friend, "is an Unrest-cure."

"An Unrest-cure? I've never heard of such a thing."

"You've heard of Rest-cures for people who've broken down under stress of too much worry and strenuous living; well, you're suffering from overmuch repose and placidity, and you need the opposite kind of treatment."

"But where would one go for such a thing?"

"Well, you might stand as an Orange candidate for Kilkenny, or do a course of district visiting in one of the Apache quarters of Paris, or give lectures in Berlin to prove that most of Wagner's music was written by Gambetta; and there's always the interior of Morocco to travel in. But, to be really effective, the Unrest-cure ought to be tried in the home. How you would do it I haven't the faintest idea."

It was at this point in the conversation that Clovis became galvanized into alert attention. After all, his two days' visit to an elderly relative at Slowborough did not promise much excitement. Before the train had stopped he had decorated his sinister shirt-cuff with the inscription, "J. P. Huddle, The Warren, Tilfield, near Slowborough."

*   *   *   *   *

Two mornings later Mr. Huddle broke in on his sister's privacy as she sat reading *Country Life* in the morning-room. It was her day and hour and place for reading *Country Life,* and the intrusion was absolutely irregular; but he bore in his hand a telegram, and in that household telegrams were recognized as happening by the hand of God. This particular telegram partook of the nature of a thunderbolt. "Bishop examining confirmation class in neighbourhood unable stay rectory on account measles invokes your hospitality sending secretary arrange."

"I scarcely know the Bishop; I've only spoken to him once," exclaimed J. P. Huddle, with the exculpating air of one who realizes too late the indiscretion of speaking to strange Bishops.

Miss Huddle was the first to rally; she disliked thunderbolts as fervently as her brother did, but the womanly instinct in her told her that thunderbolts must be fed.

"We can curry the cold duck," she said. It was not the appointed day for curry, but the little orange envelope involved a certain departure from rule and custom. Her brother said nothing, but his eyes thanked her for being brave.

"A young gentleman to see you," announced the parlour-maid.

"The secretary!" murmured the Huddles in unison; they instantly stiffened into a demeanour which proclaimed that, though they held all strangers to be guilty, they were willing to hear anything they might have to say in their defence. The young gentleman, who came into the room with a certain elegant haughtiness, was not at all Huddle's idea of a bishop's secretary; he had not supposed that the episcopal establishment could have afforded such an expensively upholstered article when there were so many other claims on its resources. The face was fleetingly familiar; if he had bestowed more attention on the fellow-traveller sitting opposite him in the railway carriage two days before he might have recognized Clovis in his present visitor.

"You are the Bishop's secretary?" asked Huddle, becoming consciously deferential.

"His confidential secretary," answered Clovis. "You may call me Stanislaus; my other name doesn't matter. The Bishop and Colonel Alberti may be here to lunch. I shall be here in any case."

It sounded rather like the programme of a Royal visit.

"The Bishop is examining a confirmation class in the neighbourhood, isn't he?" asked Miss Huddle.

"Ostensibly," was the dark reply, followed by a request for a large-scale map of the locality.

Clovis was still immersed in a seemingly profound study of the map when another telegram arrived. It was addressed to "Prince Stanislaus, care of Huddle, The Warren, etc." Clovis glanced at the contents and announced: "The Bishop and Alberti won't be here till late in the afternoon." Then he returned to his scrutiny of the map.

The luncheon was not a very festive function. The princely secretary ate and drank with fair appetite, but severely discouraged conversation. At the finish of the meal he broke suddenly into a radiant smile, thanked his hostess for a charming repast, and kissed her hand with deferential rapture. Miss Huddle was unable to decide in her mind whether the action savoured of Louis Quatorzian courtliness or the reprehensible Roman attitude towards the Sabine women. It was not her day for having a headache, but she felt that the circumstances excused her, and retired to her room to have as much headache as was possible before the Bishop's arrival. Clovis, having asked the way to the nearest telegraph office, disappeared presently down the carriage drive. Mr. Huddle met him in the hall some two hours later, and asked when the Bishop would arrive.

"He is in the library with Alberti," was the reply.

"But why wasn't I told? I never knew he had come!" exclaimed Huddle.

"No one knows he is here," said Clovis; "the quieter we can keep matters the better. And on no account disturb him in the library. Those are his orders."

"But what is all this mystery about? And who is Alberti? And isn't the Bishop going to have tea?"

"The Bishop is out for blood, not tea."

"Blood!" gasped Huddle, who did not find that the thunderbolt improved on acquaintance.

"Tonight is going to be a great night in the history of Christendom," said Clovis. "We are going to massacre every Jew in the neighbourhood."

"To massacre the Jews!" said Huddle indignantly. "Do you mean to tell me there's a general rising against them?"

"No, it's the Bishop's own idea. He's in there arranging all the details now."

"But—the Bishop is such a tolerant, humane man."

"That is precisely what will heighten the effect of his action. The sensation will be enormous."

That at least Huddle could believe.

"He will be hanged!" he exclaimed with conviction.

"A motor is waiting to carry him to the coast, where a steam yacht is in readiness."

"But there aren't thirty Jews in the whole neighbourhood," protested Huddle, whose brain, under the repeated shocks of the day, was operating with the uncertainty of a telegraph wire during earthquake disturbances.

"We have twenty-six on our list," said Clovis, referring to a bundle of notes. "We shall be able to deal with them all the more thoroughly."

"Do you mean to tell me that you are meditating violence against a man like Sir Leon Birberry," stammered Huddle; "he's one of the most respected men in the country."

"He's down on our list," said Clovis carelessly; "after all, we've got men we can trust to do our job, so we shan't have to rely on local assistance. And we've got some Boy-scouts helping us as auxiliaries."

"Boy-scouts!"

"Yes; when they understood there was real killing to be done they were even keener than the men."

"This thing will be a blot on the Twentieth Century!"

"And your house will be the blotting-pad. Have you realized that half the papers of Europe and the United States will publish pictures of it? By the way, I've sent some photographs of you and your sister, that I found in the library, to the *Matin* and *Die Woche*; I hope you don't mind. Also a sketch of the staircase; most of the killing will probably be done on the staircase."

The emotions that were surging in J. P. Huddle's brain were almost too intense to be disclosed in speech, but he managed to gasp out: "There aren't any Jews in this house."

"Not at present," said Clovis.

"I shall go to the police," shouted Huddle with sudden energy.

"In the shrubbery," said Clovis, "are posted ten men, who have orders to fire on any one who leaves the house without my signal of permission. Another armed picquet is in ambush near the front gate. The Boy-scouts watch the back premises."

At this moment the cheerful hoot of a motor-horn was heard from the drive. Huddle rushed to the hall door with the feeling of a man half-awakened from a nightmare, and beheld Sir Leon Birberry, who had driven himself over in his car. "I got your telegram," he said; "what's up?"

Telegram? It seemed to be a day of telegrams.

"Come here at once. Urgent. James Huddle," was the purport of the message displayed before Huddle's bewildered eyes.

"I see it all!" he exclaimed suddenly in a voice shaken with agitation, and with a look of agony in the direction of the shrubbery he hauled the astonished Birberry into the house. Tea had just been laid in the hall, but the now thoroughly panic-stricken Huddle dragged his protesting guest upstairs, and in a few minutes' time the entire household had been summoned to the region of momentary safety. Clovis alone graced the tea-table with his presence; the fanatics in the library were evidently too immersed in their monstrous machinations to dally with the solace of teacup and hot toast. Once the youth rose, in answer to the summons of the front-door bell, and admitted Mr. Paul Isaacs, shoemaker and parish councillor, who had also received a pressing invitation to The Warren. With an atrocious assumption of courtesy, which a Borgia could hardly have outdone, the secretary escorted this new captive of his net to the head of the stairway, where his involuntary host awaited him.

And then ensued a long ghastly vigil of watching and waiting. Once or twice Clovis left the house to stroll across to the shrubbery, returning always to the library, for the purpose evidently of making a brief report. Once he took in the letters from the evening postman, and brought them to the top of the stairs with punctilious politeness. After his next absence he came half-way up the stairs to make an announcement.

"The Boy-scouts mistook my signal, and have killed the postman. I've had very little practice in this sort of thing, you see. Another time I shall do better."

The housemaid, who was engaged to be married to the evening postman, gave way to clamorous grief.

"Remember that your mistress has a headache," said J. P. Huddle. (Miss Huddle's headache was worse.)

Clovis hastened downstairs, and after a short visit to the library returned with another message:

"The Bishop is sorry to hear that Miss Huddle has a headache. He is issuing orders that as far as possible no firearms shall be used near the house; any killing that is necessary on the premises will be done with cold steel. The Bishop does not see why a man should not be a gentleman as well as a Christian."

That was the last they saw of Clovis; it was nearly seven o'clock, and his elderly relative liked him to dress for dinner.

But, though he had left them for ever, the lurking suggestion of his presence haunted the lower regions of the house during the long hours of the wakeful night, and every creak of the stairway, every rustle of wind through the shrubbery, was fraught with horrible meaning. At about seven next morning the gardener's boy and the early postman finally convinced the watchers that the Twentieth Century was still unblotted.

"I don't suppose," mused Clovis, as an early train bore him townwards, "that they will be in the least grateful for the Unrest-cure."

THE JESTING OF ARLINGTON STRINGHAM

ARLINGTON STRINGHAM made a joke in the House of Commons. It was a thin House, and a very thin joke; something about the Anglo-Saxon race having a great many angles. It is possible that it was unintentional, but a fellow-member, who did not wish it to be supposed that he was asleep because his eyes were shut, laughed. One or two of the papers noted "a laugh" in brackets, and another, which was notorious for the carelessness of its political news, mentioned "laughter." Things often begin in that way.

"Arlington made a joke in the House last night," said Eleanor Stringham to her mother; "in all the years we've been married neither of us has made jokes, and I don't like it now. I'm afraid it's the beginning of the rift in the lute."

"What lute?" said her mother.

"It's a quotation," said Eleanor.

To say that anything was a quotation was an excellent method, in Eleanor's eyes, for withdrawing it from discussion, just as you could always defend indifferent lamb late in the season by saying "It's mutton."

And, of course, Arlington Stringham continued to tread the thorny path of conscious humour into which Fate had beckoned him.

"The country's looking very green, but, after all, that's what it's there for," he remarked to his wife two days later.

"That's very modern, and I daresay very clever, but I'm

afraid it's wasted on me," she observed coldly. If she had
known how much effort it had cost him to make the remark
she might have greeted it in a kinder spirit. It is the tragedy
of human endeavour that it works so often unseen and un-
guessed.

Arlington said nothing, not from injured pride, but because
he was thinking hard for something to say. Eleanor mistook
his silence for an assumption of tolerant superiority, and her
anger prompted her to a further gibe.

"You had better tell it to Lady Isobel. I've no doubt she
would appreciate it."

Lady Isobel was seen everywhere with a fawn-coloured
collie at a time when every one else kept nothing but Pekinese,
and she had once eaten four green apples at an afternoon tea
in the Botanical Gardens, so she was widely credited with a
rather unpleasant wit. The censorious said she slept in a hammock and understood Yeats's poems, but her family denied
both stories.

"The rift is widening to an abyss," said Eleanor to her
mother that afternoon.

"I should not tell that to any one," remarked her mother,
after long reflection.

"Naturally, I should not talk about it very much," said
Eleanor, "but why shouldn't I mention it to any one?"

"Because you can't have an abyss in a lute. There isn't
room."

Eleanor's outlook on life did not improve as the afternoon
wore on. The page-boy had brought from the library *By Mere
and Wold* instead of *By Mere Chance,* the book which every
one denied having read. The unwelcome substitute appeared
to be a collection of nature notes contributed by the author
to the pages of some Northern weekly, and when one had been
prepared to plunge with disapproving mind into a regrettable
chronicle of ill-spent lives it was intensely irritating to read
"the dainty yellow-hammers are now with us, and flaunt their
jaundiced livery from every bush and hillock." Besides, the
thing was so obviously untrue; either there must be hardly any
bushes or hillocks in those parts or the country must be fear-
fully overstocked with yellow-hammers. The thing scarcely
seemed worth telling such a lie about. And the page-boy stood
there, with his sleekly brushed and parted hair, and his air of

chaste and callous indifference to the desires and passions of the world. Eleanor hated boys, and she would have liked to have whipped this one long and often. It was perhaps the yearning of a woman who had no children of her own.

She turned at random to another paragraph. "Lie quietly concealed in the fern and bramble in the gap by the old rowan tree, and you may see, almost every evening during early summer, a pair of lesser whitethroats creeping up and down the nettles and hedge-growth that mask their nesting-place."

The insufferable monotony of the proposed recreation! Eleanor would not have watched the most brilliant performance at His Majesty's Theatre for a single evening under such uncomfortable circumstances, and to be asked to watch lesser whitethroats creeping up and down a nettle "almost every evening" during the height of the season struck her as an imputation on her intelligence that was positively offensive. Impatiently she transferred her attention to the dinner menu, which the boy had thoughtfully brought in as an alternative to the more solid literary fare. "Rabbit curry," met her eye, and the lines of disapproval deepened on her already puckered brow. The cook was a great believer in the influence of environment, and nourished an obstinate conviction that if you brought rabbit and curry-powder together in one dish a rabbit curry would be the result. And Clovis and the odious Bertie van Tahn were coming to dinner. Surely, thought Eleanor, if Arlington knew how much she had had that day to try her, he would refrain from joke-making.

At dinner that night it was Eleanor herself who mentioned the name of a certain statesman, who may be decently covered under the disguise of X.

"X," said Arlington Stringham, "has the soul of a meringue."

It was a useful remark to have on hand, because it applied equally well to four prominent statesmen of the day, which quadrupled the opportunities for using it.

"Meringues haven't got souls," said Eleanor's mother.

"It's a mercy that they haven't," said Clovis; "they would be always losing them, and people like my aunt would get up missions to meringues, and say it was wonderful how much one could teach them and how much more one could learn from them."

"What could you learn from a meringue?" asked Eleanor's mother.

"My aunt has been known to learn humility from an ex-Viceroy," said Clovis.

"I wish cook would learn to make curry, or have the sense to leave it alone," said Arlington, suddenly and savagely. Eleanor's face softened. It was like one of his old remarks in the days when there was no abyss between them.

It was during the debate on the Foreign Office vote that Stringham made his great remark that "the people of Crete unfortunately make more history than they can consume locally." It was not brilliant, but it came in the middle of a dull speech, and the House was quite pleased with it. Old gentlemen with bad memories said it reminded them of Disraeli.

It was Eleanor's friend, Gertrude Ilpton, who drew her attention to Arlington's newest outbreak. Eleanor in these days avoided the morning papers.

"It's very modern, and I suppose very clever," she observed.

"Of course it's clever," said Gertrude; "all Lady Isobel's sayings are clever, and luckily they bear repeating."

"Are you sure it's one of her sayings?" asked Eleanor.

"My dear, I've heard her say it dozens of times."

"So that is where he gets his humour," said Eleanor slowly, and the hard lines deepened round her mouth.

The death of Eleanor Stringham from an overdose of chloral, occurring at the end of a rather uneventful season, excited a certain amount of unobtrusive speculation. Clovis, who perhaps exaggerated the importance of curry in the home, hinted at domestic sorrow.

And of course Arlington never knew. It was the tragedy of his life that he should miss the fullest effect of his jesting.

SREDNI VASHTAR

CONRADIN was ten years old, and the doctor had pronounced his professional opinion that the boy would not live another five years. The doctor was silky and effete, and counted for little, but his opinion was endorsed by Mrs. De Ropp, who counted for nearly everything. Mrs. De Ropp was Conradin's cousin and guardian, and in his eyes she represented those three-fifths of the world that are necessary and disagreeable and real; the other two-fifths, in perpetual antagonism to the foregoing, were summed up in himself and his imagination. One of these days Conradin supposed he would succumb to the mastering pressure of wearisome necessary things—such as illnesses and coddling restrictions and drawn-out dullness. Without his imagination, which was rampant under the spur of loneliness, he would have succumbed long ago.

Mrs. De Ropp would never, in her honestest moments, have confessed to herself that she disliked Conradin, though she might have been dimly aware that thwarting him "for his good" was a duty which she did not find particularly irksome. Conradin hated her with a desperate sincerity which he was perfectly able to mask. Such few pleasures as he could contrive for himself gained an added relish from the likelihood that they would be displeasing to his guardian, and from the realm of his imagination she was locked out—an unclean thing, which should find no entrance.

In the dull, cheerless garden, overlooked by so many windows that were ready to open with a message not to do this or that, or a reminder that medicines were due, he found little attraction. The few fruit-trees that it contained were set jealously apart from his plucking, as though they were rare specimens of their kind blooming in an arid waste; it would probably have been difficult to find a market-gardener who would have offered ten shillings for their entire yearly produce. In a forgotten corner, however, almost hidden behind a dismal shrubbery, was a disused tool-shed of respectable proportions, and within its walls Conradin found a haven, something that took on the varying aspects of a playroom and a cathedral. He had peopled it with a legion of familiar phantoms, evoked partly from fragments of history and partly from his own brain, but it also boasted two inmates of flesh and blood. In one corner lived a ragged-plumaged Houdan hen, on which the boy lavished an affection that had scarcely another outlet. Further back in the gloom stood a large hutch, divided into two compartments, one of which was fronted with close iron bars. This was the abode of a large polecat-ferret, which a friendly butcher-boy had once smuggled, cage and all, into its present quarters, in exchange for a long-secreted hoard of small silver. Conradin was dreadfully afraid of the lithe, sharp-fanged beast, but it was his most treasured possession. Its very presence in the tool-shed was a secret and fearful joy, to be kept scrupulously from the knowledge of the Woman, as he privately dubbed his cousin. And one day, out of Heaven knows what material, he spun the beast a wonderful name, and from that moment it grew into a god and a religion. The Woman indulged in religion once a week at a church near by, and took Conradin with her, but to him the church service was an alien rite in the House of Rimmon. Every Thursday, in the dim and musty silence of the tool-shed, he worshipped with mystic and elaborate ceremonial before the wooden hutch where dwelt Sredni Vashtar, the great ferret. Red flowers in their season and scarlet berries in the winter-time were offered at his shrine, for he was a god who laid some special stress on the fierce impatient side of things, as opposed to the Woman's religion, which, as far as Conradin could observe, went to great lengths in the contrary direction. And on great festivals powdered nutmeg was strewn in front of his hutch, an important feature of the offering being that the nutmeg had to be stolen. These festivals were of irregular occurrence, and were chiefly appointed to celebrate some passing event. On one occasion, when Mrs. De Ropp suffered from acute tooth-ache for three days, Conradin kept up the festival during the entire three days, and almost succeeded in persuading himself that Sredni Vashtar was personally responsible for the tooth-ache. If the malady had lasted for another day the supply of nutmeg would have given out.

The Houdan hen was never drawn into the cult of Sredni Vashtar. Conradin had long ago settled that she was an Anabaptist. He did not pretend to have the remotest knowledge as to what an Anabaptist was, but he privately hoped that it was dashing and not very respectable. Mrs. De Ropp was the ground plan on which he based and detested all respectability.

After a while Conradin's absorption in the tool-shed began to attract the notice of his guardian. "It is not good for him to be pottering down there in all weathers," she promptly decided, and at breakfast one morning she announced that the Houdan hen had been sold and taken away overnight. With her short-sighted eyes she peered at Conradin, waiting for an

outbreak of rage and sorrow, which she was ready to rebuke
with a flow of excellent precepts and reasoning. But Conradin
said nothing: there was nothing to be said. Something perhaps
in his white set face gave her a momentary qualm, for at tea
that afternoon there was toast on the table, a delicacy which
she usually banned on the ground that it was bad for him;
also because the making of it "gave trouble," a deadly offence
in the middle-class feminine eye.

"I thought you liked toast," she exclaimed, with an injured
air, observing that he did not touch it.

"Sometimes," said Conradin.

In the shed that evening there was an innovation in the
worship of the hutch-god. Conradin had been wont to chant
his praises, tonight he asked a boon.

"Do one thing for me, Sredni Vashtar."

The thing was not specified. As Sredni Vashtar was a god
he must be supposed to know. And choking back a sob as he
looked at that other empty corner, Conradin went back to the
world he so hated.

And every night, in the welcome darkness of his bedroom,
and every evening in the dusk of the tool-shed, Conradin's
bitter litany went up: "Do one thing for me, Sredni Vashtar."

Mrs. De Ropp noticed that the visits to the shed did not
cease, and one day she made a further journey of inspection.

"What are you keeping in that locked hutch?" she asked.
"I believe it's guinea-pigs. I'll have them all cleared away."

Conradin shut his lips tight, but the Woman ransacked his
bedroom till she found the carefully hidden key, and forthwith
marched down to the shed to complete her discovery. It was a
cold afternoon, and Conradin had been bidden to keep to
the house. From the furthest window of the dining-room the
door of the shed could just be seen beyond the corner of the
shrubbery, and there Conradin stationed himself. He saw the
Woman enter, and then he imagined her opening the door
of the sacred hutch and peering down with her short-sighted
eyes into the thick straw bed where his god lay hidden. Perhaps she would prod at the straw in her clumsy impatience.
And Conradin fervently breathed his prayer for the last time.
But he knew as he prayed that he did not believe. He knew
that the Woman would come out presently with that pursed
smile he loathed so well on her face, and that in an hour or

two the gardener would carry away his wonderful god, a god no longer, but a simple brown ferret in a hutch. And he knew that the Woman would triumph always as she triumphed now, and that he would grow ever more sickly under her pestering and domineering and superior wisdom, till one day nothing would matter much more with him, and the doctor would be proved right. And in the sting and misery of his defeat, he began to chant loudly and defiantly the hymn of his threatened idol:

> Sredni Vashtar went forth,
> His thoughts were red thoughts and his teeth were white.
> His enemies called for peace, but he brought them death.
> Sredni Vashtar the Beautiful.

And then of a sudden he stopped his chanting and drew closer to the window-pane. The door of the shed still stood ajar as it had been left, and the minutes were slipping by. They were long minutes, but they slipped by nevertheless. He watched the starlings running and flying in little parties across the lawn; he counted them over and over again, with one eye always on that swinging door. A sour-faced maid came in to lay the table for tea, and still Conradin stood and waited and watched. Hope had crept by inches into his heart, and now a look of triumph began to blaze in his eyes that had only known the wistful patience of defeat. Under his breath, with a furtive exultation, he began once again the pæan of victory and devastation. And presently his eyes were rewarded: out through that doorway came a long, low, yellow-and-brown beast, with eyes a-blink at the waning daylight, and dark wet stains around the fur of jaws and throat. Conradin dropped on his knees. The great polecat-ferret made its way down to a small brook at the foot of the garden, drank for a moment, then crossed a little plank bridge and was lost to sight in the bushes. Such was the passing of Sredni Vashtar.

"Tea is ready," said the sour-faced maid; "where is the mistress?"

"She went down to the shed some time ago," said Conradin.

And while the maid went to summon her mistress to tea, Conradin fished a toasting-fork out of the sideboard drawer and proceeded to toast himself a piece of bread. And during the toasting of it and the buttering of it with much butter and the slow enjoyment of eating it, Conradin listened to the noises and silences which fell in quick spasms beyond the dining-room door. The loud foolish screaming of the maid, the answering chorus of wondering ejaculations from the kitchen region, the scuttering footsteps and hurried embassies for outside help, and then, after a lull, the scared sobbings and the shuffling tread of those who bore a heavy burden into the house.

"Whoever will break it to the poor child? I couldn't for the life of me!" exclaimed a shrill voice. And while they debated the matter among themselves, Conradin made himself another piece of toast.

THE QUEST

AN unwonted peace hung over the Villa Elsinore, broken, however, at frequent intervals, by clamorous lamentations suggestive of bewildered bereavement. The Momebys had lost their infant child; hence the peace which its absence entailed; they were looking for it in wild, undisciplined fashion, giving tongue the whole time, which accounted for the outcry which swept through house and garden whenever they returned to try the home coverts anew. Clovis, who was temporarily and unwillingly a paying guest at the villa, had been dozing in a hammock at the far end of the garden when Mrs. Momeby had broken the news to him.

"We've lost Baby," she screamed.

"Do you mean that it's dead, or stampeded, or that you staked it at cards and lost it that way?" asked Clovis lazily.

"He was toddling about quite happily on the lawn," said Mrs. Momeby tearfully, "and Arnold had just come in, and I was asking him what sort of sauce he would like with the asparagus——"

"I hope he said hollandaise," interrupted Clovis, with a show of quickened interest, "because if there's anything I hate——"

"And all of a sudden I missed Baby," continued Mrs. Momeby in a shriller tone. "We've hunted high and low, in house and garden and outside the gates, and he's nowhere to be seen."

"Is he anywhere to be heard?" asked Clovis; "if not, he must be at least two miles away."

"But where? And how?" asked the distracted mother.

"Perhaps an eagle or a wild beast has carried him off," suggested Clovis.

"There aren't eagles and wild beasts in Surrey," said Mrs. Momeby, but a note of horror had crept into her voice.

"They escape now and then from travelling shows. Sometimes I think they let them get loose for the sake of the advertisement. Think what a sensational headline it would make in the local papers: 'Infant son of prominent Nonconformist devoured by spotted hyæna.' Your husband isn't a prominent Nonconformist, but his mother came of Wesleyan stock, and you must allow the newspapers some latitude."

"But we should have found his remains," sobbed Mrs. Momeby.

"If the hyæna was really hungry and not merely toying with his food, there wouldn't be much in the way of remains. It would be like the small-boy-and-apple story—there ain't going to be no core."

Mrs. Momeby turned away hastily to seek comfort and counsel in some other direction. With the selfish absorption of young motherhood she entirely disregarded Clovis's obvious anxiety about the asparagus sauce. Before she had gone a yard, however, the click of the side gate caused her to pull up sharp. Miss Gilpet, from the Villa Peterhof, had come over to hear details of the bereavement. Clovis was already rather bored with the story, but Mrs. Momeby was equipped with that merciless faculty which finds as much joy in the ninetieth time of telling as in the first.

"Arnold had just come in; he was complaining of rheumatism——"

"There are so many things to complain of in this household that it would never have occurred to me to complain of rheumatism," murmured Clovis.

"He was complaining of rheumatism," continued Mrs. Momeby, trying to throw a chilling inflexion into a voice that was already doing a good deal of sobbing and talking at high pressure as well.

She was again interrupted.

"There is no such thing as rheumatism," said Miss Gilpet. She said it with the conscious air of defiance that a waiter adopts in announcing that the cheapest-priced claret in the wine-list is no more. She did not proceed, however, to offer the alternative of some more expensive malady, but denied the existence of them all.

Mrs. Momeby's temper began to shine out through her grief.

"I suppose you'll say next that Baby hasn't really disappeared."

"He has disappeared," conceded Miss Gilpet, "but only because you haven't sufficient faith to find him. It's only lack of faith on your part that prevents him from being restored to you safe and well."

"But if he's been eaten in the meantime by a hyæna and partly digested," said Clovis, who clung affectionately to his wild beast theory, "surely some ill-effects would be noticeable?"

Miss Gilpet was rather staggered by this complication of the question.

"I feel sure that a hyæna has not eaten him," she said lamely.

"The hyæna may be equally certain that it has. You see, it may have just as much faith as you have, and more special knowledge as to the present whereabouts of the baby."

Mrs. Momeby was in tears again. "If you have faith," she sobbed, struck by a happy inspiration, "won't you find our little Erik for us? I am sure you have powers that are denied to us."

Rose-Marie Gilpet was thoroughly sincere in her adherence to Christian Science principles; whether she understood or correctly expounded them the learned in such manners may best decide. In the present case she was undoubtedly confronted with a great opportunity, and as she started forth on her vague search she strenuously summoned to her aid every scrap of faith that she possessed. She passed out into the bare and open high road, followed by Mrs. Momeby's warning, "It's no use going there, we've searched there a dozen times." But Rose-Marie's ears were already deaf to all things save self-congratulation; for sitting in the middle of the highway, playing contentedly with the dust and some faded buttercups, was a white-pinafored baby with a mop of tow-coloured hair tied over one temple with a pale-blue ribbon. Taking first the usual feminine precaution of looking to see that no motor-car was on the distant horizon, Rose-Marie dashed at the child and bore it, despite its vigorous opposition, in through the portals of Elsinore. The child's furious screams had already announced the fact of its discovery, and the almost hysterical parents raced down the lawn to meet their restored offspring. The æsthetic value of the scene was marred in some degree by Rose-Marie's difficulty in holding the struggling infant, which was borne wrong-end foremost towards the agitated bosom of its family. "Our own little Erik come back to us," cried the Momebys in unison; as the child had rammed its fists tightly into its eye-sockets and nothing could be seen of its face but a widely gaping mouth, the recognition was in itself almost an act of faith.

"Is he glad to get back to Daddy and Mummy again?" crooned Mrs. Momeby; the preference which the child was showing for its dust and buttercup distractions was so marked that the question struck Clovis as being unnecessarily tactless.

"Give him a ride on the roly-poly," suggested the father brilliantly, as the howls continued with no sign of early abatement. In a moment the child had been placed astride the big garden roller and a preliminary tug was given to set it in motion. From the hollow depths of the cylinder came an ear-splitting roar, drowning even the vocal efforts of the squalling baby, and immediately afterwards there crept forth a white-pinafored infant with a mop of tow-coloured hair tied over one temple with a pale-blue ribbon. There was no mistaking either the features or the lung-power of the new arrival.

"Our own little Erik," screamed Mrs. Momeby, pouncing on him and nearly smothering him with kisses; "did he hide in the roly-poly to give us all a big fright?"

This was the obvious explanation of the child's sudden disappearance and equally abrupt discovery. There remained, however, the problem of the interloping baby, which now sat whimpering on the lawn in a disfavour as chilling as its previous popularity had been unwelcome. The Momebys glared at it as though it had wormed its way into their short-lived affections by heartless and unworthy pretences. Miss Gilpet's face took on an ashen tinge as she stared helplessly at the bunched-up figure that had been such a gladsome sight to her eyes a few moments ago.

"When love is over, how little of love even the lover understands," quoted Clovis to himself.

Rose-Marie was the first to break the silence.

"If that is Erik you have in your arms, who is—that?"

"That, I think, is for you to explain," said Mrs. Momeby stiffly.

"Obviously," said Clovis, "it's a duplicate Erik that your powers of faith called into being. The question is: What are you going to do with him?"

The ashen pallor deepened in Rose-Marie's cheeks. Mrs. Momeby clutched the genuine Erik closer to her side, as though she feared that her uncanny neighbour might out of sheer pique turn him into a bowl of gold-fish.

"I found him sitting in the middle of the road," said Rose-Marie weakly.

"You can't take him back and leave him there," said Clovis; "the highway is meant for traffic, not to be used as a lumber-room for disused miracles."

Rose-Marie wept. The proverb "Weep and you weep alone," broke down as badly on application as most of its kind. Both babies were wailing lugubriously, and the parent Momebys had scarcely recovered from their earlier lachrymose condition. Clovis alone maintained an unruffled cheerfulness.

"Must I keep him always?" asked Rose-Marie dolefully.

"Not always," said Clovis consolingly; "he can go into the Navy when he's thirteen." Rose-Marie wept afresh.

"Of course," added Clovis, "there may be no end of a bother about his birth certificate. You'll have to explain matters to the Admiralty, and they're dreadfully hidebound."

It was rather a relief when a breathless nursemaid from the Villa Charlottenburg over the way came running across the lawn to claim little Percy, who had slipped out of the front gate and disappeared like a twinkling from the high road.

And even then Clovis found it necessary to go in person to the kitchen to make sure about the asparagus sauce.

THE EASTER EGG

IT was distinctly hard lines for Lady Barbara, who came of good fighting stock, and was one of the bravest women of her generation, that her son should be so undisguisedly a coward. Whatever good qualities Lester Slaggby may have possessed, and he was in some respects charming, courage could certainly never be imputed to him. As a child he had suffered from childish timidity, as a boy from unboyish funk, and as a youth he had exchanged unreasoning fears for others which were more formidable from the fact of having a carefully-thought-out basis. He was frankly afraid of animals, nervous with firearms, and never crossed the Channel without mentally comparing the numerical proportion of life-belts to passengers. On horseback he seemed to require as many hands as a Hindu god, at least four for clutching the reins, and two more for patting the horse soothingly on the neck. Lady Barbara no longer pretended not to see her son's prevailing weakness; with her usual courage she faced the knowledge of it squarely, and, mother-like, loved him none the less.

Continental travel, anywhere away from the great tourist tracks, was a favoured hobby with Lady Barbara, and Lester joined her as often as possible. Eastertide usually found her at Knobaltheim, an upland township in one of those small princedoms that make inconspicuous freckles on the map of Central Europe.

A long-standing acquaintanceship with the reigning family made her a personage of due importance in the eyes of her old friend the Burgomaster, and she was anxiously consulted by that worthy on the momentous occasion when the Prince made known his intention of coming in person to open a sanatorium outside the town. All the usual items in a programme of welcome, some of them fatuous and commonplace, others quaint and charming, had been arranged for, but the Burgomaster hoped that the resourceful English lady might have something new and tasteful to suggest in the way of loyal greeting. The Prince was known to the outside world, if at all, as an old-fashioned reactionary, combating modern progress, as it were, with a wooden sword; to his own people he was known as a kindly old gentleman with a certain endearing stateliness which had nothing of standoffishness about it. Knobaltheim was anxious to do its best. Lady Barbara discussed the matter with Lester and one or two acquaintances in her little hotel, but ideas were difficult to come by.

"Might I suggest something to the Gnädige Frau?" asked a sallow, high-cheek-boned lady to whom the Englishwoman had spoken once or twice, and whom she had set down in her mind as probably a Southern Slav.

"Might I suggest something for the Reception Feast?" she went on, with a certain shy eagerness. "Our little child here, our baby, we will dress him in little white coat, with small wings, as an Easter angel, and he will carry a large white Easter egg, and inside shall be a basket of plover eggs, of which the Prince is so fond, and he shall give it to his Highness as Easter offering. It is so pretty an idea; we have seen it done once in Styria."

Lady Barbara looked dubiously at the proposed Easter angel, a fair, wooden-faced child of about four years old. She had noticed it the day before in the hotel, and wondered rather how such a tow-headed child could belong to such a dark-visaged couple as the woman and her husband; probably, she thought, an adopted baby, especially as the couple were not young.

"Of course, Gnädige Frau will escort the little child up to the Prince," pursued the woman; "but he will be quite good, and do as he is told."

"We haf some pluffers' eggs shall come fresh from Wien," said the husband.

The small child and Lady Barbara seemed equally unenthusiastic about the pretty idea; Lester was openly discouraging, but when the Burgomaster heard of it he was enchanted. The combination of sentiment and plovers' eggs appealed strongly to his Teutonic mind.

On the eventful day the Easter angel, really quite prettily and quaintly dressed, was a centre of kindly interest to the gala crowd marshalled to receive his Highness. The mother was unobtrusive and less fancy than most parents would have been under the circumstances, merely stipulating that she should place the Easter egg herself in the arms that had been carefully schooled how to hold the precious burden. Then Lady Barbara moved forward, the child marching stolidly and with grim determination at her side. It had been promised cakes and sweeties galore if it gave the egg well and truly to the kind old gentleman who was waiting to receive it. Lester had tried to convey to it privately that horrible smackings would attend any failure in its share of the proceedings, but it is doubtful if his German caused more than an immediate distress. Lady Barbara had thoughtfully provided herself with an emergency supply of chocolate sweetmeats; children may sometimes be time-servers, but they do not encourage long accounts. As they approached nearer to the princely daïs Lady Barbara stood discreetly aside, and the stolid-faced infant walked forward alone, with staggering but steadfast gait, encouraged by a murmur of elderly approval. Lester, standing in the front row of the onlookers, turned to scan the crowd for the beaming faces of the happy parents. In a side-road which led to the railway station he saw a cab; entering the cab with every appearance of furtive haste were the dark-visaged couple who had been so plausibly eager for the "pretty idea." The sharpened instinct of cowardice lit up the situation to him in one swift flash. The blood roared and surged to his head as though thousands of floodgates had been opened in his veins and arteries, and his brain was the common sluice in which all the torrents met. He saw nothing but a blur around him. Then the blood ebbed away in quick waves, till his very heart seemed drained and empty, and he stood nervelessly, helplessly, dumbly watching the child, bearing its accursed burden with slow, relentless steps nearer and nearer to the group that waited sheep-like to receive him. A fascinated curiosity compelled Lester to turn his head towards the fugitives; the cab had started at hot pace in the direction of the station.

The next moment Lester was running, running faster than any of those present had ever seen a man run, and—he was not running away. For that stray fraction of his life some unwonted impulse beset him, some hint of the stock he came from, and he ran unflinchingly towards danger. He stooped and clutched at the Easter egg as one tries to scoop up the ball in Rugby football. What he meant to do with it he had not considered, the thing was to get it. But the child had been promised cakes and sweetmeats if it safely gave the egg into the hands of the kindly old gentleman; it uttered no scream, but it held to its charge with limpet grip. Lester sank to his knees, tugging savagely at the tightly clasped burden, and angry cries rose from the scandalized onlookers. A questioning, threatening ring formed round him, then shrank back in recoil as he shrieked out one hideous word. Lady Barbara heard the word and saw the crowd race away like scattered sheep, saw the Prince forcibly hustled away by his attendants; also she saw her son lying prone in an agony of overmastering terror, his spasm of daring shattered by the child's unexpected resistance, still clutching frantically, as though for safety, at that white-satin gew-gaw, unable to crawl even from its deadly neighbourhood, able only to scream and scream and scream. In her brain she was dimly conscious of balancing, or striving to balance, the abject shame which had him now in thrall against the one compelling act of courage which had flung him grandly and madly on to the point of danger. It was only for the fraction of a minute that she stood watching the two entangled figures, the infant with its woodenly obstinate face and body tense with dogged resistance, and the boy limp and already nearly dead with a terror that almost stifled his screams; and over them the long gala streamers flapping gaily in the sunshine. She never forgot the scene; but then, it was the last she ever saw.

Lady Barbara carries her scarred face with its sightless eyes as bravely as ever in the world, but at Eastertide her friends are careful to keep from her ears any mention of the children's Easter symbol.

THE PEACE OF MOWSLE BARTON

CREFTON LOCKYER sat at his ease, an ease alike of body and soul, in the little patch of ground, half-orchard and half-garden, that abutted on the farmyard at Mowsle Barton. After the stress and noise of long years of city life, the repose and peace of the hill-begirt homestead struck on his senses with an almost dramatic intensity. Time and space seemed to lose their meaning and their abruptness; the minutes slid away into hours, and the meadows and fallows sloped away into middle distance, softly and imperceptibly. Wild weeds of the hedgerow straggled into the flower-garden, and wallflowers and garden bushes made counter-raids into farmyard and lane. Sleepy-looking hens and solemn preoccupied ducks were equally at home in yard, orchard, or roadway; nothing seemed to belong definitely to anywhere; even the gates were not necessarily to be found on their hinges. And over the whole scene brooded the sense of a peace that had almost a quality of magic in it. In the afternoon you felt that it had always been afternoon, and must always remain afternoon; in the twilight you knew that it could never have been anything else but twilight. Crefton Lockyer sat at his ease in the rustic seat beneath an old medlar tree, and decided that here was the life-anchorage that his mind had so fondly pictured and that latterly his tired and jarred senses had so often pined for. He would make a permanent lodging-place among these simple, friendly people, gradually increasing the modest comforts with which he would like to surround himself, but falling in as much as possible with their manner of living.

As he slowly matured this resolution in his mind an elderly woman came hobbling with uncertain gait through the orchard. He recognized her as a member of the farm household, the mother or possibly the mother-in-law of Mrs. Spurfield, his present landlady, and hastily formulated some pleasant remark to make to her. She forestalled him.

"There's a bit of writing chalked up on the door over yonder. What is it?"

She spoke in a dull impersonal manner, as though the question had been on her lips for years and had best be got rid of. Her eyes, however, looked impatiently over Crefton's head at the door of a small barn which formed the outpost of a straggling line of farm buildings.

"Martha Pillamon is an old witch," was the announcement that met Crefton's inquiring scrutiny, and he hesitated a moment before giving the statement wider publicity. For all he knew to the contrary, it might be Martha herself to whom he was speaking. It was possible that Mrs. Spurfield's maiden name had been Pillamon. And the gaunt, withered old dame at his side might certainly fulfil local conditions as to the outward aspect of a witch.

"It's something about some one called Martha Pillamon," he explained cautiously.

"What does it say?"

"It's very disrespectful," said Crefton; "it says she's a witch. Such things ought not to be written up."

"It's true, every word of it," said his listener with considerable satisfaction, adding as a special descriptive note of her own, "the old toad."

And as she hobbled away through the farmyard she shrilled out in her cracked voice, "Martha Pillamon is an old witch!"

"Did you hear what she said?" mumbled a weak, angry voice somewhere behind Crefton's shoulder. Turning hastily, he beheld another old crone, thin and yellow and wrinkled, and evidently in a high state of displeasure. Obviously this was Martha Pillamon in person. The orchard seemed to be a favourite promenade for the aged women of the neighbourhood.

" 'Tis lies, 'tis sinful lies," the weak voice went on. " 'Tis Betsy Croot is the old witch. She an' her daughter, the dirty rat. I'll put a spell on 'em, the old nuisances."

As she limped slowly away her eye caught the chalk inscription on the barn door.

"What's written up there?" she demanded, wheeling round on Crefton.

"Vote for Soarker," he responded, with the craven boldness of the practised peacemaker.

The old woman grunted, and her mutterings and her faded red shawl lost themselves gradually among the tree-trunks. Crefton rose presently and made his way towards the farmhouse. Somehow a good deal of the peace seemed to have slipped out of the atmosphere.

The cheery bustle of tea-time in the old farm kitchen, which Crefton had found so agreeable on previous afternoons, seemed to have soured today into a certain uneasy melancholy. There was a dull, dragging silence around the board, and the tea itself, when Crefton came to taste it, was a flat, lukewarm concoction that would have driven the spirit of revelry out of a carnival.

"It's no use complaining of the tea," said Mrs. Spurfield hastily, as her guest stared with an air of polite inquiry at his cup. "The kettle won't boil, that's the truth of it."

Crefton turned to the hearth, where an unusually fierce fire was banked up under a big black kettle, which sent a thin wreath of steam from its spout, but seemed otherwise to ignore the action of the roaring blaze beneath it.

"It's been there more than an hour, an' boil it won't," said Mrs. Spurfield, adding, by way of complete explanation, "we're bewitched."

"It's Martha Pillamon as has done it," chimed in the old mother; "I'll be even with the old toad. I'll put a spell on her."

"It must boil in time," protested Crefton, ignoring the suggestions of foul influences. "Perhaps the coal is damp."

"It won't boil in time for supper, nor for breakfast tomorrow morning, not if you was to keep the fire a-going all night for it," said Mrs. Spurfield. And it didn't. The household subsisted on fried and baked dishes, and a neighbour obligingly brewed tea and sent it across in a moderately warm condition.

"I suppose you'll be leaving us, now that things has turned up uncomfortable," Mrs. Spurfield observed at breakfast; "there are folks as deserts one as soon as trouble comes."

Crefton hurriedly disclaimed any immediate change of plans; he observed, however, to himself that the earlier heartiness of manner had in a large measure deserted the household. Suspicious looks, sulky silences, or sharp speeches had become the order of the day. As for the old mother, she sat about the kitchen or the garden all day, murmuring threats and spells against Martha Pillamon. There was something alike terrifying and piteous in the spectacle of these frail old morsels of humanity consecrating their last flickering energies to the task of making each other wretched. Hatred seemed to be the one faculty which had survived in undiminished vigour and intensity where all else was dropping into ordered and symmetrical decay. And the uncanny part of it was that some horrid unwholesome power seemed to be distilled from their spite and their cursings. No amount of sceptical explanation could remove the undoubted fact that neither kettle nor saucepan would come to boiling-point over the hottest fire. Crefton clung as long as possible to the theory of some defect in the coals, but a wood fire gave the same result, and when a small spirit-lamp kettle, which he ordered out by carrier, showed the same obstinate refusal to allow its contents to boil, he felt that he had come suddenly into contact with some unguessed-at and very evil aspect of hidden forces. Miles away, down through an opening in the hills, he could catch glimpses of a road where motor-cars sometimes passed, and yet here, so little removed from the arteries of the latest civilization, was a bat-haunted old homestead, where something unmistakably like witchcraft seemed to hold a very practical sway.

Passing out through the farm garden on his way to the lanes beyond, where he hoped to recapture the comfortable sense of peacefulness that was so lacking around house and hearth—especially hearth—Crefton came across the old mother, sitting mumbling to herself in the seat beneath the medlar tree. "Let un sink as swims, let un sink as swims," she was repeating over and over again, as a child repeats a half-learned lesson. And now and then she would break off into a shrill laugh, with a note of malice in it that was not pleasant to hear. Crefton was glad when he found himself out of earshot, in the quiet and seclusion of the deep overgrown lanes that seemed to lead away to nowhere; one, narrower and deeper than the rest, attracted his footsteps, and he was almost annoyed when he found that it really did act as a miniature roadway to a human dwelling. A forlorn-looking cottage with a scrap of ill-tended cabbage garden and a few aged apple trees stood at an angle where a swift-flowing stream widened out for a space into a decent-sized pond before hurrying away again through the willows that had checked its course. Crefton leaned against a tree-trunk and looked across the swirling eddies of the pond at the humble little homestead opposite him; the only sign of life came from a small procession of dingy-looking ducks that marched in single file down to the water's edge. There is always something rather taking in the way a duck changes itself in an instant from a slow, clumsy waddler of the earth to a graceful, buoyant swimmer of the waters, and Crefton waited with a certain arrested attention to watch the leader of the file launch itself on to the surface of the pond. He was aware at the same time of a curious warning instinct that something strange and unpleasant was about to happen. The duck flung itself confidently forward into the water, and rolled immediately under the surface. Its head appeared for a moment and went under again, leaving a train of bubbles in its wake, while wings and legs churned the water in a helpless swirl of flapping and kicking. The bird was obviously drowning. Crefton thought at first that it had caught itself in some weeds, or was being attacked from below by a pike or water-rat. But no blood floated to the surface, and the wildly bobbing body made the circuit of the pond current without hindrance from any entanglement. A second duck had by this time launched itself into the pond, and a second struggling body rolled and twisted under the surface. There was something peculiarly piteous in the sight of the gasping beaks that showed now and again above the water, as though in terrified protest at this treachery of a trusted and familiar element. Crefton gazed with something like horror as a third duck poised itself on the bank and splashed in, to share the fate of the other two. He felt almost relieved when the remainder of the flock, taking tardy alarm from the commotion of the slowly drowning bodies, drew themselves up with tense outstretched necks, and sidled away from the scene of danger, quacking a deep note of disquietude as they went. At the same moment Crefton became aware that he was not the only human witness of the scene; a bent and withered old woman, whom he recognized at once as Martha Pillamon, of sinister reputation, had limped down the cottage path to the water's edge, and was gazing fixedly at the gruesome whirligig of dying birds that went in horrible procession round the pool. Presently her voice rang out in a shrill note of quavering rage:

" 'Tis Betsy Croot adone it, the old rat. I'll put a spell on her, see if I don't."

Crefton slipped quietly away, uncertain whether or no the old woman had noticed his presence. Even before she had proclaimed the guiltiness of Betsy Croot, the latter's muttered incantation "Let un sink as swims" had flashed uncomfortably across his mind. But it was the final threat of a retaliatory spell which crowded his mind with misgiving to the exclusion of all other thoughts or fancies. His reasoning powers could no longer afford to dismiss these old-wives' threats as empty bickerings. The household at Mowsle Barton lay under the displeasure of a vindictive old woman who seemed able to materialize her personal spites in a very practical fashion, and there was no saying what form her revenge for three drowned ducks might not take. As a member of the household Crefton might find himself involved in some general and highly disagreeable visitation of Martha Pillamon's wrath. Of course he knew that he was giving way to absurd fancies, but the behaviour of the spirit-lamp kettle and the subsequent scene at the pond had considerably unnerved him. And the vagueness of his alarm added to its terrors; when once you have taken the Impossible into your calculations its possibilities become practically limitless.

Crefton rose at his usual early hour the next morning, after one of the least restful nights he had spent at the farm. His sharpened senses quickly detected that subtle atmosphere of things-being-not-altogether-well that hangs over a stricken household. The cows had been milked, but they stood huddled about in the yard, waiting impatiently to be driven out afield, and the poultry kept up an importunate querulous reminder of deferred feeding-time; the yard pump, which usually made discordant music at frequent intervals during the early morning, was today ominously silent. In the house itself there was a coming and going of scuttering footsteps, a rushing and dying away of hurried voices, and long, uneasy stillnesses. Crefton finished his dressing and made his way to the head of a narrow staircase. He could hear a dull, complaining voice, a voice into which an awed hush had crept, and recognized the speaker as Mrs. Spurfield.

"He'll go away, for sure," the voice was saying; "there are those as runs away from one as soon as real misfortune shows itself."

Crefton felt that he probably was one of "those," and that

there were moments when it was advisable to be true to type.

He crept back to his room, collected and packed his few belongings, placed the money due for his lodgings on a table, and made his way out by a back door into the yard. A mob of poultry surged expectantly towards him; shaking off their interested attentions, he hurried along under cover of cow-stall, piggery, and hayricks till he reached the lane at the back of the farm. A few minutes' walk, which only the burden of his portmanteaux restrained from developing into an undisguised run, brought him to a main road, where the early carrier soon overtook him and sped him onward to the neighbouring town. At a bend of the road he caught a last glimpse of the farm; the old gabled roofs and thatched barns, the straggling orchard, and the medlar tree, with its wooden seat, stood out with an almost spectral clearness in the early morning light, and over it all brooded that air of magic possession which Crefton had once mistaken for peace.

The bustle and roar of Paddington Station smote on his ears with a welcome protective greeting.

"Very bad for our nerves, all this rush and hurry," said a fellow-traveller; "give me the peace and quiet of the country."

Crefton mentally surrendered his share of the desired commodity. A crowded, brilliantly over-lighted music-hall, where an exuberant rendering of "1812" was being given by a strenuous orchestra, came nearest to his ideal of a nerve sedative.

THE TALKING-OUT OF TARRINGTON

"HEAVENS!" exclaimed the aunt of Clovis, "here's some one I know bearing down on us. I can't remember his name, but he lunched with us once in Town. Tarrington—yes, that's it. He's heard of the picnic I'm giving for the Princess, and he'll cling to me like a lifebelt till I give him an invitation; then he'll ask if he may bring all his wives and mothers and sisters with him. That's the worst of these small watering-places; one can't escape from anybody."

"I'll fight a rearguard action for you if you like to do a bolt now," volunteered Clovis; "you've a clear ten yards' start if you don't lose time."

The aunt of Clovis responded gamely to the suggestion, and churned away like a Nile steamer, with a long brown ripple of Pekingese spaniel trailing in her wake.

"Pretend you don't know him," was her parting advice, tinged with the reckless courage of the non-combatant.

The next moment the overtures of an affably disposed gentleman were being received by Clovis with a "silent-upon-a-peak-in-Darien" stare which denoted an absence of all previous acquaintance with the object scrutinized.

"I expect you don't know me with my moustache," said the new-comer, "I've only grown it during the last two months."

"On the contrary," said Clovis, "the moustache is the only thing about you that seemed familiar to me. I felt certain that I had met it somewhere before."

"My name is Tarrington," resumed the candidate for recognition.

"A very useful kind of name," said Clovis; "with a name of that sort no one would blame you if you did nothing in particular heroic or remarkable, would they? And yet if you were to raise a troop of light horse in a moment of national emergency, 'Tarrington's Light Horse' would sound quite appropriate and pulse-quickening; whereas if you were called Spoopin, for instance, the thing would be out of the question. No one, even in a moment of national emergency, could possibly belong to Spoopin's Horse."

The new-comer smiled weakly, as one who is not to be put off by mere flippancy, and began again with patient persistence :

"I think you ought to remember my name——"

"I shall," said Clovis, with an air of immense sincerity. "My aunt was asking me only this morning to suggest names for four young owls she's just had sent her as pets. I shall call them all Tarrington; then if one or two of them die or fly away, or leave us in any of the ways that pet owls are prone to, there will be always one or two left to carry on your name. And my aunt won't *let* me forget it; she will always be asking 'Have the Tarringtons had their mice?' and questions of that sort. She says if you keep wild creatures in captivity you ought to see after their wants, and of course she's quite right there."

"I met you at luncheon at your aunt's house once——" broke in Mr. Tarrington, pale but still resolute.

"My aunt never lunches," said Clovis; "she belongs to the National Anti-Luncheon League, which is doing quite a lot of good work in a quiet, unobtrusive way. A subscription of half a crown per quarter entitles you to go without ninety-two luncheons."

"This must be something new," exclaimed Tarrington.

"It's the same aunt that I've always had," said Clovis coldly.

"I perfectly well remember meeting you at a luncheon-party given by your aunt," persisted Tarrington, who was beginning to flush an unhealthy shade of mottled pink.

"What was there for lunch?" asked Clovis.

"Oh, well, I don't remember that——"

"How nice of you to remember my aunt when you can no longer recall the names of the things you ate. Now my memory works quite differently. I can remember a menu long after I've forgotten the hostess that accompanied it. When I was seven years old I recollect being given a peach at a garden-party by some Duchess or other; I can't remember a thing about her, except that I imagine our acquaintance must have been of the slightest, as she called me a 'nice little boy,' but I have unfading memories of that peach. It was one of those exuberant peaches that meet you half-way, so to speak, and are all over you in a moment. It was a beautiful unspoiled product of a hothouse, and yet it managed quite successfully to give itself the airs of a compôte. You had to bite it and imbibe it at the same time. To me there has always been something charming and mystic in the thought of that delicate velvet globe of fruit, slowly ripening and warming to perfection through the long summer days and perfumed nights, and then coming suddenly athwart my life in the supreme moment of its existence. I can never forget it, even if I wished to. And when I had devoured all that was edible of it, there still remained the stone, which a heedless, thoughtless child would doubtless have thrown away; I put it down the neck of a young friend who was wearing a very *décolleté* sailor suit. I told him it was a scorpion, and from the way he wriggled and screamed he evidently believed it, though where the silly kid imagined I could procure a live scorpion at a garden-party I don't know. Altogether, that peach is for me an unfading and happy memory——"

The defeated Tarrington had by this time retreated out of car-shot, comforting himself as best he might with the reflection that a picnic which included the presence of Clovis might prove a doubtfully agreeable experience.

"I shall certainly go in for a Parliamentary career," said Clovis to himself as he turned complacently to rejoin his aunt. "As a talker-out of inconvenient bills I should be invaluable."

THE SECRET SIN OF SEPTIMUS BROPE

"Who and what is Mr. Brope?" demanded the aunt of Clovis suddenly.

Mrs. Riversedge, who had been snipping off the heads of defunct roses, and thinking of nothing in particular, sprang hurriedly to mental attention. She was one of those old-fashioned hostesses who consider that one ought to know something about one's guests, and that the something ought to be to their credit.

"I believe he comes from Leighton Buzzard," she observed by way of preliminary explanation.

"In these days of rapid and convenient travel," said Clovis, who was dispersing a colony of green-fly with visitations of cigarette smoke, "to come from Leighton Buzzard does not necessarily denote any great strength of character. It might only mean mere restlessness. Now if he had left it under a cloud, or as a protest against the incurable and heartless frivolity of its inhabitants, that would tell us something about the man and his mission in life."

"What does he do?" pursued Mrs. Troyle magisterially.

"He edits the *Cathedral Monthly*," said her hostess, "and he's enormously learned about memorial brasses and transepts and the influence of Byzantine worship on modern liturgy, and all those sort of things. Perhaps he is just a little bit heavy and immersed in one range of subjects, but it takes all sorts to make a good house-party, you know. You don't find him *too* dull, do you?"

"Dullness I could overlook," said the aunt of Clovis; "what I cannot forgive is his making love to my maid."

"My dear Mrs. Troyle," gasped the hostess, "what an extraordinary idea! I assure you Mr. Brope would not dream of doing such a thing."

"His dreams are a matter of indifference to me; for all I care his slumbers may be one long indiscretion of unsuitable erotic advances, in which the entire servants' hall may be involved. But in his waking hours he shall not make love to my maid. It's no use arguing about it, I'm firm on the point."

"But you must be mistaken," persisted Mrs. Riversedge; "Mr. Brope would be the last person to do such a thing."

"He is the first person to do such a thing, as far as my information goes, and if I have any voice in the matter he certainly shall be the last. Of course, I am not referring to respectably-intentioned lovers."

"I simply cannot think that a man who writes so charmingly and informingly about transepts and Byzantine influences would behave in such an unprincipled manner," said Mrs. Riversedge; "what evidence have you that he's doing anything of the sort? I don't want to doubt your word, of course, but we mustn't be too ready to condemn him unheard, must we?"

"Whether we condemn him or not, he has certainly not been unheard. He has the room next to my dressing-room, and on two occasions, when I daresay he thought I was absent, I have plainly heard him announcing through the wall, 'I love you, Florrie.' Those partition walls upstairs are very thin; one can almost hear a watch ticking in the next room."

"Is your maid called Florence?"

"Her name is Florinda."

"What an extraordinary name to give a maid!"

"I did not give it to her; she arrived in my service already christened."

"What I mean is," said Mrs. Riversedge, "that when I get maids with unsuitable names I call them Jane; they soon get used to it."

"An excellent plan," said the aunt of Clovis coldly, "unfortunately I have got used to being called Jane myself. It happens to be my name."

She cut short Mrs. Riversedge's flood of apologies by abruptly remarking:

"The question is not whether I'm to call my maid Florinda, but whether Mr. Brope is to be permitted to call her Florrie. I am strongly of opinion that he shall not."

"He may have been repeating the words of some song," said Mrs. Riversedge hopefully; "there are lots of those sorts of silly refrains with girls' names," she continued, turning to Clovis as a possible authority on the subject. " 'You mustn't call me Mary——' "

"I shouldn't think of doing so," Clovis assured her; "in the first place, I've always understood that your name was Henrietta; and then I hardly know you well enough to take such a liberty."

"I mean there's a *song* with that refrain," hurriedly explained Mrs. Riversedge, "and there's 'Rhoda, Rhoda kept a pagoda,' and 'Maisie is a daisy,' and heaps of others. Certainly it doesn't sound like Mr. Brope to be singing such songs, but I think we ought to give him the benefit of the doubt."

"I had already done so," said Mrs. Troyle, "until further evidence came my way."

She shut her lips with the resolute finality of one who enjoys the blessed certainty of being implored to open them again.

"Further evidence!" exclaimed her hostess; "do tell me!"

"As I was coming upstairs after breakfast Mr. Brope was just passing my room. In the most natural way in the world a piece of paper dropped out of a packet that he held in his hand and fluttered to the ground just at my door. I was going to call out to him 'You've dropped something,' and then for some reason I held back and didn't show myself till he was safely in his room. You see it occurred to me that I was very seldom in my room just at that hour, and that Florinda was almost always there tidying up things about that time. So I picked up that innocent-looking piece of paper."

Mrs. Troyle paused again, with the self-applauding air of one who has detected an asp lurking in an apple-charlotte.

Mrs. Riversedge snipped vigorously at the nearest rose bush, incidentally decapitating a Viscountess Folkestone that was just coming into bloom.

"What was on the paper?" she asked.

"Just the words in pencil, 'I love you, Florrie,' and then underneath, crossed out with a faint line, but perfectly plain to read, 'Meet me in the garden by the yew.' "

"There *is* a yew tree at the bottom of the garden," admitted Mrs. Riversedge.

"At any rate he appears to be truthful," commented Clovis.

"To think that a scandal of this sort should be going on under my roof!" said Mrs. Riversedge indignantly.

"I wonder why it is that scandal seems so much worse under a roof," observed Clovis; "I've always regarded it as a proof of the superior delicacy of the cat tribe that it conducts most of its scandals above the slates."

"Now I come to think of it," resumed Mrs. Riversedge, "there are things about Mr. Brope that I've never been able to account for. His income, for instance: he only gets two hundred a year as editor of the *Cathedral Monthly,* and I know that his people are quite poor, and he hasn't any private means. Yet he manages to afford a flat somewhere in Westminster, and he goes abroad to Bruges and those sort of places every year, and always dresses well, and gives quite nice luncheon-parties in the season. You can't do all that on two hundred a year, can you?"

"Does he write for any other papers?" queried Mrs. Troyle.

"No, you see he specializes so entirely on liturgy and ecclesiastical architecture that his field is rather restricted. He once tried the *Sporting and Dramatic* with an article on church edifices in famous fox-hunting centres, but it wasn't considered of sufficient general interest to be accepted. No, I don't see how he can support himself in his present style merely by what he writes."

"Perhaps he sells spurious transepts to American enthusiasts," suggested Clovis.

"How could you sell a transept?" said Mrs. Riversedge; "such a thing would be impossible."

"Whatever he may do to eke out his income," interrupted Mrs. Troyle, "he is certainly not going to fill in his leisure moments by making love to my maid."

"Of course not," agreed her hostess; "that must be put a stop to at once. But I don't quite know what we ought to do."

"You might put a barbed wire entanglement round the yew tree as a precautionary measure," said Clovis.

"I don't think that the disagreeable situation that has arisen is improved by flippancy," said Mrs. Riversedge; "a good maid is a treasure——"

"I am sure I don't know what I should do without Florinda," admitted Mrs. Troyle; "she understands my hair. I've long ago given up trying to do anything with it myself. I regard one's hair as I regard husbands: as long as one is seen together in public one's private divergences don't matter. Surely that was the luncheon gong."

Septimus Brope and Clovis had the smoking-room to themselves after lunch. The former seemed restless and preoccupied, the latter quietly observant.

"What is a lorry?" asked Septimus suddenly; "I don't mean the thing on wheels, of course I know what that is, but isn't there a bird with a name like that, the larger form of a lorikeet?"

"I fancy it's a lory, with one 'r'," said Clovis lazily, "in which case it's no good to you."

Septimus Brope stared in some astonishment.

"How do you mean, no good to me?" he asked, with more than a trace of uneasiness in his voice.

"Won't rhyme with Florrie," explained Clovis briefly.

Septimus sat upright in his chair, with unmistakable alarm on his face.

"How did you find out? I mean, how did you know I was trying to get a rhyme to Florrie?" he asked sharply.

"I didn't know," said Clovis, "I only guessed. When you wanted to turn the prosaic lorry of commerce into a feathered poem flitting through the verdure of a tropical forest, I knew you must be working up a sonnet, and Florrie was the only female name that suggested itself as rhyming with lorry."

Septimus still looked uneasy.

"I believe you know more," he said.

Clovis laughed quietly, but said nothing.

"How much do you know?" Septimus asked desperately.

"The yew tree in the garden," said Clovis.

"There! I felt certain I'd dropped it somewhere. But you must have guessed something before. Look here, you have surprised my secret. You won't give me away, will you? It is nothing to be ashamed of, but it wouldn't do for the editor of the *Cathedral Monthly* to go in openly for that sort of thing, would it?"

"Well, I suppose not," admitted Clovis.

"You see," continued Septimus, "I get quite a decent lot of money out of it. I could never live in the style I do on what I get as editor of the *Cathedral Monthly*."

Clovis was even more startled than Septimus had been earlier in the conversation, but he was better skilled in repressing surprise.

"Do you mean to say you get money out of—Florrie?" he asked.

"Not out of Florrie, as yet," said Septimus; "in fact, I don't mind saying that I'm having a good deal of trouble over Florrie. But there are a lot of others."

Clovis's cigarette went out.

"This is *very* interesting," he said slowly. And then, with Septimus Brope's next words, illumination dawned on him.

"There are heaps of others; for instance:

" '*Cora with the lips of coral,*
You and I will never quarrel.'

That was one of my earliest successes, and it still brings me in royalties. And then there is—'Esmeralda, when I first beheld her,' and 'Fair Teresa, how I love to please her,' both of those have been fairly popular. And there is one rather

dreadful one," continued Septimus, flushing deep carmine,
"which has brought me in more money than any of the others:

> " *'Lively little Lucie*
> *With her naughty nez retrousse.'*

Of course, I loathe the whole lot of them; in fact, I'm rapidly
becoming something of a woman-hater under their influence,
but I can't afford to disregard the financial aspect of the matter.
And at the same time you can understand that my position as
an authority on ecclesiastical architecture and liturgical subjects would be weakened, if not altogether ruined, if it once
got about that I was the author of 'Cora with the lips of coral'
and all the rest of them."

Clovis had recovered sufficiently to ask in a sympathetic,
if rather unsteady, voice what was the special trouble with
"Florrie."

"I can't get her into lyric shape, try as I will," said Septimus mournfully. "You see, one has to work in a lot of
sentimental, sugary compliment with a catchy rhyme, and a
certain amount of personal biography or prophecy. They've
all of them got to have a long string of past successes recorded
about them, or else you've got to foretell blissful things about
them and yourself in the future. For instance, there is:

> " *'Dainty little girlie Mavis,*
> *She is such a rara avis,*
> *All the money I can save is*
> *All to be for Mavis mine.'*

It goes to a sickening namby-pamby waltz time, and for
months nothing else was sung and hummed in Blackpool and
other popular centres."

This time Clovis's self-control broke down badly.

"Please excuse me," he gurgled, "but I can't help it when
I remember the awful solemnity of that article of yours that
you so kindly read us last night, on the Coptic Church in its
relation to early Christian worship."

Septimus groaned.

"You see how it would be," he said; "as soon as people
knew me to be the author of that miserable sentimental

twaddle, all respect for the serious labours of my life would be gone. I dare say I know more about memorial brasses than anyone living, in fact I hope one day to publish a monograph on the subject, but I should be pointed out everywhere as the man whose ditties were in the mouths of nigger minstrels along the entire coast-line of our Island home. Can you wonder that I positively hate Florrie all the time that I'm trying to grind out sugar-coated rhapsodies about her?"

"Why not give free play to your emotions and be brutally abusive? An uncomplimentary refrain would have an instant success as a novelty if you were sufficiently out-spoken."

"I've never thought of that," said Septimus, "and I'm afraid I couldn't break away from the habit of fulsome adulation and suddenly change my style."

"You needn't change your style in the least," said Clovis; "merely reverse the sentiment and keep to the inane phrase-ology of the thing. If you'll do the body of the song I'll knock off the refrain, which is the thing that principally matters, I believe. I shall charge half-shares in the royalties, and throw in my silence as to your guilty secret. In the eyes of the world you shall still be the man who has devoted his life to the study of transepts and Byzantine ritual; only sometimes, in the long winter evenings, when the wind howls drearily down the chimney and the rain beats against the windows, I shall think of you as the author of 'Cora with the lips of coral.' Of course, if in sheer gratitude at my silence you like to take me for a much-needed holiday to the Adriatic or some-where equally interesting, paying all expenses, I shouldn't dream of refusing."

Later in the afternoon Clovis found his aunt and Mrs. Riversedge indulging in gentle exercise in the Jacobean garden.

"I've spoken to Mr. Brope about F.," he announced.

"How splendid of you! What did he say?" came in a quick chorus from the two ladies.

"He was quite frank and straightforward with me when he saw that I knew his secret," said Clovis, "and it seems that his intentions were quite serious, if slightly unsuitable. I tried to show him the impracticability of the course that he was following. He said he wanted to be understood, and he seemed to think that Florinda would excel in that requirement, but I pointed out that there were probably dozens of delicately nurtured, pure-hearted young English girls who would be capable of understanding him, while Florinda was the only person in the world who understood my aunt's hair. That rather weighed with him, for he's not really a selfish animal, if you take him in the right way, and when I appealed to the memory of his happy childish days, spent amid the daisied fields of Leighton Buzzard (I suppose daisies do grow there), he was obviously affected. Anyhow, he gave me his word that he would put Florinda absolutely out of his mind, and he has agreed to go for a short trip abroad as the best distraction for his thoughts. I am going with him as far as Ragusa. If my aunt should wish to give me a really nice scarf-pin (to be chosen by myself), as a small recognition of the very considerable service I have done her, I shouldn't dream of refusing. I'm not one of those who think that because one is abroad one can go about dressed anyhow."

A few weeks later in Blackpool and places where they sing, the following refrain held undisputed sway:

> *"How you bore me, Florrie,*
> *With those eyes of vacant blue;*
> *You'll be very sorry, Florrie,*
> *If I marry you.*
> *Though I'm easy-goin', Florrie,*
> *This I swear is true,*
> *I'll throw you down a quarry, Florrie,*
> *If I marry you."*

B & S - B)
(1914)
C

THE SHE-WOLF

LEONARD BILSITER was one of those people who have failed
to find this world attractive or interesting, and who have sought
compensation in an "unseen world" of their own experience
or imagination—or invention. Children do that sort of thing
successfully, but children are content to convince themselves,
and do not vulgarize their beliefs by trying to convince other
people. Leonard Bilsiter's beliefs were for "the few," that is
to say, any one who would listen to him.

His dabblings in the unseen might not have carried him
beyond the customary platitudes of the drawing-room vision-
ary if accident had not reinforced his stock-in-trade of mysti-
cal lore. In company with a friend, who was interested in
a Ural mining concern, he had made a trip across Eastern
Europe at a moment when the great Russian railway strike
was developing from a threat to a reality; its outbreak caught
him on the return journey, somewhere on the further side of
Perm, and it was while waiting for a couple of days at a
wayside station in a state of suspended locomotion that he
made the acquaintance of a dealer in harness and metalware,
who profitably whiled away the tedium of the long halt by
initiating his English travelling companion in a fragmentary
system of folk-lore that he had picked up from Trans-Baikal
traders and natives. Leonard returned to his home circle
garrulous about his Russian strike experiences, but oppressively
reticent about certain dark mysteries, which he alluded to under
the resounding title of Siberian Magic. The reticence wore
off in a week or two under the influence of an entire lack of
general curiosity, and Leonard began to make more detailed
allusions to the enormous powers which this new esoteric force,
to use his own description of it, conferred on the initiated few
who knew how to wield it. His aunt, Cecilia Hoops, who
loved sensation perhaps rather better than she loved the truth,
gave him as clamorous an advertisement as any one could wish
for by retailing an account of how he had turned a vegetable
marrow into a wood-pigeon before her very eyes. As a mani-
festation of the possession of supernatural powers, the story

was discounted in some quarters by the respect accorded to Mrs. Hoops' powers of imagination.

However divided opinion might be on the question of Leonard's status as a wonder-worker or a charlatan, he certainly arrived at Mary Hampton's house-party with a reputation for pre-eminence in one or other of those professions, and he was not disposed to shun such publicity as might fall to his share. Esoteric forces and unusual powers figured largely in whatever conversation he or his aunt had a share in, and his own performances, past and potential, were the subject of mysterious hints and dark avowals.

"I wish you would turn me into a wolf, Mr. Bilsiter," said his hostess at luncheon the day after his arrival.

"My dear Mary," said Colonel Hampton, "I never knew you had a craving in that direction."

"A she-wolf, of course," continued Mrs. Hampton; "it would be too confusing to change one's sex as well as one's species at a moment's notice."

"I don't think one should jest on these subjects," said Leonard.

"I'm not jesting. I'm quite serious, I assure you. Only don't do it today; we have only eight available bridge players, and it would break up one of our tables. Tomorrow we shall be a larger party. Tomorrow night, after dinner——"

"In our present imperfect understanding of these hidden forces I think one should approach them with humbleness rather than mockery," observed Leonard, with such severity that the subject was forthwith dropped.

Clovis Sangrail had sat unusually silent during the discussion on the possibilities of Siberian magic; after lunch he sidetracked Lord Pabham into the comparative seclusion of the billiard-room and delivered himself of a searching question.

"Have you such a thing as a she-wolf in your collection of wild animals? A she-wolf of moderately good temper?"

Lord Pabham considered. "There is Louisa," he said, "a rather fine specimen of the timber-wolf. I got her two years ago in exchange for some Arctic foxes. Most of my animals get to be fairly tame before they've been with me very long; I think I can say Louisa has an angelic temper, as she-wolves go. Why do you ask?"

"I was wondering whether you would lend her to me for

tomorrow night," said Clovis, with a careless solicitude of one who borrows a collar stud or a tennis racquet.

"Tomorrow night?"

"Yes, wolves are nocturnal animals, so the late hours won't hurt her," said Clovis, with the air of one who has taken everything into consideration; "one of your men could bring her over from Pabham Park after dusk, and with a little help he ought to be able to smuggle her into the conservatory at the same moment that Mary Hampton makes an unobtrusive exit."

Lord Pabham stared at Clovis for a moment in pardonable bewilderment; then his face broke into a wrinkled network of laughter.

"Oh, that's your game, is it? You are going to do a little Siberian magic on your own account. And is Mrs. Hampton willing to be a fellow-conspirator?"

"Mary is pledged to see me through with it, if you will guarantee Louisa's temper."

"I'll answer for Louisa," said Lord Pabham.

By the following day the house-party had swollen to larger proportions, and Bilsiter's instinct for self-advertisement expanded duly under the stimulant of an increased audience. At dinner that evening he held forth at length on the subject of unseen forces and untested powers, and his flow of impressive eloquence continued unabated while coffee was being served in the drawing-room preparatory to a general migration to the card-room. His aunt ensured a respectful hearing for his utterances, but her sensation-loving soul hankered after something more dramatic than mere vocal demonstration.

"Won't you do something to *convince* them of your powers, Leonard?" she pleaded. "Change something into another shape. He can, you know, if he only chooses to," she informed the company.

"Oh, do," said Mavis Pellington earnestly, and her request was echoed by nearly every one present. Even those who were not open to conviction were perfectly willing to be entertained by an exhibition of amateur conjuring.

Leonard felt that something tangible was expected of him.

"Has any one present," he asked, "got a three-penny bit or some small object of no particular value——?"

"You're surely not going to make coins disappear, or something primitive of that sort?" said Clovis contemptuously.

"I think it is very unkind of you not to carry out my sugges-tion of turning me into a wolf," said Mary Hampton, as she crossed over to the conservatory to give her macaws their usual tribute from the dessert dishes.

"I have already warned you of the danger of treating these powers in a mocking spirit," said Leonard solemnly.

"I don't believe you can do it," laughed Mary provocatively from the conservatory; "I dare you to do it if you can. I defy you to turn me into a wolf."

As she said this she was lost to view behind a clump of azaleas.

"Mrs. Hampton——" began Leonard with increased solem-nity, but he got no further. A breath of chill air seemed to rush across the room, and at the same time the macaws broke forth into ear-splitting screams.

"What on earth is the matter with those confounded birds, Mary?" exclaimed Colonel Hampton; at the same moment an even more piercing scream from Mavis Pellington stam-peded the entire company from their seats. In various attitudes of helpless horror or instinctive defence they confronted the evil-looking grey beast that was peering at them from amid a setting of fern and azalea.

Mrs. Hoops was the first to recover from the general chaos of fright and bewilderment.

"Leonard!" she screamed shrilly to her nephew, "turn it back into Mrs. Hampton at once! It may fly at us at any moment. Turn it back!"

"I—I don't know how to," faltered Leonard, who looked more scared and horrified than any one.

"What!" shouted Colonel Hampton, "you've taken the abominable liberty of turning my wife into a wolf, and now you stand there calmly and say you can't turn her back again!"

To do strict justice to Leonard, calmness was not a distin-guishing feature of his attitude at the moment.

"I assure you I didn't turn Mrs. Hampton into a wolf; nothing was farther from my intentions," he protested.

"Then where is she, and how came that animal into the conservatory?" demanded the Colonel.

"Of course we must accept your assurance that you didn't

turn Mrs. Hampton into a wolf," said Clovis politely, "but you will agree that appearances are against you."

"Are we to have all these recriminations with that beast standing there ready to tear us to pieces!" wailed Mavis indignantly.

"Lord Pabham, you know a good deal about wild beasts——" suggested Colonel Hampton.

"The wild beasts that I have been accustomed to," said Lord Pabham, "have come with proper credentials from well-known dealers, or have been bred in my own menagerie. I've never before been confronted with an animal that walks unconcernedly out of an azalea bush, leaving a charming and popular hostess unaccounted for. As far as one can judge from *outward* characteristics," he continued, "it has the appearance of a well-grown female of the North American timber-wolf, a variety of the common species *canis lupus*."

"Oh, never mind its Latin name," screamed Mavis, as the beast came a step or two further into the room; "can't you entice it away with food, and shut it up where it can't do any harm?"

"If it is really Mrs. Hampton, who has just had a very good dinner, I don't suppose food will appeal to it very strongly," said Clovis.

"Leonard," beseeched Mrs. Hoops tearfully, "even if this *is* none of your doing, can't you use your great powers to turn this dreadful beast into something harmless before it bites us all—a rabbit or something?"

"I don't suppose Colonel Hampton would care to have his wife turned into a succession of fancy animals as though we were playing a round game with her," interposed Clovis.

"I absolutely forbid it," thundered the Colonel.

"Most wolves that I've had anything to do with have been inordinately fond of sugar," said Lord Pabham; "if you like I'll try the effect on this one."

He took a piece of sugar from the saucer of his coffee cup and flung it to the expectant Louisa, who snapped it in mid-air. There was a sigh of relief from the company; a wolf that ate sugar when it might at the least have been employed in tearing macaws to pieces had already shed some of its terrors. The sigh deepened to a gasp of thanksgiving when Lord Pabham decoyed the animal out of the room by a pretended largesse of further sugar. There was an instant rush to the vacated conservatory. There was no trace of Mrs. Hampton except the plate containing the macaw's supper.

"The door is locked on the inside!" exclaimed Clovis, who had deftly turned the key as he affected to test it.

Every one turned towards Bilsiter.

"If you haven't turned my wife into a wolf," said Colonel Hampton, "will you kindly explain where she has disappeared to, since she obviously could not have gone through a locked door? I will not press you for an explanation of how a North American timber-wolf suddenly appeared in the conservatory, but I think I have some right to inquire what has become of Mrs. Hampton."

Bilsiter's reiterated disclaimer was met with a general murmur of impatient disbelief.

"I refuse to stay another hour under this roof," declared Mavis Pellington.

"If our hostess has really vanished out of human form," said Mrs. Hoops, "none of the ladies of the party can very well remain. I absolutely decline to be chaperoned by a wolf!"

"It's a she-wolf," said Clovis soothingly.

The correct etiquette to be observed under the unusual circumstances received no further elucidation. The sudden entry of Mary Hampton deprived the discussion of its immediate interest.

"Some one has mesmerized me," she exclaimed crossly; "I found myself in the game larder, of all places, being fed with sugar by Lord Pabham. I hate being mesmerized, and the doctor has forbidden me to touch sugar."

The situation was explained to her, as far as it permitted of anything that could be called explanation.

"Then you *really* did turn me into a wolf, Mr. Bilsiter?" she exclaimed excitedly.

But Leonard had burned the boat in which he might now have embarked on a sea of glory. He could only shake his head feebly.

"It was I who took that liberty," said Clovis; "you see, I happen to have lived for a couple of years in North-eastern Russia, and I have more than a tourist's acquaintance with the magic craft of that region. One does not care to speak about these strange powers, but once in a way, when one hears a lot of nonsense being talked about them, one is tempted to show what Siberian magic can accomplish in the hands of some one who really understands it. I yielded to that temptation. May I have some brandy? The effort has left me rather faint."

If Leonard Bilsiter could at that moment have transformed Clovis into a cockroach and then have stepped on him he would gladly have performed both operations.

THE BOAR-PIG

"THERE is a back way on to the lawn," said Mrs. Philidore Stossen to her daughter, "through a small grass paddock and then through a walled fruit garden full of gooseberry bushes. I went all over the place last year when the family were away. There is a door that opens from the fruit garden into a shrubbery, and once we emerge from there we can mingle with the guests as if we had come in by the ordinary way. It's much safer than going in by the front entrance and running the risk of coming bang up against the hostess; that would be so awkward when she doesn't happen to have invited us."

"Isn't it a lot of trouble to take for getting admittance to a garden party?"

"To a garden party, yes; to *the* garden party of the season, certainly not. Every one of any consequence in the county, with the exception of ourselves, has been asked to meet the Princess, and it would be far more troublesome to invent explanations as to why we weren't there than to get in by a roundabout way. I stopped Mrs. Cuvering in the road yesterday and talked very pointedly about the Princess. If she didn't choose to take the hint and send me an invitation it's not my fault, is it? Here we are: we just cut across the grass and through that little gate into the garden."

Mrs. Stossen and her daughter, suitably arrayed for a county garden party function with an infusion of *Almanack de Gotha,* sailed through the narrow grass paddock and the ensuing gooseberry garden with the air of state barges making an unofficial progress along a rural trout stream. There was a certain amount of furtive haste mingled with the stateliness of their advance as though hostile searchlights might be turned on them at any moment; and, as a matter of fact, they were not unobserved. Matilda Cuvering, with the alert eyes of thirteen years and the added advantage of an exalted position in the branches of a medlar tree, had enjoyed a good view of the Stossen flanking movement and had foreseen exactly where it would break down in execution.

"They'll find the door locked, and they'll jolly well have to go back the way they came," she remarked to herself. "Serves them right for not coming in by the proper entrance. What a pity Tarquin Superbus isn't loose in the paddock. After all, as every one else is enjoying themselves, I don't see why Tarquin shouldn't have an afternoon out."

Matilda was of an age when thought is action; she slid down from the branches of the medlar tree, and when she clambered back again, Tarquin, the huge white Yorkshire boar-pig, had exchanged the narrow limits of his sty for the wider range of the grass paddock. The discomfited Stossen expedition, returning in recriminatory but otherwise orderly retreat from the unyielding obstacle of the locked door, came to a sudden halt at the gate dividing the paddock from the gooseberry garden.

"What a villainous-looking animal," exclaimed Mrs. Stossen; "it wasn't there when we came in."

"It's there now, anyhow," said her daughter. "What on earth are we to do? I wish we had never come."

The boar-pig had drawn nearer to the gate for a closer inspection of the human intruders, and stood champing his jaws and blinking his small red eyes in a manner that was doubtless intended to be disconcerting, and, as far as the Stossens were concerned, thoroughly achieved that result.

"Shoo! Hist! Hist! Shoo!" cried the ladies in chorus.

"If they think they're going to drive him away by reciting lists of the kings of Israel and Judah they're laying themselves out for disappointment," observed Matilda from her seat in the medlar tree. As she made the observation aloud Mrs. Stossen became for the first time aware of her presence. A moment or two earlier she would have been anything but pleased at the discovery that the garden was not as deserted as it looked, but now she hailed the fact of the child's presence on the scene with absolute relief.

"Little girl, can you find some one to drive away——" she began hopefully.

"*Comment? Comprends pas,*" was the response.

"Oh, are you French? *Êtes vous française?*"

"*Pas de tout. 'Suis anglaise.*"

"Then why not talk English? I want to know if——"

"*Permettez-moi expliquer.* You see, I'm rather under a cloud," said Matilda. "I'm staying with my aunt, and I was told I must behave particularly well today, as lots of people were coming for a garden party, and I was told to imitate Claude, that's my young cousin, who never does anything wrong except by accident, and then is always apologetic about it. It seems they thought I ate too much raspberry trifle at lunch, and they said Claude never eats too much raspberry trifle. Well, Claude always goes to sleep for half an hour after lunch, because he's told to, and I waited till he was asleep, and tied his hands and started forcible feeding with a whole bucketful of raspberry trifle that they were keeping for the garden party. Lots of it went on to his sailor-suit and some of it on to the bed, but a good deal went down Claude's throat, and they can't say again that he has never been known to eat too much raspberry trifle. That is why I am not allowed to go to the party, and as an additional punishment I must speak French all the afternoon. I've had to tell you all this in English, as there were words like 'forcible feeding' that I didn't know the French for; of course I could have invented them, but if I had said *nourriture obligatoire* you wouldn't have had the least idea what I was talking about. *Mais maintenant, nous parlons français.*"

"Oh, very well, *très bien,*" said Mrs. Stossen reluctantly; in moments of flurry such French as she knew was not under very good control. "*Là à l'autre côté de la porte, est un cochon——*"

"*Un cochon? Ah, le petit charmant!*" exclaimed Matilda with enthusiasm.

"*Mais non, pas du tout petit, et pas tout charmant; un bête féroce——*"

"*Une bête,*" corrected Matilda; "a pig is masculine as long as you call it a pig, but if you lose your temper with it and call it a ferocious beast it becomes one of us at once. French is a dreadfully unsexing language."

"For goodness' sake let us talk English then," said Mrs. Stossen. "Is there any way out of this garden except through the paddock where the pig is?"

"I always go over the wall, by way of the plum tree," said Matilda.

"Dressed as we are, we could hardly do that," said Mrs. Stossen; it was difficult to imagine her doing it in any costume.

"Do you think you could go and get some one who would drive the pig away?" asked Miss Stossen.

"I promised my aunt I would stay here till five o'clock; it's not four yet."

"I am sure, under the circumstances, your aunt would permit——"

"My conscience would not permit," said Matilda with cold dignity.

"We can't stay here till five o'clock," exclaimed Mrs. Stossen with growing exasperation.

"Shall I recite to you to make the time pass quicker?" asked Matilda obligingly. " 'Belinda, the little Breadwinner,' is considered my best piece, or, perhaps, it ought to be something in French. Henri Quartre's address to his soldiers is the only thing I really know in that language."

"If you will go and fetch some one to drive that animal away I will give you something to buy yourself a nice present," said Mrs. Stossen.

Matilda came several inches lower down the medlar tree.

"That is the most practical suggestion you have made yet for getting out of the garden," she remarked cheerfully; "Claude and I are collecting money for the Children's Fresh Air Fund, and we are seeing which of us can collect the biggest sum."

"I shall be very glad to contribute half a crown, very glad indeed," said Mrs. Stossen, digging that coin out of the depths of a receptacle which formed a detached outwork of her toilet.

"Claude is a long way ahead of me at present," continued Matilda, taking no notice of the suggested offering; "you see, he's only eleven, and has golden hair, and those are enormous advantages when you're on the collecting job. Only the other day a Russian lady gave him ten shillings. Russians understand the art of giving far better than we do. I expect Claude will net quite twenty-five shillings this afternoon; he'll have the field to himself, and he'll be able to do the pale, fragile, not-long-for-this-world business to perfection after his raspberry trifle experience. Yes, he'll be *quite* two pounds ahead of me by now."

With much probing and plucking and many regretful murmurs the beleaguered ladies managed to produce seven-and-sixpence between them.

"I am afraid this is all we've got," said Mrs. Stossen.

Matilda showed no sign of coming down either to the earth or to their figure.

"I could not do violence to my conscience for anything less than ten shillings," she announced stiffly.

Mother and daughter muttered certain remarks under their breath, in which the word "beast" was prominent, and probably had no reference to Tarquin.

"I find I *have* got another half-crown," said Mrs. Stossen in a shaking voice; "here you are. Now please fetch some one quickly."

Matilda slipped down from the tree, took possession of the donation, and proceeded to pick up a handful of over-ripe medlars from the grass at her feet. Then she climbed over the gate and addressed herself affectionately to the boar-pig.

"Come, Tarquin, dear old boy; you know you can't resist medlars when they're rotten and squashy."

Tarquin couldn't. By dint of throwing the fruit in front of him at judicious intervals Matilda decoyed him back to his sty, while the delivered captives hurried across the paddock.

"Well, I never! The little minx!" exclaimed Mrs. Stossen when she was safely on the high road. "The animal wasn't savage at all, and as for the ten shillings, I don't believe the Fresh Air Fund will see a penny of it!"

There she was unwarrantably harsh in her judgment. If you examine the books of the fund you will find the acknowledgment: "Collected by Miss Matilda Cuvering, 2*s*. 6*d*."

THE BROGUE

THE hunting season had come to an end, and the Mullets had not succeeded in selling the Brogue. There had been a kind of tradition in the family for the past three or four years, a sort of fatalistic hope, that the Brogue would find a purchaser before the hunting was over; but seasons came and went without anything happening to justify such ill-founded optimism. The animal had been named Berserker in the earlier stages of its career; it had been rechristened the Brogue later on, in recognition of the fact that, once acquired, it was extremely difficult to get rid of. The unkinder wits of the neighbourhood had been known to suggest that the first letter of its name was superfluous. The Brogue had been variously described in sale catalogues as a light-weight hunter, a lady's hack, and, more simply, but still with a touch of imagination, as a useful brown gelding, standing 15.1. Toby Mullet had ridden him for four seasons with the West Wessex; you can ride almost any sort of horse with the West Wessex as long as it is an animal that knows the country. The Brogue knew the country intimately, having personally created most of the gaps that were to be met with in banks and hedges for many miles round. His manners and characteristics were not ideal in the hunting field, but he was probably rather safer to ride to hounds than he was as a hack on country roads. According to the Mullet family, he was not really road-shy, but there were one or two objects of dislike that brought on sudden attacks of what Toby called swerving sickness. Motors and cycles he treated with tolerant disregard, but pigs, wheel-barrows, piles of stones by the roadside, perambulators in a village street, gates painted too aggressively white, and sometimes, but not always, the newer kind of beehives, turned him aside from his tracks in vivid imitation of the zigzag course of forked lightning. If a pheasant rose noisily from the other side of a hedgerow the Brogue would spring into the air at the same moment, but this may have been due to a desire to be companionable. The Mullet family contradicted the widely prevalent report that the horse was a confirmed crib-biter.

It was about the third week in May that Mrs. Mullet, relict of the late Sylvester Mullet, and mother of Toby and a bunch of daughters, assailed Clovis Sangrail on the outskirts of the village with a breathless catalogue of local happenings.

"You know our new neighbour, Mr. Penricarde?" she vociferated; "awfully rich, owns tin mines in Cornwall, middle-aged and rather quiet. He's taken the Red House on a long lease and spent a lot of money on alterations and improvements. Well, Toby's sold him the Brogue!"

Clovis spent a moment or two in assimilating the astonishing news; then he broke out into unstinted congratulation. If he had belonged to a more emotional race he would probably have kissed Mrs. Mullet.

"How wonderfully lucky to have pulled it off at last! Now you can buy a decent animal. I've always said that Toby was clever. Ever so many congratulations."

"Don't congratulate me. It's the most unfortunate thing that could have happened!" said Mrs. Mullet dramatically.

Clovis stared at her in amazement.

"Mr. Penricarde," said Mrs. Mullet, sinking her voice to what she imagined to be an impressive whisper, though it rather resembled a hoarse, excited squeak, "Mr. Penricarde has just begun to pay attentions to Jessie. Slight at first, but now unmistakable. I was a fool not to have seen it sooner. Yesterday, at the Rectory garden party, he asked her what her favourite flowers were, and she told him carnations, and today a whole stack of carnations has arrived, clove and malmaison and lovely dark-red ones, regular exhibition blooms, and a box of chocolates that he must have got on purpose from London. And he's asked her to go round the links with him tomorrow. And now, just at this critical moment, Toby has sold him that animal. It's a calamity!"

"But you've been trying to get the horse off your hands for years," said Clovis.

"I've got a houseful of daughters," said Mrs. Mullet, "and I've been trying—well, not to get them off my hands, of course, but a husband or two wouldn't be amiss among the lot of them; there are six of them, you know."

"I don't know," said Clovis, "I've never counted, but I expect you're right as to the numbers; mothers generally know these things."

"And now," continued Mrs. Mullet, in her tragic whisper, "when there's a rich husband-in-prospect imminent on the horizon Toby goes and sells him that miserable animal. It will probably kill him if he tries to ride it; anyway, it will kill any affection he might have felt towards any member of our family. What is to be done? We can't very well ask to have the horse back; you see, we praised it up like anything when we thought there was a chance of his buying it, and said it was just the animal to suit him."

"Couldn't you steal it out of his stable and send it to grass at some farm miles away?" suggested Clovis. "Write 'Votes for Women' on the stable door, and the thing would pass for a Suffragette outrage. No one who knew the horse could possibly suspect you of wanting to get it back again."

"Every newspaper in the country would ring with the affair," said Mrs. Mullet; "can't you imagine the headline, 'Valuable Hunter Stolen by Suffragettes'? The police would scour the countryside till they found the animal."

"Well, Jessie must try and get it back from Penricarde on the plea that it's an old favourite. She can say it was only sold because the stable had to be pulled down under the terms of an old repairing lease, and that now it has been arranged that the stable is to stand for a couple of years longer."

"It sounds a queer proceeding to ask for a horse back when you've just sold him," said Mrs. Mullet, "but something must be done, and done at once. The man is not used to horses, and I believe I told him it was as quiet as a lamb. After all, lambs go kicking and twisting about as if they were demented, don't they?"

"The lamb has an entirely unmerited character for sedateness," agreed Clovis.

Jessie came back from the golf links next day in a state of mingled elation and concern.

"It's all right about the proposal," she announced, "he came out with it at the sixth hole. I said I must have time to think it over. I accepted him at the seventh."

"My dear," said her mother, "I think a little more maidenly reserve and hesitation would have been advisable, as you've known him so short a time. You might have waited till the ninth hole."

"The seventh is a very long hole," said Jessie; "besides, the tension was putting us both off our game. By the time we'd got to the ninth hole we'd settled lots of things. The honeymoon is to be spent in Corsica, with perhaps a flying visit to Naples if we feel like it, and a week in London to wind up with. Two of his nieces are to be asked to be bridesmaids, so with our lot there will be seven, which is rather a lucky number. You are to wear your pearl grey, with any amount of Honiton lace jabbed into it. By the way, he's coming over this evening to ask your consent to the whole affair. So far all's well, but about the Brogue it's a different matter. I told him the legend about the stable, and how keen we were about buying the horse back, but he seems equally keen on keeping it. He said he must have horse exercise now that he's living in the country, and he's going to start riding tomorrow. He's ridden a few times in the Row on an animal that was accustomed to carry octogenarians and people undergoing rest cures, and that's about all his experience in the saddle—oh, and he rode a pony once in Norfolk, when he was fifteen and the pony twenty-four; and tomorrow he's going to ride the Brogue! I shall be a widow before I'm married, and I do so want to see what Corsica's like; it looks so silly on the map."

Clovis was sent for in haste, and the developments of the situation put before him.

"Nobody can ride that animal with any safety," said Mrs. Mullet, "except Toby, and he knows by long experience what it is going to shy at, and manages to swerve at the same time."

"I did hint to Mr. Penricarde—to Vincent, I should say— that the Brogue didn't like white gates," said Jessie.

"White gates!" exclaimed Mrs. Mullet; "did you mention what effect a pig has on him? He'll have to go past Lockyer's farm to get to the high road, and there's sure to be a pig or two grunting about in the lane."

"He's taken rather a dislike to turkeys lately," said Toby.

"It's obvious that Penricarde mustn't be allowed to go out on that animal," said Clovis, "at least not till Jessie has married him, and tired of him. I tell you what; ask him to a picnic tomorrow, starting at an early hour; he's not the sort to go out for a ride before breakfast. The day after I'll get the rector to drive him over to Crowleigh before lunch, to see the new cottage hospital they're building there. The Brogue will be standing idle in the stable and Toby can offer to exercise it;

then it can pick up a stone or something of the sort and go conveniently lame. If you hurry on the wedding a bit the lameness fiction can be kept up till the ceremony is safely over."

Mrs. Mullet belonged to an emotional race, and she kissed Clovis.

It was nobody's fault that the rain came down in torrents the next morning, making a picnic a fantastic impossibility. It was also nobody's fault, but sheer ill-luck, that the weather cleared up sufficiently in the afternoon to tempt Mr. Penricarde to make his first essay with the Brogue. They did not get as far as the pigs at Lockyer's farm; the Rectory gate was painted a dull unobtrusive green, but it had been white a year or two ago, and the Brogue never forgot that he had been in the habit of making a violent curtsy, a back-pedal and a swerve at this particular point of the road. Subsequently, there being apparently no further call on his services, he broke his way into the Rectory orchard, where he found a hen turkey in a coop; later visitors to the orchard found the coop almost intact, but very little left of the turkey.

Mr. Penricarde, a little stunned and shaken, and suffering from a bruised knee and some minor damages, good-naturedly ascribed the accident to his own inexperience with horses and country roads, and allowed Jessie to nurse him back into complete recovery and golf-fitness within something less than a week.

In the list of wedding presents which the local newspaper published a fortnight or so later appeared the following item:

"Brown saddle-horse, 'The Brogue,' bridegroom's gift to bride."

"Which shows," said Toby Mullet, "that he knew nothing."

"Or else," said Clovis, "that he has a very pleasing wit."

THE OPEN WINDOW

"My aunt will be down presently, Mr. Nuttel," said a very self-possessed young lady of fifteen; "in the meantime you must try and put up with me."

Framton Nuttel endeavoured to say the correct something which should duly flatter the niece of the moment without unduly discounting the aunt that was to come. Privately he doubted more than ever whether these formal visits on a succession of total strangers would do much towards helping the nerve cure which he was supposed to be undergoing.

"I know how it will be," his sister had said when he was preparing to migrate to this rural retreat; "you will bury yourself down there and not speak to a living soul, and your nerves will be worse than ever from moping. I shall just give you letters of introduction to all the people I know there. Some of them, as far as I can remember, were quite nice."

Framton wondered whether Mrs. Sappleton, the lady to whom he was presenting one of the letters of introduction, came into the nice division.

"Do you know many of the people round here?" asked the niece, when she judged that they had had sufficient silent communion.

"Hardly a soul," said Framton. "My sister was staying here, at the Rectory, you know, some four years ago, and she gave me letters of introduction to some of the people here."

He made the last statement in a tone of distinct regret.

"Then you know practically nothing about my aunt?" pursued the self-possessed young lady.

"Only her name and address," admitted the caller. He was wondering whether Mrs. Sappleton was in the married or widowed state. An undefinable something about the room seemed to suggest masculine habitation.

"Her great tragedy happened just three years ago," said the child; "that would be since your sister's time."

"Her tragedy?" asked Framton; somehow in this restful country spot tragedies seemed out of place.

"You may wonder why we keep that window wide open on

an October afternoon," said the niece, indicating a large French window that opened on to a lawn.

"It is quite warm for the time of the year," said Framton; "but has that window got anything to do with the tragedy?"

"Out through that window, three years ago to a day, her husband and her two young brothers went off for their day's shooting. They never came back. In crossing the moor to their favourite snipe-shooting ground they were all three engulfed in a treacherous piece of bog. It had been that dreadful wet summer, you know, and places that were safe in other years gave way suddenly without warning. Their bodies were never recovered. That was the dreadful part of it." Here the child's voice lost its self-possessed note and became falteringly human. "Poor aunt always thinks that they will come back some day, they and the little brown spaniel that was lost with them, and walk in at that window just as they used to do. That is why the window is kept open every evening till it is quite dusk. Poor dear aunt, she has often told me how they went out, her husband with his white waterproof coat over his arm, and Ronnie, her youngest brother, singing, 'Bertie, why do you bound?' as he always did to tease her, because she said it got on her nerves. Do you know, sometimes on still, quiet evenings like this, I almost get a creepy feeling that they will all walk in through that window——"

She broke off with a little shudder. It was a relief to Framton when the aunt bustled into the room with a whirl of apologies for being late in making her appearance.

"I hope Vera has been amusing you?" she said.

"She has been very interesting," said Framton.

"I hope you don't mind the open window," said Mrs. Sappleton briskly; "my husband and brothers will be home directly from shooting, and they always come in this way. They've been out for snipe in the marshes today, so they'll make a fine mess over my poor carpets. So like you men-folk, isn't it?"

She rattled on cheerfully about the shooting and the scarcity of birds, and the prospects for duck in the winter. To Framton it was all purely horrible. He made a desperate but only partially successful effort to turn the talk on to a less ghastly topic; he was conscious that his hostess was giving him only a fragment of her attention, and her eyes were constantly straying past him to the open window and the lawn beyond. It was certainly an unfortunate coincidence that he should have paid his visit on this tragic anniversary.

"The doctors agree in ordering me complete rest, an absence of mental excitement, and avoidance of anything in the nature of violent physical exercise," announced Framton, who laboured under the tolerably wide-spread delusion that total strangers and chance acquaintances are hungry for the least detail of one's ailments and infirmities, their cause and cure. "On the matter of diet they are not so much in agreement," he continued.

"No?" said Mrs. Sappleton, in a voice which only replaced a yawn at the last moment. Then she suddenly brightened into alert attention—but not to what Framton was saying.

"Here they are at last!" she cried. "Just in time for tea, and don't they look as if they were muddy up to the eyes!"

Framton shivered slightly and turned towards the niece with a look intended to convey sympathetic comprehension. The child was staring out through the open window with dazed horror in her eyes. In a chill shock of nameless fear Framton swung round in his seat and looked in the same direction.

In the deepening twilight three figures were walking across the lawn towards the window; they all carried guns under their arms, and one of them was additionally burdened with a white coat hung over his shoulders. A tired brown spaniel kept close to their heels. Noiselessly they neared the house, and then a hoarse young voice chanted out of the dusk: "I said, Bertie, why do you bound?"

Framton grabbed wildly at his stick and hat; the hall-door, the gravel-drive, and the front gate were dimly noted stages in his headlong retreat. A cyclist coming along the road had to run into the hedge to avoid imminent collision.

"Here we are, my dear," said the bearer of the white mackintosh, coming in through the window; "fairly muddy, but most of it's dry. Who was that who bolted out as we came up?"

"A most extraordinary man, a Mr. Nuttel," said Mrs. Sappleton; "could only talk about his illnesses, and dashed off without a word of good-bye or apology when you arrived. One would think he had seen a ghost."

"I expect it was the spaniel," said the niece calmly; "he told me he had a horror of dogs. He was once hunted into a cemetery somewhere on the banks of the Ganges by a pack of pariah dogs, and had to spend the night in a newly dug grave with the creatures snarling and grinning and foaming just above him. Enough to make any one lose their nerve."

Romance at short notice was her speciality.

THE SCHARTZ-METTERKLUME METHOD

LADY CARLOTTA stepped out on to the platform of the small wayside station and took a turn or two up and down its uninteresting length, to kill time till the train should be pleased to proceed on its way. Then, in the roadway beyond, she saw a horse struggling with a more than ample load, and a carter of the sort that seems to bear a sullen hatred against the animal that helps him to earn a living. Lady Carlotta promptly betook her to the roadway, and put rather a different complexion on the struggle. Certain of her acquaintances were wont to give her plentiful admonition as to the undesirability of interfering on behalf of a distressed animal, such interference being "none of her business." Only once had she put the doctrine of non-interference into practice, when one of its most eloquent exponents had been besieged for nearly three hours in a small and extremely uncomfortable may-tree by an angry boar-pig, while Lady Carlotta, on the other side of the fence, had proceeded with the water-colour sketch she was engaged on, and refused to interfere between the boar and his prisoner. It is to be feared that she lost the friendship of the ultimately rescued lady. On this occasion she merely lost the train, which gave way to the first sign of impatience it had shown throughout the journey, and steamed off without her. She bore the desertion with philosophical indifference; her friends and relations were thoroughly well used to the fact of her luggage arriving without her. She wired a vague noncommittal message to her destination to say that she was coming on "by another train." Before she had time to think what her next move might be, she was confronted by an imposingly attired lady, who seemed to be taking a prolonged mental inventory of her clothes and looks.

"You must be Miss Hope, the governess I've come to meet," said the apparition, in a tone that admitted of very little argument.

"Very well, if I must I must," said Lady Carlotta to herself with dangerous meekness.

"I am Mrs. Quabarl," continued the lady; "and where, pray, is your luggage?"

"It's gone astray," said the alleged governess, falling in with the excellent rule of life that the absent are always to blame; the luggage had, in point of fact, behaved with perfect correctitude. "I've just telegraphed about it," she added, with a nearer approach to truth.

"How provoking," said Mrs. Quabarl; "these railway companies are so careless. However, my maid can lend you things for the night," and she led the way to her car.

During the drive to the Quabarl mansion Lady Carlotta was impressively introduced to the nature of the charge that had been thrust upon her; she learned that Claude and Wilfrid were delicate, sensitive young people, that Irene had the artistic temperament highly developed, and that Viola was something or other else of a mould equally commonplace among children of that class and type in the twentieth century.

"I wish them not only to be *taught*," said Mrs. Quabarl, "but *interested* in what they learn. In their history lessons, for instance, you must try to make them feel that they are being introduced to the life-stories of men and women who really lived, not merely committing a mass of names and dates to memory. French, of course, I shall expect you to talk at meal-times several days in the week."

"I shall talk French four days of the week and Russian in the remaining three."

"Russian? My dear Miss Hope, no one in the house speaks or understands Russian."

"That will not embarrass me in the least," said Lady Carlotta coldly.

Mrs. Quabarl, to use a colloquial expression, was knocked off her perch. She was one of those imperfectly self-assured individuals who are magnificent and autocratic as long as they are not seriously opposed. The least show of unexpected resistance goes a long way towards rendering them cowed and apologetic. When the new governess failed to express wondering admiration of the large newly purchased and expensive car, and lightly alluded to the superior advantages of one or two makes which had just been put on the market, the discomfiture of her patroness became almost abject. Her feelings were those which might have animated a general of ancient warfaring days, on beholding his heaviest battle-elephant ignominiously driven off the field by slingers and javelin throwers.

At dinner that evening, although reinforced by her husband, who usually duplicated her opinions and lent her moral support generally, Mrs. Quabarl regained none of her lost ground. The governess not only helped herself well and truly to wine, but held forth with considerable show of critical knowledge on various vintage matters, concerning which the Quabarls were in no wise able to pose as authorities. Previous governesses had limited their conversation on the wine topic to a respectful and doubtless sincere expression of a preference for water. When this one went as far as to recommend a wine firm in whose hands you could not go very far wrong Mrs. Quabarl thought it time to turn the conversation into more usual channels.

"We got very satisfactory references about you from Canon Teep," she observed; "a very estimable man, I should think."

"Drinks like a fish and beats his wife, otherwise a very lovable character," said the governess imperturbably.

"My *dear* Miss Hope! I trust you are exaggerating," exclaimed the Quabarls in unison.

"One must in justice admit that there is some provocation," continued the romancer. "Mrs. Teep is quite the most irritating bridge-player that I have ever sat down with; her leads and declarations would condone a certain amount of brutality in her partner, but to souse her with the contents of the only soda-water syphon in the house on a Sunday afternoon, when one couldn't get another, argues an indifference to the comfort of others which I cannot altogether overlook. You may think me hasty in my judgments, but it was practically on account of the syphon incident that I left."

"We will talk of this some other time," said Mrs. Quabarl hastily.

"I shall never allude to it again," said the governess with decision.

Mr. Quabarl made a welcome diversion by asking what studies the new instructress proposed to inaugurate on the morrow.

"History to begin with," she informed him.

"Ah, history," he observed sagely; "now in teaching them history you must take care to interest them in what they learn. You must make them feel that they are being introduced to the life-stories of men and women who really lived——"

"I've told her all that," interposed Mrs. Quabarl.

"I teach history on the Schartz-Metterklume method," said the governess loftily.

"Ah, yes," said her listeners, thinking it expedient to assume an acquaintance at least with the name.

"What are you children doing out here?" demanded Mrs. Quabarl the next morning, on finding Irene sitting rather glumly at the head of the stairs, while her sister was perched in an attitude of depressed discomfort on the window-seat behind her, with a wolf-skin rug almost covering her.

"We are having a history lesson," came the unexpected reply. "I am supposed to be Rome, and Viola up there is the she-wolf; not a real wolf, but the figure of one that the Romans used to set store by—I forget why. Claude and Wilfrid have gone to fetch the shabby women."

"The shabby women?"

"Yes, they've got to carry them off. They didn't want to, but Miss Hope got one of father's fives-bats and said she'd give them a number nine spanking if they didn't, so they've gone to do it."

A loud, angry screaming from the direction of the lawn drew Mrs. Quabarl thither in hot haste, fearful lest the threatened castigation might even now be in process of infliction. The outcry, however, came principally from the two small daughters of the lodge-keeper, who were being hauled and pushed towards the house by the panting and dishevelled Claude and Wilfrid, whose task was rendered even more arduous by the incessant, if not very effectual, attacks of the captured maidens' small brother. The governess, fives-bat in hand, sat negligently on the stone balustrade, presiding over the scene with the cold impartiality of a Goddess of Battles. A furious and repeated chorus of "I'll tell muvver" rose from the lodge children, but the lodge-mother, who was hard of hearing, was for the moment immersed in the preoccupation of her washtub. After an apprehensive glance in the direction of the lodge (the good woman was gifted with the highly militant temper which is sometimes the privilege of deafness) Mrs. Quabarl flew indignantly to the rescue of the struggling captives.

"Wilfrid! Claude! Let those children go at once. Miss Hope, what on earth is the meaning of this scene?"

"Early Roman history; the Sabine women, don't you know? It's the Schartz-Metterklume method to make children understand history by acting it themselves; fixes it in their memory, you know. Of course, if, thanks to your interference, your boys go through life thinking that the Sabine women ultimately escaped, I really cannot be held responsible."

"You may be very clever and modern, Miss Hope," said Mrs. Quabarl firmly, "but I should like you to leave here by the next train. Your luggage will be sent after you as soon as it arrives."

"I'm not certain exactly where I shall be for the next few days," said the dismissed instructress of youth; "you might keep my luggage till I wire my address. There are only a couple of trunks and some golf-clubs and a leopard cub."

"A leopard cub!" gasped Mrs. Quabarl. Even in her departure this extraordinary person seemed destined to leave a trail of embarrassment behind her.

"Well, it's rather left off being a cub; it's more than half-grown, you know. A fowl every day and a rabbit on Sundays is what it usually gets. Raw beef makes it too excitable. Don't trouble about getting the car for me, I'm rather inclined for a walk."

And Lady Carlotta strode out of the Quabarl horizon.

The advent of the genuine Miss Hope, who had made a mistake as to the day on which she was due to arrive, caused a turmoil which that good lady was quite unused to inspiring. Obviously the Quabarl family had been woefully befooled, but a certain amount of relief came with the knowledge.

"How tiresome for you, dear Carlotta," said her hostess, when the overdue guest ultimately arrived; "how very tiresome losing your train and having to stop overnight in a strange place."

"Oh, dear, no," said Lady Carlotta; "not at all tiresome—for me."

THE SEVENTH PULLET

"IT'S not the daily grind that I complain of," said Blenkinthrope resentfully; "it's the dull grey sameness of my life outside of office hours. Nothing of interest comes my way, nothing remarkable or out of the common. Even the little things that I do try to find some interest in don't seem to interest other people. Things in my garden, for instance."

"The potato that weighed just over two pounds," said his friend Gorworth.

"Did I tell you about that?" said Blenkinthrope; "I was telling the others in the train this morning. I forget if I'd told you."

"To be exact, you told me that it weighed just under two pounds, but I took into account the fact that abnormal vegetables and freshwater fish have an after-life, in which growth is not arrested."

"You're just like the others," said Blenkinthrope sadly, "you only make fun of it."

"The fault is with the potato, not with us," said Gorworth; "we are not in the least interested in it because it is not in the least interesting. The men you go up in the train with every day are just in the same case as yourself; their lives are commonplace and not very interesting to themselves, and they certainly are not going to wax enthusiastic over the commonplace events in other men's lives. Tell them something startling, dramatic, piquant, that has happened to yourself or to some one in your family, and you will capture their interest at once. They will talk about you with a certain personal pride to all their acquaintances. 'Man I know intimately, fellow called Blenkinthrope, lives down my way, had two of his fingers clawed clean off by a lobster he was carrying home to supper. Doctor says entire hand may have to come off.' Now that is conversation of a very high order. But imagine walking into a tennis club with the remark 'I know a man who has grown a potato weighing two and a quarter pounds.'"

"But hang it all, my dear fellow," said Blenkinthrope impatiently, "haven't I just told you that nothing of a remarkable nature ever happens to me?"

"Invent something," said Gorworth. Since winning a prize for excellence in Scriptural knowledge at a preparatory school he had felt licensed to be a little more unscrupulous than the circle he moved in. Much might surely be excused to one who in early life could give a list of seventeen trees mentioned in the Old Testament.

"What sort of thing?" asked Blenkinthrope, somewhat snappishly.

"A snake got into your hen-run yesterday morning and killed six out of seven pullets, first mesmerizing them with its eyes and then biting them as they stood helpless. The seventh pullet was one of that French sort, with feathers all over its eyes, so it escaped the mesmeric snare, and just flew at what it could see of the snake and pecked it to pieces."

"Thank you," said Blenkinthrope stiffly, "it's a very clever invention. If such a thing had really happened in my poultry-run I admit I should have been proud and interested to tell people about it. But I'd rather stick to fact, even if it is plain fact." All the same his mind dwelt wistfully on the story of the Seventh Pullet. He could picture himself telling it in the train amid the absorbed interest of his fellow-passengers. Unconsciously all sorts of little details and improvements began to suggest themselves.

Wistfulness was still his dominant mood when he took his seat in the railway carriage the next morning. Opposite him sat Stevenham, who had attained to a recognized brevet of importance through the fact of an uncle having dropped dead in the act of voting at a Parliamentary election. That had happened three years ago, but Stevenham was still deferred to on all questions of home and foreign politics.

"Hullo, how's the giant mushroom, or whatever it was?" was all the notice Blenkinthrope got from his fellow travellers.

Young Duckby, whom he mildly disliked, speedily monopolized the general attention by an account of a domestic bereavement.

"Had four young pigeons carried off last night by a whacking big rat. Oh, a monster he must have been; you could tell by the size of the hole he made breaking into the loft."

No moderate-sized rat ever seemed to carry out any preda-

tory operations in these regions; they were all enormous in
their enormity.

"Pretty hard lines that," continued Duckby, seeing that he
had secured the attention and respect of the company;
"four squeakers carried off at one swoop. You'd find it
rather hard to match that in the way of unlooked-for bad
luck."

"I had six pullets out of a pen of seven killed by a snake
yesterday afternoon," said Blenkinthrope, in a voice which he
hardly recognized as his own.

"By a snake?" came in excited chorus.

"It fascinated them with its deadly, glittering eyes, one after
the other, and struck them down while they stood helpless.
A bedridden neighbour, who wasn't able to call for assistance,
witnessed it all from her bedroom window."

"Well, I never!" broke in the chorus, with variations.

"The interesting part of it is about the seventh pullet, the
one that didn't get killed," resumed Blenkinthrope, slowly
lighting a cigarette. His diffidence had left him, and he was
beginning to realize how safe and easy depravity can seem
once one has the courage to begin. "The six dead birds were
Minorcas; the seventh was a Houdan with a mop of feathers
all over its eyes. It could hardly see the snake at all, so of
course it wasn't mesmerized like the others. It just could see
something wriggling on the ground, and went for it and pecked
it to death."

"Well, I'm blessed!" exclaimed the chorus.

In the course of the next few days Blenkinthrope discovered
how little the loss of one's self-respect affects one when one
has gained the esteem of the world. His story found its way
into one of the poultry papers, and was copied thence into a
daily news-sheet as a matter of general interest. A lady wrote
from the North of Scotland recounting a similar episode which
she had witnessed as occurring between a stoat and a blind
grouse. Somehow a lie seems so much less reprehensible when
one can call it a lee.

For a while the adapter of the Seventh Pullet story enjoyed
to the full his altered standing as a person of consequence, one
who had had some share in the strange events of his times.
Then he was thrust once again into the cold grey background
by the sudden blossoming into importance of Smith-Paddon,

a daily fellow traveller, whose little girl had been knocked down and nearly hurt by a car belonging to a musical-comedy actress. The actress was not in the car at the time, but she was in numerous photographs which appeared in the illustrated papers of Zoto Dobreen inquiring after the well-being of Maisie, daughter of Edmund Smith-Paddon, Esq. With this new human interest to absorb them the travelling companions were almost rude when Blenkinthrope tried to explain his contrivance for keeping vipers and peregrine falcons out of his chicken-run.

Gorworth, to whom he unburdened himself in private, gave him the same counsel as theretofore.

"Invent something."

"Yes, but what?"

The ready affirmative coupled with the question betrayed a significant shifting of the ethical standpoint.

It was a few days later that Blenkinthrope revealed a chapter of family history to the customary gathering in the railway carriage.

"Curious thing happened to my aunt, the one who lives in Paris," he began. He had several aunts, but they were all geographically distributed over Greater London.

"She was sitting on a seat in the Bois the other afternoon, after lunching at the Roumanian Legation."

Whatever the story gained in picturesqueness for the dragging-in of diplomatic "atmosphere," it ceased from the moment to command any acceptance as a record of current events. Gorworth had warned his neophyte that this would be the case, but the traditional enthusiasm of the neophyte had triumphed over discretion.

"She was feeling rather drowsy, the effect probably of the champagne, which she's not in the habit of taking in the middle of the day."

A subdued murmur of admiration went round the company. Blenkinthrope's aunts were not used to taking champagne in the middle of the year, regarding it exclusively as a Christmas and New Year accessory.

"Presently a rather portly gentleman passed by her seat and paused an instant to light a cigar. At that moment a youngish man came up behind him, drew the blade from a swordstick, and stabbed him half a dozen times through and through.

'Scoundrel,' he cried to his victim, 'you do not know me. My name is Henri Leturc.' The elder man wiped away some of the blood that was spattering his clothes, turned to his assailant, and said: 'And since when has an attempted assassination been considered an introduction?' Then he finished lighting his cigar and walked away. My aunt had intended screaming for the police, but seeing the indifference with which the principal in the affair treated the matter she felt that it would be an impertinence on her part to interfere. Of course I need hardly say she put the whole thing down to the effects of a warm, drowsy afternoon and the Legation champagne. Now comes the astonishing part of my story. A fortnight later a bank manager was stabbed to death with a swordstick in that very part of the Bois. His assassin was the son of a charwoman formerly working at the bank, who had been dismissed from her job by the manager on account of chronic intemperance. His name was Henri Leturc."

From that moment Blenkinthrope was tacitly accepted as the Munchausen of the party. No effort was spared to draw him out from day to day in the exercise of testing their powers of credulity, and Blenkinthrope, in the false security of an assured and receptive audience, waxed industrious and ingenious in supplying the demand for marvels. Duckby's satirical story of a tame otter that had a tank in the garden to swim in, and whined restlessly whenever the water-rate was overdue, was scarcely an unfair parody of some of Blenkinthrope's wilder efforts. And then one day came Nemesis.

Returning to his villa one evening Blenkinthrope found his wife sitting in front of a pack of cards, which she was scrutinizing with unusual concentration.

"The same old patience-game?" he asked carelessly.

"No, dear; this is the Death's Head patience, the most difficult of them all. I've never got it to work out, and somehow I should be rather frightened if I did. Mother only got it out once in her life; she was afraid of it, too. Her great-aunt had done it once and fallen dead from excitement the next moment, and Mother always had a feeling that she would die if she ever got it out. She died the same night that she did it. She was in bad health at the time, certainly, but it was a strange coincidence."

"Don't do it if it frightens you," was Blenkinthrope's practical comment as he left the room. A few minutes later his wife called to him.

"John, it gave me such a turn, I nearly got it out. Only the five of diamonds held me up at the end. I really thought I'd done it."

"Why, you can do it," said Blenkinthrope, who had come back to the room; "if you shift the eight of clubs on to that open nine the five can be moved on to the six."

His wife made the suggested move with hasty, trembling fingers, and piled the outstanding cards on to their respective packs. Then she followed the example of her mother and great-grand-aunt.

Blenkinthrope had been genuinely fond of his wife, but in the midst of his bereavement one dominant thought obtruded itself. Something sensational and real had at last come into his life; no longer was it a grey, colourless record. The head-lines which might appropriately describe his domestic tragedy kept shaping themselves in his brain. "Inherited presentiment comes true." "The Death's Head patience: Card-game that justified its sinister name in three generations." He wrote out a full story of the fatal occurrence for the *Essex Vedette*, the editor of which was a friend of his, and to another friend he gave a condensed account, to be taken up to the office of one of the halfpenny dailies. But in both cases his reputation as a romancer stood fatally in the way of the fulfilment of his ambitions. "Not the right thing to be Munchausening in a time of sorrow," agreed his friends among themselves, and a brief note of regret at the "sudden death of the wife of our respected neighbour, Mr. John Blenkinthrope, from heart failure," appearing in the news column of the local paper was the forlorn outcome of his visions of widespread publicity.

Blenkinthrope shrank from the society of his erstwhile travelling companions and took to travelling townwards by an earlier train. He sometimes tries to enlist the sympathy and attention of a chance acquaintance in details of the whistling prowess of his best canary or the dimensions of his largest beetroot; he scarcely recognizes himself as the man who was once spoken about and pointed out as the owner of the Seventh Pullet.

CLOVIS ON PARENTAL
RESPONSIBILITIES

MARION EGGELBY sat talking to Clovis on the only subject that she ever willingly talked about—her offspring and their varied perfections and accomplishments. Clovis was not in what could be called a receptive mood; the younger generation of Eggelby, depicted in the glowing improbable colours of parent impressionism, aroused in him no enthusiasm. Mrs. Eggelby, on the other hand, was furnished with enthusiasm enough for two.

"You would like Eric," she said, argumentatively rather than hopefully. Clovis had intimated very unmistakably that he was unlikely to care extravagantly for either Amy or Willie. "Yes, I feel sure you would like Eric. Every one takes to him at once. You know, he always reminds me of that famous picture of the youthful David—I forget who it's by, but it's very well known."

"That would be sufficient to set me against him, if I saw much of him," said Clovis. "Just imagine at auction bridge, for instance, when one was trying to concentrate one's mind on what one's partner's original declaration had been, and to remember what suits one's opponents had originally discarded, what it would be like to have some one persistently reminding one of a picture of the youthful David. It would be simply maddening. If Eric did that I should detest him."

"Eric doesn't play bridge," said Mrs. Eggelby with dignity.

"Doesn't he?" asked Clovis; "why not?"

"None of my children have been brought up to play card games," said Mrs. Eggelby; "draughts and halma and those sort of games I encourage. Eric is considered quite a wonderful draughts-player."

"You are strewing dreadful risks in the path of your family," said Clovis; "a friend of mine who is a prison chaplain told me that among the worst criminal cases that have come under his notice, men condemned to death or to long periods of penal servitude, there was not a single bridge-player. On the other hand, he knew at least two expert draughts-players among them."

"I really don't see what my boys have got to do with the criminal classes," said Mrs. Eggelby resentfully. "They have been most carefully brought up, I can assure you that."

"That shows that you were nervous as to how they would turn out," said Clovis. "Now, my mother never bothered about bringing me up. She just saw to it that I got whacked at decent intervals and was taught the difference between right and wrong; there is some difference, you know, but I've forgotten what it is."

"Forgotten the difference between right and wrong!" exclaimed Mrs. Eggelby.

"Well, you see, I took up natural history and a whole lot of other subjects at the same time, and one can't remember everything, can one? I used to know the difference between the Sardinian dormouse and the ordinary kind, and whether the wryneck arrives at our shores earlier than the cuckoo, or the other way round, and how long the walrus takes in growing to maturity; I dare say you knew all those sort of things once, but I bet you've forgotten them."

"Those things are not important," said Mrs. Eggelby, "but——"

"The fact that we've both forgotten them proves that they *are* important," said Clovis; "you must have noticed that it's always the important things that one forgets, while the trivial, unnecessary facts of life stick in one's memory. There's my cousin, Editha Clubberly, for instance; I can never forget that her birthday is on the twelfth of October. It's a matter of utter indifference to me on what date her birthday falls, or whether she was born at all; either fact seems to me absolutely trivial, or unnecessary—I've heaps of other cousins to go on with. On the other hand, when I'm staying with Hildegarde Shrubley I can never remember the important circumstance whether her first husband got his unenviable reputation on the Turf or the Stock Exchange, and that uncertainty rules Sport and Finance out of the conversation at once. One can never mention travel, either, because her second husband had to live permanently abroad."

"Mrs. Shrubley and I move in very different circles," said Mrs. Eggelby stiffly.

"No one who knows Hildegarde could possibly accuse her of moving in a circle," said Clovis; "her view of life seems to be a non-stop run with an inexhaustible supply of petrol. If she can get some one else to pay for the petrol so much the better. I don't mind confessing to you that she has taught me more than any other woman I can think of."

"What kind of knowledge?" demanded Mrs. Eggelby, with the air a jury might collectively wear when finding a verdict without leaving the box.

"Well, among other things, she's introduced me to at least four different ways of cooking lobster," said Clovis gratefully. "That, of course, wouldn't appeal to you; people who abstain from the pleasures of the card-table never really appreciate the finer possibilities of the dining-table. I suppose their powers of enlightened enjoyment get atrophied from disuse."

"An aunt of mine was very ill after eating a lobster," said Mrs. Eggelby.

"I dare say, if we knew more of her history, we should find out that she'd often been ill before eating the lobster. Aren't you concealing the fact that she'd had measles and influenza and nervous headache and hysteria, and other things that aunts do have, long before she ate the lobster? Aunts that have never known a day's illness are very rare; in fact, I don't personally know of any. Of course if she ate it as a child of two weeks old it might have been her first illness— and her last. But if that was the case I think you should have said so."

"I must be going," said Mrs. Eggelby, in a tone which had been thoroughly sterilized of even perfunctory regret.

Clovis rose with an air of graceful reluctance.

"I have so enjoyed our little talk about Eric," he said; "I quite look forward to meeting him some day."

"Good-bye," said Mrs. Eggelby frostily; the supplementary remark which she made at the back of her throat was:

"I'll take care that you never shall!"

A HOLIDAY TASK

KENELM JERTON entered the dining-hall of the Golden Galleon Hotel in the full crush of the luncheon hour. Nearly every seat was occupied, and small additional tables had been brought in, where floor space permitted, to accommodate late-comers, with the result that many of the tables were almost touching each other. Jerton was beckoned by a waiter to the only vacant table that was discernible, and took his seat with the uncomfortable and wholly groundless idea that nearly every one in the room was staring at him. He was a youngish man of ordinary appearance, quiet of dress and unobtrusive of manner, and he could never wholly rid himself of the idea that a fierce light of public scrutiny beat on him as though he had been a notability or a super-nut. After he had ordered his lunch there came the unavoidable interval of waiting, with nothing to do but to stare at the flower-vase on his table and to be stared at (in imagination) by several flappers, some maturer beings of the same sex, and a satirical-looking Jew. In order to carry off the situation with some appearance of unconcern he became spuriously interested in the contents of the flower-vase.

"What is the name of those roses, d'you know?" he asked the waiter. The waiter was ready at all times to conceal his ignorance concerning items of the wine-list or *menu*; he was frankly ignorant as to the specific name of the roses.

"*Amy Silvester Partington,*" said a voice at Jerton's elbow.

The voice came from a pleasant-faced, well-dressed young woman who was sitting at a table that almost touched Jerton's. He thanked her hurriedly and nervously for the information, and made some inconsequent remark about the flowers.

"It is a curious thing," said the young woman, "that I should be able to tell you the name of those roses without an effort of memory, because if you were to ask me my name I should be utterly unable to give it to you."

Jerton had not harboured the least intention of extending his thirst for name-labels to his neighbour. After her rather remarkable announcement, however, he was obliged to say something in the way of polite inquiry.

"Yes," answered the lady, "I suppose it is a case of partial loss of memory. I was in the train coming down here; my ticket told me that I had come from Victoria and was bound for this place. I had a couple of five-pound notes and a sovereign on me, no visiting cards or any other means of identification, and no idea as to who I am. I can only hazily recollect that I have a title; I am Lady Somebody—beyond that my mind is a blank."

"Hadn't you any luggage with you?" asked Jerton.

"That is what I didn't know. I knew the name of this hotel and made up my mind to come here, and when the hotel porter who meets the trains asked if I had any luggage I had to invent a dressing-bag and dress-basket; I could always pretend that they had gone astray. I gave him the name of Smith, and presently he emerged from a confused pile of luggage and passengers with a dressing-bag and dress-basket labelled Kestrel-Smith. I had to take them; I don't see what else I could have done."

Jerton said nothing, but he rather wondered what the lawful owner of the baggage would do.

"Of course it was dreadful arriving at a strange hotel with the name of Kestrel-Smith, but it would have been worse to have arrived without luggage. Anyhow, I hate causing trouble."

Jerton had visions of harassed railway officials and distraught Kestrel-Smiths, but he made no attempt to clothe his mental picture in words. The lady continued her story.

"Naturally, none of my keys would fit the things, but I told an intelligent page-boy that I had lost my key-ring, and he had the locks forced in a twinkling. Rather too intelligent, that boy; he will probably end in Dartmoor. The Kestrel-Smith toilet tools aren't up to much, but they are better than nothing."

"If you feel sure that you have a title," said Jerton, "why not get hold of a peerage and go right through it?"

"I tried that. I skimmed through the list of the House of Lords in *Whitaker*, but a mere printed string of names conveys awfully little to one, you know. If you were an army officer and had lost your identity you might pore over the Army List for months without finding out who you were. I'm going on another tack; I'm trying to find out by various little tests who I am *not*—that will narrow the range of uncertainty down a bit. You may have noticed, for instance, that I'm lunching principally off lobster Newburg."

Jerton had not ventured to notice anything of the sort.

"It's an extravagance, because it's one of the most expensive dishes on the *menu*, but at any rate it proves that I'm not Lady Starping; she never touches shell-fish, and poor Lady Braddleshrub has no digestion at all; if I am *her* I shall certainly die in agony in the course of the afternoon, and the duty of finding out who I am will devolve on the Press and the police and those sort of people; I shall be past caring. Lady Knewford doesn't know one rose from another and she hates men, so she wouldn't have spoken to you in any case; and Lady Mousehilton flirts with every man she meets—I haven't flirted with you, have I?"

Jerton hastily gave the required assurance.

"Well, you see," continued the lady, "that knocks four off the list at once."

"It'll be rather a lengthy process bringing the list down to one," said Jerton.

"Oh, but, of course, there are heaps of them that I couldn't possibly be—women who've got grandchildren or sons old enough to have celebrated their coming of age. I've only got to consider the ones about my own age. I tell you how you might help me this afternoon, if you don't mind; go through any of the back numbers of *Country Life* and those sort of papers that you can find in the smoking-room, and see if you come across my portrait with infant son or anything of that sort. It won't take you ten minutes. I'll meet you in the lounge about tea-time. Thanks awfully."

And the Fair Unknown, having graciously pressed Jerton into the search for her lost identity, rose and left the room. As she passed the young man's table she halted for a moment and whispered:

"Did you notice that I tipped the waiter a shilling? We can cross Lady Ulwight off the list; she would have died rather than do that."

At five o'clock Jerton made his way to the hotel lounge; he had spent a diligent but fruitless quarter of an hour among the illustrated weeklies in the smoking-room. His new acquaintance was seated at a small tea-table, with a waiter hovering in attendance.

"China tea or Indian?" she asked as Jerton came up.

"China, please, and nothing to eat. Have you discovered anything?"

"Only negative information. I'm not Lady Befnal. She disapproves dreadfully of any form of gambling, so when I recognized a well-known bookmaker in the hotel lobby I went and put a tenner on an unnamed filly by William the Third out of Mitrovitza for the three-fifteen race. I suppose the fact of the animal being nameless was what attracted me."

"Did it win?" asked Jerton.

"No, came in fourth, the most irritating thing a horse can do when you've backed it win or place. Anyhow, I know now that I'm not Lady Befnal."

"It seems to me that the knowledge was rather dearly bought," commented Jerton.

"Well, yes, it has rather cleared me out," admitted the identity-seeker; "a florin is about all I've got left on me. The lobster Newburg made my lunch rather an expensive one, and, of course, I had to tip that boy for what he did to the Kestrel-Smith locks. I've got rather a useful idea, though. I feel certain that I belong to the Pivot Club; I'll go back to town and ask the hall porter there if there are any letters for me. He knows all the members by sight, and if there are any letters or telephone messages waiting for me, of course that will solve the problem. If he says there aren't any, I shall say: 'You know who I am, don't you?' so I'll find out anyway."

The plan seemed a sound one; a difficulty in its execution suggested itself to Jerton.

"Of course," said the lady, when he hinted at the obstacle, "there's my fare back to town, and my bill here and cabs and things. If you lend me three pounds that ought to see me through comfortably. Thanks ever so. Then there is the question of that luggage: I don't want to be saddled with that for the rest of my life. I'll have it brought down to the hall and you can pretend to mount guard over it while I'm writing a letter. Then I shall just slip away to the station, and you can wander off to the smoking-room, and they can do what they like with the things. They'll advertise them after a bit and the owner can claim them."

Jerton acquiesced in the manœuvre, and duly mounted guard over the luggage while its temporary owner slipped unobtrusively out of the hotel. Her departure was not, however, altogether unnoticed. Two gentlemen were strolling past Jerton, and one of them remarked to the other:

"Did you see that tall young woman in grey who went out just now? She is the Lady——"

His promenade carried him out of earshot at the critical moment when he was about to disclose the elusive identity. The Lady Who? Jerton could scarcely run after a total stranger, break into his conversation, and ask him for information concerning a chance passer-by. Besides, it was desirable that he should keep up the appearance of looking after the luggage. In a minute or two, however, the important personage, the man who knew, came strolling back alone. Jerton summoned up all his courage and waylaid him.

"I think I heard you say you knew the lady who went out of the hotel a few minutes ago, a tall lady, dressed in grey. Excuse me for asking if you could tell me her name; I've been talking to her for half an hour; she—er—she knows all my people and seems to know me, so I suppose I've met her somewhere before, but I'm blest if I can put a name to her. Could you——?"

"Certainly. She's a Mrs. Stroope."

"*Mrs.?*" queried Jerton.

"Yes, she's the Lady Champion at golf in my part of the world. An awful good sort, and goes about a good deal in Society, but she has an awkward habit of losing her memory every now and then, and gets into all sorts of fixes. She's furious, too, if you make any allusion to it afterwards. Good day, sir."

The stranger passed on his way, and before Jerton had had time to assimilate his information he found his whole attention centred on an angry-looking lady who was making loud and fretful-seeming inquiries of the hotel clerks.

"Has any luggage been brought here from the station by mistake, a dress-basket and dressing-case, with the name Kestrel-Smith? It can't be traced anywhere. I saw it put in at Victoria, that I'll swear. Why—there *is* my luggage! and the locks have been tampered with!"

Jerton heard no more. He fled down to the Turkish bath, and stayed there for hours.

↖ THE STALLED OX

THEOPHIL ESHLEY was an artist by profession, a cattle painter by force of environment. It is not to be supposed that he lived on a ranch or a dairy farm, in an atmosphere pervaded with horn and hoof, milking-stool, and branding-iron. His home was in a park-like, villa-dotted district that only just escaped the reproach of being suburban. On one side of his garden there abutted a small, picturesque meadow, in which an enter-prising neighbour pastured some small picturesque cows of the Channel Island persuasion. At noonday in summertime the cows stood knee-deep in tall meadow-grass under the shade of a group of walnut trees, with the sunlight falling in dappled patches on their mouse-sleek coats. Eshley had conceived and executed a dainty picture of two reposeful milch-cows in a setting of walnut tree and meadow-grass and filtered sun-beam, and the Royal Academy had duly exposed the same on the walls of its Summer Exhibition. The Royal Academy encourages orderly, methodical habits in its children. Eshley had painted a successful and acceptable picture of cattle drowsing picturesquely under walnut trees, and as he had begun, so, of necessity, he went on. His "Noontide Peace," a study of two dun cows under a walnut tree, was followed by "A Mid-day Sanctuary," a study of a walnut tree, with two dun cows under it. In due succession there came "Where the Gad-Flies Cease from Troubling," "The Haven of the Herd," and "A Dream in Dairyland," studies of walnut trees and dun cows. His two attempts to break away from his own tradition were signal failures: "Turtle Doves Alarmed by Sparrow-hawk" and "Wolves on the Roman Campagna" came back to his studio in the guise of abominable heresies, and Eshley climbed back into grace and the public gaze with "A Shaded Nook Where Drowsy Milkers Dream."

On a fine afternoon in late autumn he was putting some finishing touches to a study of meadow weeds when his neigh-bour, Adela Pingsford, assailed the outer door of his studio with loud peremptory knockings.

"There is an ox in my garden," she announced, in explanation of the tempestuous intrusion.

"An ox," said Eshley blankly, and rather fatuously; "what kind of ox?"

"Oh, I don't know what kind," snapped the lady. "A common or garden ox, to use the slang expression. It is the garden part of it that I object to. My garden has just been put straight for the winter, and an ox roaming about in it won't improve matters. Besides, there are the chrysanthemums just coming into flower."

"How did it get into the garden?" asked Eshley.

"I imagine it came in by the gate," said the lady impatiently; "it couldn't have climbed the walls, and I don't suppose anyone dropped it from an aeroplane as a Bovril advertisement. The immediately important question is not how it got in, but how to get it out."

"Won't it go?" said Eshley.

"If it was anxious to go," said Adela Pingsford rather angrily, "I should not have come here to chat with you about it. I'm practically all alone; the housemaid is having her afternoon out and the cook is lying down with an attack of neuralgia. Anything that I may have learned at school or in after life about how to remove a large ox from a small garden seems to have escaped from my memory now. All I could think of was that you were a near neighbour and a cattle painter, presumably more or less familiar with the subjects that you painted, and that you might be of some slight assistance. Possibly I was mistaken."

"I paint dairy cows, certainly," admitted Eshley, "but I cannot claim to have had any experience in rounding up stray oxen. I've seen it done on a cinema film, of course, but there were always horses and lots of other accessories; besides, one never knows how much of those pictures are faked."

Adela Pingsford said nothing, but led the way to her garden. It was normally a fair-sized garden, but it looked small in comparison with the ox, a huge mottled brute, dull red about the head and shoulders, passing to dirty white on the flanks and hind-quarters, with shaggy ears and large blood-shot eyes. It bore about as much resemblance to the dainty paddock heifers that Eshley was accustomed to paint as the chief of a Kurdish nomad clan would to a Japanese tea-shop girl. Eshley stood very near the gate while he studied the animal's appearance and demeanour. Adela Pingsford continued to say nothing.

"It's eating a chrysanthemum," said Eshley at last, when the silence had become unbearable.

"How observant you are," said Adela bitterly. "You seem to notice everything. As a matter of fact, it has got six chrysanthemums in its mouth at the present moment."

The necessity for doing something was becoming imperative. Eshley took a step or two in the direction of the animal, clapped his hands, and made noises of the "Hish" and "Shoo" variety. If the ox heard them, it gave no outward indication of the fact.

"If any hens should ever stray into my garden," said Adela, "I should certainly send for you to frighten them out. You 'shoo' beautifully. Meanwhile, do you mind trying to drive that ox away? That is a *Mademoiselle Louise Bichot* that he's begun on now," she added in icy calm, as a glowing orange head was crushed into the huge munching mouth.

"Since you have been so frank about the variety of the chrysanthemums," said Eshley, "I don't mind telling you that this is an Ayrshire ox."

The icy calm broke down; Adela Pingsford used language that sent the artist instinctively a few feet nearer to the ox. He picked up a pea-stick and flung it with some determination against the animal's mottled flanks. The operation of mashing *Mademoiselle Louise Bichot* into a petal salad was suspended for a long moment, while the ox gazed with concentrated inquiry at the stick-thrower. Adela gazed with equal concentration and more obvious hostility at the same focus. As the beast neither lowered its head nor stamped its feet, Eshley ventured on another javelin exercise with another pea-stick. The ox seemed to realize at once that it was to go; it gave a hurried final pluck at the bed where the chrysanthemums had been, and strode swiftly up the garden. Eshley ran to head it towards the gate, but only succeeded in quickening its pace from a walk to a lumbering trot. With an air of inquiry, but with no real hesitation, it crossed the tiny strip of turf that the charitable called the croquet lawn, and pushed its way through the open French window into the morning-room. Some chrysanthemums and other autumn herbage stood about the room in vases, and the animal resumed its browsing operations;

all the same, Eshley fancied that the beginnings of a hunted look had come into its eyes, a look that counselled respect. He discontinued his attempt to interfere with its choice of surroundings.

"Mr. Eshley," said Adela in a shaking voice, "I asked you to drive that beast out of my garden, but I did not ask you to drive it into my house. If I must have it anywhere on the premises, I prefer the garden to the morning-room."

"Cattle drives are not in my line," said Eshley; "if I remember, I told you so at the outset."

"I quite agree," retorted the lady, "painting pretty pictures of pretty little cows is what you're suited for. Perhaps you'd like to do a nice sketch of that ox making itself at home in my morning-room?"

This time it seemed as if the worm had turned; Eshley began striding away.

"Where are you going?" screamed Adela.

"To fetch implements," was the answer.

"Implements? I won't have you use a lasso. The room will be wrecked if there's a struggle."

But the artist marched out of the garden. In a couple of minutes he returned, laden with easel, sketching-stool, and painting materials.

"Do you mean to say that you're going to sit quietly down and paint that brute while it's destroying my morning-room?" gasped Adela.

"It was your suggestion," said Eshley, setting his canvas in position.

"I forbid it; I absolutely forbid it!" stormed Adela.

"I don't see what standing you have in the matter," said the artist; "you can hardly pretend that it's your ox, even by adoption."

"You seem to forget that it's in my morning-room, eating my flowers," came the raging retort.

"You seem to forget that the cook has neuralgia," said Eshley; "she may be just dozing off into a merciful sleep and your outcry will waken her. Consideration for others should be the guiding principle of people in our station of life."

"The man is mad!" exclaimed Adela tragically. A moment later it was Adela herself who appeared to go mad. The ox had finished the vase-flowers and the cover of *Israel Kalisch,* and appeared to be thinking of leaving its rather restricted quarters. Eshley noticed its restlessness and promptly flung it some bunches of Virginia creeper leaves as an inducement to continue the sitting.

"I forget how the proverb runs," he observed; "something about 'better a dinner of herbs than a stalled ox where hate is.' We seem to have all the ingredients for the proverb ready to hand."

"I shall go to the Public Library and get them to telephone for the police," announced Adela, and, raging audibly, she departed.

Some minutes later the ox, awakening probably to the suspicion that oil cake and chopped mangold was waiting for it in some appointed byre, stepped with much precaution out of the morning-room, stared with grave inquiry at the no longer obtrusive and pea-stick-throwing human, and then lumbered heavily but swiftly out of the garden. Eshley packed up his tools and followed the animal's example and "Larkdene" was left to neuralgia and the cook.

The episode was the turning-point in Eshley's artistic career. His remarkable picture, "Ox in a Morning-room, Late Autumn," was one of the sensations and successes of the next Paris Salon, and when it was subsequently exhibited at Munich it was bought by the Bavarian Government, in the teeth of the spirited bidding of three meat-extract firms. From that moment his success was continuous and assured, and the Royal Academy was thankful, two years later, to give a conspicuous position on its walls to his large canvas "Barbary Apes Wrecking a Boudoir."

Eshley presented Adela Pingsford with a new copy of *Israel Kalisch,* and a couple of finely flowering plants of *Madame André Blusset,* but nothing in the nature of a real reconciliation has taken place between them.

THE STORY-TELLER

IT was a hot afternoon, and the railway carriage was correspondingly sultry, and the next stop was at Templecombe, nearly an hour ahead. The occupants of the carriage were a small girl, and a smaller girl, and a small boy. An aunt belonging to the children occupied one corner seat, and the further corner seat on the opposite side was occupied by a bachelor who was a stranger to their party, but the small girls and the small boy emphatically occupied the compartment. Both the aunt and the children were conversational in a limited, persistent way, reminding one of the attentions of a housefly that refused to be discouraged. Most of the aunt's remarks seemed to begin with "Don't," and nearly all of the children's remarks began with "Why?" The bachelor said nothing out loud.

"Don't, Cyril, don't," exclaimed the aunt, as the small boy began smacking the cushions of the seat, producing a cloud of dust at each blow.

"Come and look out of the window," she added.

The child moved reluctantly to the window. "Why are those sheep being driven out of that field?" he asked.

"I expect they are being driven to another field where there is more grass," said the aunt weakly.

"But there is lots of grass in that field," protested the boy; "there's nothing else but grass there. Aunt, there's lots of grass in that field."

"Perhaps the grass in the other field is better," suggested the aunt fatuously.

"Why is it better?" came the swift, inevitable question.

"Oh, look at those cows!" exclaimed the aunt. Nearly every field along the line had contained cows or bullocks, but she spoke as though she were drawing attention to a rarity.

"Why is the grass in the other field better?" persisted Cyril.

The frown on the bachelor's face was deepening to a scowl. He was a hard, unsympathetic man, the aunt decided in her mind. She was utterly unable to come to any satisfactory decision about the grass in the other field.

The smaller girl created a diversion by beginning to recite "On the Road to Mandalay." She only knew the first line, but she put her limited knowledge to the fullest possible use. She repeated the line over and over again in a dreamy but resolute and very audible voice; it seemed to the bachelor as though some one had had a bet with her that she could not repeat the line aloud two thousand times without stopping. Whoever it was who had made the wager was likely to lose his bet.

"Come over here and listen to a story," said the aunt, when the bachelor had looked twice at her and once at the communication cord.

The children moved listlessly towards the aunt's end of the carriage. Evidently her reputation as a story-teller did not rank high in their estimation.

In a low, confidential voice, interrupted at frequent intervals by loud, petulant questions from her listeners, she began an unenterprising and deplorably uninteresting story about a little girl who was good, and made friends with every one on account of her goodness, and was finally saved from a mad bull by a number of rescuers who admired her moral character.

"Wouldn't they have saved her if she hadn't been good?" demanded the bigger of the small girls. It was exactly the question that the bachelor had wanted to ask.

"Well, yes," admitted the aunt lamely, "but I don't think they would have run quite so fast to her help if they had not liked her so much."

"It's the stupidest story I've ever heard," said the bigger of the small girls, with immense conviction.

"I didn't listen after the first bit, it was so stupid," said Cyril.

The smaller girl made no actual comment on the story, but she had long ago recommenced a murmured repetition of her favourite line.

"You don't seem to be a success as a story-teller," said the bachelor suddenly from his corner.

The aunt bristled in instant defence at this unexpected attack.

"It's a very difficult thing to tell stories that children can both understand and appreciate," she said stiffly.

"I don't agree with you," said the bachelor.

"Perhaps *you* would like to tell them a story," was the aunt's retort.

"Tell us a story," demanded the bigger of the small girls.

"Once upon a time," began the bachelor, "there was a little girl called Bertha, who was extraordinarily good."

The children's momentarily-aroused interest began at once to flicker; all stories seemed dreadfully alike, no matter who told them.

"She did all that she was told, she was always truthful, she kept her clothes clean, ate milk puddings as though they were jam tarts, learned her lessons perfectly, and was polite in her manners."

"Was she pretty?" asked the bigger of the small girls.

"Not as pretty as any of you," said the bachelor, "but she was horribly good."

There was a wave of reaction in favour of the story; the word horrible in connection with goodness was a novelty that commended itself. It seemed to introduce a ring of truth that was absent from the aunt's tales of infant life.

"She was so good," continued the bachelor, "that she won several medals for goodness, which she always wore, pinned on to her dress. There was a medal for obedience, another medal for punctuality, and a third for good behaviour. They were large metal medals and they clicked against one another as she walked. No other child in the town where she lived had as many as three medals, so everybody knew that she must be an extra good child."

"Horribly good," quoted Cyril.

"Everybody talked about her goodness, and the Prince of the country got to hear about it, and he said that as she was so very good she might be allowed once a week to walk in his park, which was just outside the town. It was a beautiful park, and no children were ever allowed in it, so it was a great honour for Bertha to be allowed to go there."

"Were there any sheep in the park?" demanded Cyril.

"No," said the bachelor, "there were no sheep."

"Why weren't there any sheep?" came the inevitable question arising out of that answer.

The aunt permitted herself a smile, which might almost have been described as a grin.

"There were no sheep in the park," said the bachelor, "because the Prince's mother had once had a dream that her son would either be killed by a sheep or else by a clock falling on him. For that reason the Prince never kept a sheep in his park or a clock in his palace."

The aunt suppressed a gasp of admiration.

"Was the Prince killed by a sheep or by a clock?" asked Cyril.

"He is still alive, so we can't tell whether the dream will come true," said the bachelor unconcernedly; "anyway, there were no sheep in the park, but there were lots of little pigs running all over the place."

"What colour were they?"

"Black with white faces, white with black spots, black all over, grey with white patches, and some were white all over."

The story-teller paused to let a full idea of the park's treasures sink into the children's imaginations; then he resumed:

"Bertha was rather sorry to find that there were no flowers in the park. She had promised her aunts, with tears in her eyes, that she would not pick any of the kind Prince's flowers, and she had meant to keep her promise, so of course it made her feel silly to find that there were no flowers to pick."

"Why weren't there any flowers?"

"Because the pigs had eaten them all," said the bachelor promptly. "The gardeners had told the Prince that you couldn't have pigs and flowers, so he decided to have pigs and no flowers."

There was a murmur of approval at the excellence of the Prince's decision; so many people would have decided the other way.

"There were lots of other delightful things in the park. There were ponds with gold and blue and green fish in them, and trees with beautiful parrots that said clever things at a moment's notice, and humming birds that hummed all the popular tunes of the day. Bertha walked up and down and enjoyed herself immensely, and thought to herself: 'If I were not so extraordinarily good I should not have been allowed to come into this beautiful park and enjoy all that there is to be seen in it,' and her three medals clinked against one another as she walked and helped to remind her how very good she really was. Just then an enormous wolf came prowling into the park to see if it could catch a fat little pig for its supper."

"What colour was it?" asked the children, amid an immediate quickening of interest.

"Mud-colour all over, with a black tongue and pale grey eyes that gleamed with unspeakable ferocity. The first thing that it saw in the park was Bertha; her pinafore was so spotlessly white and clean that it could be seen from a great distance. Bertha saw the wolf and saw that it was stealing towards her, and she began to wish that she had never been allowed to come into the park. She ran as hard as she could, and the wolf came after her with huge leaps and bounds. She managed to reach a shrubbery of myrtle bushes and she hid herself in one of the thickest of the bushes. The wolf came sniffing among the branches, its black tongue lolling out of its mouth and its pale grey eyes glaring with rage. Bertha was terribly frightened, and thought to herself: 'If I had not been so extraordinarily good I should have been safe in the town at this moment.' However, the scent of the myrtle was so strong that the wolf could not sniff out where Bertha was hiding, and the bushes were so thick that he might have hunted about in them for a long time without catching sight of her, so he thought he might as well go off and catch a little pig instead. Bertha was trembling very much at having the wolf prowling and sniffing so near her, and as she trembled the medal for obedience clinked against the medals for good conduct and punctuality. The wolf was just moving away when he heard the sound of the medals clinking and stopped to listen; they clinked again in a bush quite near him. He dashed into the bush, his pale grey eyes gleaming with ferocity and triumph and dragged Bertha out and devoured her to the last morsel. All that was left of her were her shoes, bits of clothing, and the three medals for goodness."

"Were any of the little pigs killed?"

"No, they all escaped."

"The story began badly," said the smaller of the small girls, "but it had a beautiful ending."

"It is the most beautiful story that I ever heard," said the bigger of the small girls, with immense decision.

"It is the *only* beautiful story I have ever heard," said Cyril.

A dissentient opinion came from the aunt.

"A most improper story to tell to young children! You have undermined the effect of years of careful teaching."

"At any rate," said the bachelor, collecting his belongings preparatory to leaving the carriage, "I kept them quiet for ten minutes, which was more than you were able to do."

"Unhappy woman!" he observed to himself as he walked down the platform of Templecombe station; "for the next six months or so those children will assail her in public with demands for an improper story!"

A DEFENSIVE DIAMOND

TREDDLEFORD sat in an easeful arm-chair in front of a slumberous fire, with a volume of verse in his hand and the comfortable consciousness that outside the club windows the rain was dripping and pattering with persistent purpose. A chill, wet October afternoon was emerging into a black, wet October evening, and the club smoking-room seemed warmer and cosier by contrast. It was an afternoon on which to be wafted away from one's climatic surroundings, and *The Golden Journey to Samarkand* promised to bear Treddleford well and bravely into other lands and under other skies. He had already migrated from London the rain-swept to Baghdad the Beautiful, and stood by the Sun Gate "in the olden time" when an icy breath of imminent annoyance seemed to creep between the book and himself. Amblecope, the man with the restless, prominent eyes and the mouth ready mobilized for conversational openings, had planted himself in a neighbouring arm-chair. For a twelve-month and some odd weeks Treddleford had skilfully avoided making the acquaintance of his voluble fellow-clubman; he had marvellously escaped from the infliction of his relentless record of tedious personal achievements, or alleged achievements, on golf links, turf, and gaming table, by flood and field and covert-side. Now his season of immunity was coming to an end. There was no escape; in another moment he would be numbered among those who knew Amblecope to speak to—or rather, to suffer being spoken to.

The intruder was armed with a copy of *Country Life,* not for purposes of reading, but as an aid to conversational ice-breaking.

"Rather a good portrait of Throstlewing," he remarked explosively, turning his large challenging eyes on Treddleford; "somehow it reminds me very much of Yellowstep, who was supposed to be such a good thing for the Grand Prix in 1903. Curious race that was; I suppose I've seen every race for the Grand Prix for the last——"

"Be kind enough never to mention the Grand Prix in my hearing," said Treddleford desperately; "it awakens acutely distressing memories. I can't explain why without going into a long and complicated story."

"Oh, certainly, certainly," said Amblecope hastily; long and complicated stories that were not told by himself were abominable in his eyes. He turned the pages of *Country Life* and became spuriously interested in the picture of a Mongolian pheasant.

"Not a bad representation of the Mongolian variety," he exclaimed, holding it up for his neighbour's inspection. "They do very well in some coverts. Take some stopping too once they're fairly on the wing. I suppose the biggest bag I ever made in two successive days——"

"My aunt, who owns the greater part of Lincolnshire," broke in Treddleford, with dramatic abruptness, "possesses perhaps the most remarkable record in the way of a pheasant bag that has ever been achieved. She is seventy-five and can't hit a thing, but she always goes out with the guns. When I say she can't hit a thing, I don't mean to say that she doesn't occasionally endanger the lives of her fellow-guns, because that wouldn't be true. In fact, the chief Government Whip won't allow Ministerial M.P.s to go out with her; 'We don't want to incur by-elections needlessly,' he quite reasonably observed. Well, the other day she winged a pheasant, and brought it to earth with a feather or two knocked out of it; it was a runner, and my aunt saw herself in danger of being done out of about the only bird she'd hit during the present reign. Of course she wasn't going to stand for that; she followed it through bracken and brushwood, and when it took to the open country and started across a ploughed field she jumped on to the shooting pony and went after it. The chase was a long one, and when my aunt at last ran the bird to a standstill she was nearer home than she was to the shooting party; she had left that some five miles behind her."

"Rather a long run for a wounded pheasant," snapped Amblecope.

"The story rests on my aunt's authority," said Treddleford coldly, "and she is local vice-president of the Young Women's Christian Association. She trotted three miles or so to her home, and it was not till the middle of the afternoon that it was discovered that the lunch for the entire shooting party was in a pannier attached to the pony's saddle. Anyway, she got her bird."

"Some birds, of course, take a lot of killing," said Amblecope; "so do some fish. I remember once I was fishing in the Exe, lovely trout stream, lots of fish, though they don't run to any great size——"

"One of them did," announced Treddleford, with emphasis. "My uncle, the Bishop of Southmolton, came across a giant trout in a pool just off the main stream of the Exe near Ugworthy; he tried it with every kind of fly and worm every day for three weeks without an atom of success, and then Fate intervened on his behalf. There was a low stone bridge just over this pool, and on the last day of his fishing holiday a motor van ran violently into the parapet and turned completely over; no one was hurt, but part of the parapet was knocked away, and the entire load that the van was carrying was pitched over and fell a little way into the pool. In a couple of minutes the giant trout was flapping and twisting on bare mud at the bottom of a waterless pool, and my uncle was able to walk down to him and fold him to his breast. The van-load consisted of blotting-paper, and every drop of water in that pool had been sucked up into the mass of spilt cargo."

There was silence for nearly half a minute in the smoking-room, and Treddleford began to let his mind steal back towards the golden road that led to Samarkand. Amblecope, however, rallied, and remarked in a rather tired and dispirited voice:

"Talking of motor accidents, the narrowest squeak I ever had was the other day, motoring with old Tommy Yarby in

North Wales. Awfully good sort, old Yarby, thorough good sportsman, and the best——"

"It was in North Wales," said Treddleford, "that my sister met with her sensational carriage accident last year. She was on her way to a garden-party at Lady Nineveh's, about the only garden-party that ever comes to pass in those parts in the course of the year, and therefore a thing that she would have been very sorry to miss. She was driving a young horse that she'd only bought a week or two previously, warranted to be perfectly steady with motor traffic, bicycles, and other common objects of the roadside. The animal lived up to its reputation, and passed the most explosive of motor-bikes with an indifference that almost amounted to apathy. However, I suppose we all draw the line somewhere, and this particular cob drew it at travelling wild beast shows. Of course my sister didn't know that, but she knew it very distinctly when she turned a sharp corner and found herself in a mixed company of camels, piebald horses, and canary-coloured vans. The dog-cart was overturned in a ditch and kicked to splinters, and the cob went home across country. Neither my sister nor the groom was hurt, but the problem of how to get to the Nineveh garden-party, some three miles distant, seemed rather difficult to solve; once there, of course, my sister would easily find someone to drive her home. 'I suppose you wouldn't care for the loan of a couple of my camels?' the showman suggested, in humorous sympathy. 'I would,' said my sister, who had ridden camel-back in Egypt, and she overruled the objections of the groom, who hadn't. She picked out two of the most presentable-looking of the beasts and had them dusted and made as tidy as was possible at short notice, and set out for the Nineveh mansion. You may imagine the sensation that her small but imposing caravan created when she arrived at the hall door. The entire garden-party flocked up to gape. My sister was rather glad to slip down from her camel, and the groom was thankful to scramble down from his. Then young Billy Doulton, of the Dragoon Guards, who has been a lot at Aden and thinks he knows camel-language backwards, thought he would show off by making the beasts kneel down in orthodox fashion. Unfortunately camel words-of-command are not the same all the world over; these were magnificent Turkestan camels, accustomed to stride up the stony terraces of mountain passes, and when Doulton shouted at them they went side by side up the front steps, into the entrance hall, and up the grand staircase. The German governess met them just at the turn of the corridor. The Ninevehs nursed her with devoted attention for weeks, and when I last heard from them she was well enough to go about her duties again, but the doctor says she will always suffer from Hagenbeck heart."

Amblecope got up from his chair and moved to another part of the room. Treddleford reopened his book and betook himself once more across—

The dragon-green, the luminous, the dark, the serpent-haunted sea.

For a blessed half-hour he disported himself in imagination by the "gay Aleppo-Gate," and listened to the bird-voiced singing-man. Then the world of today called him back; a page summoned him to speak with a friend on the telephone.

As Treddleford was about to pass out of the room he encountered Amblecope, also passing out, on his way to the billiard-room, where, perchance, some luckless wight might be secured and held fast to listen to the number of his attendances at the Grand Prix, with subsequent remarks on Newmarket and the Cambridgeshire. Amblecope made as if to pass out first, but a new-born pride was surging in Treddleford's breast and he waved him back.

"I believe I take precedence," he said coldly; "you are merely the club Bore; I am the club Liar."

THE ELK

TERESA, Mrs. Thropplestance, was the richest and most intractable old woman in the county of Woldshire. In her dealings with the world in general her manner suggested a blend between a Mistress of the Robes and a Master of Foxhounds, with the vocabulary of both. In her domestic circle she comported herself in the arbitrary style that one attributes, probably without the least justification, to an American political Boss in the bosom of his caucus. The late Theodore Thropple-

stance had left her, some thirty-five years ago, in absolute
possession of a considerable fortune, a large landed property,
and a gallery full of valuable pictures. In those intervening
years she had outlived her son and quarrelled with her elder
grandson, who had married without her consent or approval.
Bertie Thropplestance, her younger grandson, was the heir-
designate to her property, and as such he was a centre of interest and concern to some half-hundred ambitious mothers
with daughters of marriageable age. Bertie was an amiable,
easy-going young man, who was quite ready to marry anyone
who was favourably recommended to his notice, but he was
not going to waste his time in falling in love with anyone
who would come under his grandmother's veto. The favourable recommendation would have to come from Mrs. Thropplestance.

Teresa's house-parties were always rounded off with a
plentiful garnishing of presentable young women and alert,
attendant mothers, but the old lady was emphatically discouraging whenever any one of her girl guests became at all
likely to outbid the others as a possible granddaughter-in-law.
It was the inheritance of her fortune and estate that was in
question, and she was evidently disposed to exercise and enjoy
her powers of selection and rejection to the utmost. Bertie's
preferences did not greatly matter; he was of the sort who can
be stolidly happy with any kind of wife; he had cheerfully put
up with his grandmother all his life, so he was not likely to
fret and fume over anything that might befall him in the way
of a helpmate.

The party that gathered under Teresa's roof in Christmas
week of the year nineteen-hundred-and-something was of
smaller proportions than usual, and Mrs. Yonelet, who formed
one of the party, was inclined to deduce hopeful augury from
this circumstance. Dora Yonelet and Bertie were so obviously
made for one another, she confided to the vicar's wife, and if
the old lady were accustomed to seeing them about a lot together she might adopt the view that they would make a suitable married couple.

"People soon get used to an idea if it is dangled constantly
before their eyes," said Mrs. Yonelet hopefully, "and the
more often Teresa sees those young people together, happy
in each other's company, the more she will get to take a

kindly interest in Dora as a possible and desirable wife for
Bertie."

"My dear," said the vicar's wife resignedly, "my own Sybil
was thrown together with Bertie under the most romantic
circumstances—I'll tell you about it some day—but it made
no impression whatever on Teresa; she put her foot down in
the most uncompromising fashion, and Sybil married an Indian
civilian."

"Quite right of her," said Mrs. Yonelet with vague approval; "it's what any girl of spirit would have done. Still,
that was a year or two ago, I believe; Bertie is older now, and
so is Teresa. Naturally she must be anxious to see him settled."

The vicar's wife reflected that Teresa seemed to be the one
person who showed no immediate anxiety to supply Bertie
with a wife, but she kept the thought to herself.

Mrs. Yonelet was a woman of resourceful energy and
generalship; she involved the other members of the house-
party, the deadweight, so to speak, in all manner of exercises
and occupations that segregated them from Bertie and Dora,
who were left to their own devisings—that is to say, to Dora's
devisings and Bertie's accommodating acquiescence. Dora
helped in the Christmas decorations of the parish church, and
Bertie helped her to help. Together they fed the swans, till the
birds went on a dyspepsia-strike, together they played bil-
liards, together they photographed the village almshouses, and,
at a respectful distance, the tame elk that browsed in solitary
aloofness in the park. It was "tame" in the sense that it had
long ago discarded the least vestige of fear of the human race;
nothing in its record encouraged its human neighbours to feel
a reciprocal confidence.

Whatever sport or exercise or occupation Bertie and Dora
indulged in together was unfailingly chronicled and advertised by Mrs. Yonelet for the due enlightenment of Bertie's
grandmother.

"Those two inseparables have just come in from a bicycle
ride," she would announce; "quite a picture they make, so
fresh and glowing after their spin."

"A picture needing words," would be Teresa's private comment, and as far as Bertie was concerned she was determined
that the words should remain unspoken.

On the afternoon after Christmas Day Mrs. Yonelet dashed

into the drawing-room, where her hostess was sitting amid a
circle of guests and tea-cups and muffin-dishes. Fate had placed
what seemed like a trump-card in the hands of the patiently
manœuvring mother. With eyes blazing with excitement and
a voice heavily escorted with exclamation marks she made a
dramatic announcement.

"Bertie has saved Dora from the elk!"

In swift, excited sentences, broken with maternal emotion,
she gave supplementary information as to how the treacherous
animal had ambushed Dora as she was hunting for a strayed
golf ball, and how Bertie had dashed to her rescue with a
stable fork and driven the beast off in the nick of time.

"It was touch and go! She threw her niblick at it, but that
didn't stop it. In another moment she would have been crushed
beneath its hoofs," panted Mrs. Yonelet.

"The animal is not safe," said Teresa, handing her agitated
guest a cup of tea. "I forget if you take sugar. I suppose the
solitary life it leads has soured its temper. There are muffins
in the grate. It's not my fault; I've tried to get it a mate for
ever so long. You don't know of anyone with a lady elk for
sale or exchange, do you?" she asked the company generally.

But Mrs. Yonelet was in no humour to listen to talk of
elk marriages. The mating of two human beings was the subject uppermost in her mind, and the opportunity for advancing
her pet project was too valuable to be neglected.

"Teresa," she exclaimed impressively, "after those two
young people have been thrown together so dramatically,
nothing can be quite the same again between them. Bertie has
done more than save Dora's life; he has earned her affection.
One cannot help feeling that Fate has consecrated them for
one another."

"Exactly what the vicar's wife said when Bertie saved Sybil
from the elk a year or two ago," observed Teresa placidly;
"I pointed out to her that he had rescued Mirabel Hicks
from the same predicament a few months previously, and that
priority really belonged to the gardener's boy, who had been
rescued in the January of that year. There is a good deal of
sameness in country life, you know."

"It seems to be a very dangerous animal," said one of the
guests.

"That's what the mother of the gardener's boy said," remarked Teresa; "she wanted me to have it destroyed, but I pointed out to her that she had eleven children and I had only one elk. I also gave her a black silk skirt; she said that though there hadn't been a funeral in her family, she felt as if there had been. Anyhow, we parted friends. I can't offer you a silk skirt, Emily, but you may have another cup of tea. As I have already remarked, there are muffins in the grate."

Teresa closed the discussion, having deftly conveyed the impression that she considered the mother of the gardener's boy had shown a far more reasonable spirit than the parents of other elk-assaulted victims.

"Teresa is devoid of feeling," said Mrs. Yonelet afterwards to the vicar's wife; "to sit there, talking of muffins, with an appalling tragedy only narrowly averted——"

"Of course you know whom she really intends Bertie to marry?" asked the vicar's wife; "I've noticed it for some time. The Bickelbys' German governess."

"A German governess! What an idea!" gasped Mrs. Yonelet.

"She's of quite good family, I believe," said the vicar's wife, "and not at all the mouse-in-the-background sort of person that governesses are usually supposed to be. In fact, next to Teresa, she's about the most assertive and combative personality in the neighbourhood. She's pointed out to my husband all sorts of errors in his sermons, and she gave Sir Laurence a public lecture on how he ought to handle the hounds. You know how sensitive Sir Laurence is about any criticism of his Mastership, and to have a governess laying down the law to him nearly drove him into a fit. She's behaved like that to everyone, except, of course, Teresa, and everyone has been defensively rude to her in return. The Bickelbys are simply too afraid of her to get rid of her. Now isn't that exactly the sort of woman whom Teresa would take a delight in installing as her successor? Imagine the discomfort and awkwardness in the county if we suddenly found that she was to be the future hostess at the Hall. Teresa's only regret will be that she won't be alive to see it."

"But," objected Mrs. Yonelet, "surely Bertie hasn't shown the least sign of being attracted in that quarter?"

"Oh, she's quite nice-looking in a way, and dresses well, and plays a good game of tennis. She often comes across the park with messages from the Bickelby mansion, and one of these days Bertie will rescue her from the elk, which has become almost a habit with him, and Teresa will say that Fate has consecrated them to one another. Bertie might not be disposed to pay much attention to the consecrations of Fate, but he would not dream of opposing his grandmother."

The vicar's wife spoke with the quiet authority of one who has intuitive knowledge, and in her heart of hearts Mrs. Yonelet believed her.

Six months later the elk had to be destroyed. In a fit of exceptional moroseness it had killed the Bickelbys' German governess. It was an irony of its fate that it should achieve popularity in the last moments of its career; at any rate, it established the record of being the only living thing that had permanently thwarted Teresa Thropplestance's plans.

Dora Yonelet broke off her engagement with an Indian civilian, and married Bertie three months after his grandmother's death—Teresa did not long survive the German governess fiasco. At Christmas-time every year young Mrs. Thropplestance hangs an extra large festoon of evergreens on the elk horns that decorate the hall.

"It was a fearsome beast," she observed to Bertie, "but I always feel that it was instrumental in bringing us together."

Which, of course, was true.

THE LUMBER-ROOM

THE children were to be driven, as a special treat, to the sands at Jagborough. Nicholas was not to be of the party; he was in disgrace. Only that morning he had refused to eat his wholesome bread-and-milk on the seemingly frivolous ground that there was a frog in it. Older and wiser and better people had told him that there could not possibly be a frog in his bread-and-milk and that he was not to talk nonsense; he continued, nevertheless, to talk what seemed the veriest nonsense, and described with much detail the coloration and markings of the alleged frog. The dramatic part of the incident was that there really was a frog in Nicholas' basin of bread-and-milk; he had put it there himself, so he felt entitled to know something about it. The sin of taking a frog from the garden and putting it into a bowl of wholesome bread-and-milk was enlarged on at great length, but the fact that stood out clearest in the whole affair, as it presented itself to the mind of Nicholas, was that the older, wiser, and better people had been proved to be profoundly in error in matters about which they had expressed the utmost assurance.

"You said there couldn't possibly be a frog in my bread-and-milk; there *was* a frog in my bread-and-milk," he repeated, with the insistence of a skilled tactician who does not intend to shift from favourable ground.

So his boy-cousin and girl-cousin and his quite uninteresting younger brother were to be taken to Jagborough sands that afternoon and he was to stay at home. His cousins' aunt, who insisted, by an unwarranted stretch of imagination, in styling herself his aunt also, had hastily invented the Jagborough expedition in order to impress on Nicholas the delights that he had justly forfeited by his disgraceful conduct at the breakfast-table. It was her habit, whenever one of the children fell from grace, to improvise something of a festival nature from which the offender would be rigorously debarred; if all the children sinned collectively they were suddenly informed of a circus in a neighbouring town, a circus of unrivalled merit and uncounted elephants, to which, but for their depravity, they would have been taken that very day.

A few decent tears were looked for on the part of Nicholas when the moment for the departure of the expedition arrived. As a matter of fact, however, all the crying was done by his girl-cousin, who scraped her knee rather painfully against the step of the carriage as she was scrambling in.

"How she did howl," said Nicholas cheerfully, as the party drove off without any of the elation of high spirits that should have characterized it.

"She'll soon get over that," said the *soi-disant* aunt; "it will be a glorious afternoon for racing about over those beautiful sands. How they will enjoy themselves."

"Bobby won't enjoy himself much, and he won't race much either," said Nicholas with a grim chuckle; "his boots are hurting him. They're too tight."

"Why didn't he tell me they were hurting?" asked the aunt with some asperity.

"He told you twice, but you weren't listening. You often don't listen when we tell you important things."

"You are not to go into the gooseberry garden," said the aunt, changing the subject.

"Why not?" demanded Nicholas.

"Because you are in disgrace," said the aunt loftily.

Nicholas did not admit the flawlessness of the reasoning; he felt perfectly capable of being in disgrace and in a gooseberry garden at the same moment. His face took on an expression of considerable obstinacy. It was clear to his aunt that he was determined to get into the gooseberry garden, "only," as she remarked to herself, "because I have told him he is not to."

Now the gooseberry garden had two doors by which it might be entered, and once a small person like Nicholas could slip in there he could effectually disappear from view amid the masking growth of artichokes, raspberry canes, and fruit bushes. The aunt had many other things to do that afternoon, but she spent an hour or two in trivial gardening operations among flower beds and shrubberies, whence she could keep a watchful eye on the two doors that led to the forbidden paradise. She was a woman of few ideas, with immense powers of concentration.

Nicholas made one or two sorties into the front garden, wriggling his way with obvious stealth of purpose towards one or other of the doors, but never able for a moment to evade the aunt's watchful eye. As a matter of fact, he had no intention of trying to get into the gooseberry garden, but it was extremely convenient for him that his aunt should believe that he had; it was a belief that would keep her on self-imposed sentry-duty for the greater part of the afternoon. Having thoroughly confirmed and fortified her suspicions, Nicholas slipped back into the house and rapidly put into execution a plan of action that had long germinated in his brain. By standing on a chair in the library one could reach a shelf on which reposed a fat, important-looking key. The key was as important as it looked; it was the instrument which kept the mysteries of the lumber-room secure from unauthorized intrusion, which opened a way only for aunts and such-like privileged persons. Nicholas had not had much experience of the art of fitting keys into keyholes and turning locks, but for some days past he had practised with the key of the school-room door; he did not believe in trusting too much to luck and accident. The key turned stiffly in the lock, but it turned. The door opened, and Nicholas was in an unknown land, compared with which the gooseberry garden was a stale delight, a mere material pleasure.

Often and often Nicholas had pictured to himself what the lumber-room might be like, that region that was so carefully sealed from youthful eyes and concerning which no questions were ever answered. It came up to his expectations. In the first place it was large and dimly lit, one high window opening on to the forbidden garden being its only source of illumination. In the second place it was a storehouse of unimagined treasures. The aunt-by-assertion was one of those people who think that things spoil by use and consign them to dust and damp by way of preserving them. Such parts of the house as Nicholas knew best were rather bare and cheerless, but here there were wonderful things for the eye to feast on. First and foremost there was a piece of framed tapestry that was evidently meant to be a fire-screen. To Nicholas it was a living, breathing story; he sat down on a roll of Indian hangings, glowing in wonderful colours beneath a layer of dust, and took in all the details of the tapestry picture. A man, dressed in the hunting costume of some remote period, had just transfixed a stag with an arrow; it could not have been a difficult shot because the stag was only one or two paces away from him; in the thickly growing vegetation that the picture suggested it would not have been difficult to creep up to a feeding stag, and the two spotted dogs that were springing forward to join in the chase had evidently been trained to keep to heel till the arrow was discharged. That part of the picture was simple, if interesting, but did the huntsman see, what Nicholas saw, that four galloping wolves were coming in his direction through the wood? There might be more than four of them hidden behind the trees, and in any case would the man and his dogs be able to cope with the four wolves if they made an attack? The man had only two arrows left in his quiver, and he might miss with one or both of them; all one knew about his skill in shooting was that he could hit a large stag at a ridiculously short range. Nicholas sat for many golden minutes revolving the possibilities of the scene; he was inclined to think that there were more than four wolves and that the man and his dogs were in a tight corner.

But there were other objects of delight and interest claiming his instant attention; there were quaint twisted candlesticks in the shape of snakes, and a teapot fashioned like a china duck, out of whose open beak the tea was supposed to come. How dull and shapeless the nursery teapot seemed in comparison! And there was a carved sandal-wood box packed tight with aromatic cotton-wool, and between the layers of cotton-wool were little brass figures, hump-necked bulls, and peacocks and goblins, delightful to see and to handle. Less promising in appearance was a large square book with plain black covers; Nicholas peeped into it, and, behold, it was full of coloured pictures of birds. And such birds! In the garden, and in the lanes when he went for a walk, Nicholas came across a few birds, of which the largest were an occasional magpie or wood-pigeon; here were herons and bustards, kites, toucans, tiger-bitterns, brush turkeys, ibises, golden pheasants, a whole portrait gallery of undreamed-of creatures. And as he was admiring the colouring of the mandarin duck and assigning a life-history to it, the voice of his aunt in shrill vociferation of his name came from the gooseberry garden without. She had grown suspicious at his long disappearance, and had leapt to the conclusion that he had climbed over the wall behind the sheltering screen of the lilac bushes; she was now engaged in energetic and rather hopeless search for him among the artichokes and raspberry canes.

"Nicholas, Nicholas!" she screamed, "you are to come out of this at once. It's no use trying to hide there; I can see you all the time."

It was probably the first time for twenty years that anyone had smiled in that lumber-room.

Presently the angry repetitions of Nicholas' name gave way to a shriek, and a cry for somebody to come quickly. Nicholas shut the book, restored it carefully to its place in a corner, and shook some dust from a neighbouring pile of newspapers over it. Then he crept from the room, locked the door, and replaced the key exactly where he had found it. His aunt was still calling his name when he sauntered into the front garden.

"Who's calling?" he asked.

"Me," came the answer from the other side of the wall;

"didn't you hear me? I've been looking for you in the gooseberry garden, and I've slipped into the rain-water tank. Luckily there's no water in it, but the sides are slippery and I can't get out. Fetch the little ladder from under the cherry tree——"

"I was told I wasn't to go into the gooseberry garden," said Nicholas promptly.

"I told you not to, and now I tell you that you may," came the voice from the rain-water tank, rather impatiently.

"Your voice doesn't sound like Aunt's," objected Nicholas; "you may be the Evil One tempting me to be disobedient. Aunt often tells me that the Evil One tempts me and that I always yield. This time I'm not going to yield."

"Don't talk nonsense," said the prisoner in the tank; "go and fetch the ladder."

"Will there be strawberry jam for tea?" asked Nicholas innocently.

"Certainly there will be," said the aunt, privately resolving that Nicholas should have none of it.

"Now I know that you are the Evil One and not Aunt," shouted Nicholas gleefully; "when we asked Aunt for strawberry jam yesterday she said there wasn't any. I know there are four jars of it in the store cupboard, because I looked, and of course you know it's there, but *she* doesn't, because she said there wasn't any. Oh, Devil, you *have* sold yourself!"

There was an unusual sense of luxury in being able to talk to an aunt as though one was talking to the Evil One, but Nicholas knew, with childish discernment, that such luxuries were not to be over-indulged in. He walked noisily away, and it was a kitchenmaid, in search of parsley, who eventually rescued the aunt from the rain-water tank.

Tea that evening was partaken of in a fearsome silence. The tide had been at its highest when the children had arrived at Jagborough Cove, so there had been no sands to play on—a circumstance that the aunt had overlooked in the haste of organizing her punitive expedition. The tightness of Bobby's boots had had disastrous effect on his temper the whole of the afternoon, and altogether the children could not have been said to have enjoyed themselves. The aunt maintained the frozen muteness of one who has suffered undignified and unmerited detention in a rain-water tank for thirty-five minutes.

As for Nicholas, he, too, was silent, in the absorption of one who has much to think about; it was just possible, he considered, that the huntsman would escape with his hounds while the wolves feasted on the stricken stag.

TTsf P
((1923)

LOUISE

"THE tea will be quite cold, you'd better ring for some more," said the Dowager Lady Beanford.

Susan Lady Beanford was a vigorous old woman who had coquetted with imaginary ill-health for the greater part of a lifetime; Clovis Sangrail irreverently declared that she had caught a chill at the Coronation of Queen Victoria and had never let it go again. Her sister, Jane Thropplestance, who was some years her junior, was chiefly remarkable for being the most absent-minded woman in Middlesex.

"I've really been unusually clever this afternoon," she remarked gaily, as she rang for the tea. "I've called on all the people I meant to call on, and I've done all the shopping that I set out to do. I even remembered to try and match that silk for you at Harrod's, but I'd forgotten to bring the pattern with me, so it was no use. I really think that was the only important thing I forgot during the whole afternoon. Quite wonderful for me, isn't it?"

"What have you done with Louise?" asked her sister. "Didn't you take her out with you? You said you were going to."

"Good gracious," exclaimed Jane, "what *have* I done with Louise? I must have left her somewhere."

"But where?"

"That's just it. Where have I left her? I can't remember if the Carrywoods were at home or if I just left cards. If they were at home I may have left Louise there to play bridge. I'll go and telephone to Lord Carrywood and find out."

"Is that you, Lord Carrywood?" she queried over the telephone; "it's me, Jane Thropplestance. I want to know, have you seen Louise?"

" 'Louise,' " came the answer, "it's been my fate to see it three times. At first, I must admit, I wasn't impressed by it, but the music grows on one after a bit. Still, I don't think I want to see it again just at present. Were you going to offer me a seat in your box?"

"Not the opera 'Louise'—my niece, Louise Thropplestance. I thought I might have left her at your house."

"You left cards on us this afternoon, I understand, but I don't think you left a niece. The footman would have been sure to have mentioned it if you had. Is it going to be a fashion to leave nieces on people as well as cards? I hope not; some of these houses in Berkeley Square have practically no accommodation for that sort of thing."

"She's not at the Carrywoods'," announced Jane, returning to her tea; "now I come to think of it, perhaps I left her at the silk counter at Selfridge's. I may have told her to wait there a moment while I went to look at the silks in a better light, and I may easily have forgotten about her when I found I hadn't your pattern with me. In that case she's still sitting there. She wouldn't move unless she was told to; Louise has no initiative."

"You said you tried to match the silk at Harrod's," interjected the dowager.

"Did I? Perhaps it was Harrod's. I really don't remember. It was one of those places where everyone is so kind and sympathetic and devoted that one almost hates to taken even a reel of cotton away from such pleasant surroundings."

"I think you might have taken Louise away. I don't like the idea of her being there among a lot of strangers. Supposing some unprincipled person was to get into conversation with her."

"Impossible. Louise has no conversation. I've never discovered a single topic on which she'd anything to say beyond 'Do you think so? I dare say you're right.' I really thought her reticence about the fall of the Ribot Ministry was ridiculous, considering how much her dear mother used to visit Paris. This bread and butter is cut far too thin; it crumbles away long before you can get it to your mouth. One feels so absurd, snapping at one's food in mid-air, like a trout leaping at may-fly."

"I am rather surprised," said the dowager, "that you can sit there making a hearty tea when you've just lost a favourite niece."

"You talk as if I'd lost her in a churchyard sense, instead of having temporarily mislaid her. I'm sure to remember presently where I left her."

"You didn't visit any place of devotion, did you? If you've left her mooning about Westminster Abbey or St. Peter's, Eaton Square, without being able to give any satisfactory reason why she's there, she'll be seized under the Cat and Mouse Act and sent to Reginald McKenna."

"That would be extremely awkward," said Jane, meeting an irresolute piece of bread and butter halfway, "we hardly know the McKennas, and it would be very tiresome having to telephone to some unsympathetic private secretary, describing Louise to him and asking to have her sent back in time for dinner. Fortunately, I didn't go to any place of devotion, though I did get mixed up with a Salvation Army procession. It was quite interesting to be at close quarters with them, they're so absolutely different to what they used to be when I first remember them in the 'eighties. They used to go about then unkempt and dishevelled, in a sort of smiling rage with the world, and now they're spruce and jaunty and flamboyantly decorative, like a geranium bed with religious convictions. Laura Kettleway was going on about them in the lift of the Dover Street Tube the other day, saying what a lot of good work they did, and what a loss it would have been if they'd never existed. 'If they had never existed,' I said, 'Granville Barker would have been certain to have invented something that looked exactly like them.' If you say things like that, quite loud, in a Tube lift, they always sound like epigrams."

"I think you ought to do something about Louise," said the dowager.

"I'm trying to think whether she was with me when I called on Ada Spelvexit. I rather enjoyed myself there. Ada was trying, as usual, to ram that odious Koriatoffski woman down my throat, knowing perfectly well that I detest her, and in an unguarded moment she said: 'She's leaving her present house and going to Lower Seymour Street.' 'I dare say she will, if she stays there long enough,' I said. Ada didn't see it for about three minutes, and then she was positively uncivil. No, I am certain I didn't leave Louise there."

"If you could manage to remember where you *did* leave

her, it would be more to the point than these negative assurances," said Lady Beanford; "so far, all that we know is that she is not at the Carrywoods', or Ada Spelvexit's, or Westminster Abbey."

"That narrows the search down a bit," said Jane hopefully; "I rather fancy she must have been with me when I went to Mornay's. I know I went to Mornay's, because I remember meeting that delightful Malcolm What's-his-name there—you know whom I mean. That's the great advantage of people having unusual first names, you needn't try and remember what their other name is. Of course I know one or two other Malcolms, but none that could possibly be described as delightful. He gave me two tickets for the Happy Sunday Evenings in Sloane Square. I've probably left them at Mornay's, but still it was awfully kind of him to give them to me."

"Do you think you left Louise there?"

"I might telephone and ask. Oh, Robert, before you clear the tea-things away I wish you'd ring up Mornay's, in Regent Street, and ask if I left two theatre tickets and one niece in their shop this afternoon."

"A niece, ma'am?" asked the footman.

"Yes, Miss Louise didn't come home with me, and I'm not sure where I left her."

"Miss Louise has been upstairs all the afternoon, ma'am, reading to the second kitchenmaid, who has the neuralgia. I took up tea to Miss Louise at a quarter to five o'clock, ma'am."

"Of course, how silly of me. I remember now, I asked her to read the *Faërie Queene* to poor Emma, to try to send her to sleep. I always get some one to read the *Faërie Queene* to me when I have neuralgia, and it usually sends me to sleep. Louise doesn't seem to have been successful, but one can't say she hasn't tried. I expect after the first hour or so the kitchenmaid would rather have been left alone with her neuralgia, but of course Louise wouldn't leave off till someone told her to. Anyhow, you can ring up Mornay's, Robert, and ask whether I left two theatre tickets there. Except for your silk, Susan, those seem to be the only things I've forgotten this afternoon. Quite wonderful for me."

THE GUESTS

"THE landscape seen from our windows is certainly charming," said Annabel; "those cherry orchards and green meadows, and the river winding along the valley, and the church tower peeping out among the elms, thcy all make a most effective picture. There's something dreadfully sleepy and languorous about it, though; stagnation seems to be the dominant note. Nothing ever happens here; seedtime and harvest, an occasional outbreak of measles or a mildly destructive thunderstorm, and a little election excitement about once in five years, that is all that we have to modify the monotony of our existence. Rather dreadful, isn't it?"

"On the contrary," said Matilda, "I find it soothing and restful; but then, you see, I've lived in countries where things do happen, ever so many at a time, when you're not ready for them happening all at once."

"That, of course, makes a difference," said Annabel.

"I have never forgotten," said Matilda, "the occasion when the Bishop of Bequar paid us an unexpected visit; he was on his way to lay the foundation-stone of a mission-house or something of the sort."

"I thought that out there you were always prepared for emergency guests turning up," said Annabel.

"I was quite prepared for half a dozen bishops," said Matilda, "but it was rather disconcerting to find out after a little conversation that this particular one was a distant cousin of mine, belonging to a branch of the family that had quarrelled bitterly and offensively with our branch about a Crown Derby dessert service; they got it, and we ought to have got it, in some legacy, or else we got it and they thought they ought to have it, I forget which; anyhow, I know they behaved disgracefully. Now here was one of them turning up in the odour of sanctity, so to speak, and claiming the traditional hospitality of the East."

"It was rather trying, but you could have left your husband to do most of the entertaining."

"My husband was fifty miles up-country, talking sense, or

what he imagined to be sense, to a village community that fancied one of their leading men was a were-tiger."

"A what tiger?"

"A were-tiger; you've heard of were-wolves, haven't you, a mixture of wolf and human being and demon? Well, in those parts they have were-tigers, or think they have, and I must say that in this case, so far as sworn and uncontested evidence went, they had every ground for thinking so. However, as we gave up witchcraft prosecutions about three hundred years ago, we don't like to have other people keeping on our discarded practices; it doesn't seem respectful to our mental and moral position."

"I hope you weren't unkind to the Bishop," said Annabel.

"Well, of course he was my guest, so I had to be outwardly polite to him, but he was tactless enough to rake up the incidents of the old quarrel, and to try to make out that there was something to be said for the way his side of the family had behaved; even if there was, which I don't for a moment admit, my house was not the place in which to say it. I didn't argue the matter, but I gave my cook a holiday to go and visit his aged parents some ninety miles away. The emergency cook was not a specialist in curries; in fact, I don't think cooking in any shape or form could have been one of his strong points. I believe he originally came to us in the guise of a gardener, but as we never pretended to have anything that could be considered a garden he was utilized as assistant goatherd, in which capacity, I understand, he gave every satisfaction. When the Bishop heard that I had sent away the cook on a special and unnecessary holiday, he saw the inwardness of the manœuvre, and from that moment we were scarcely on speaking terms. If you have ever had a Bishop with whom you were not on speaking terms staying in your house, you will appreciate the situation."

Annabel confessed that her life-story had never included such a disturbing experience.

"Then," continued Matilda, "to make matters more complicated, the Gwadlipichee overflowed its banks, a thing it did every now and then when the rains were unduly prolonged, and the lower part of the house and all the out-buildings were submerged. We managed to get the ponies loose in time, and the syce swam the whole lot of them off to the nearest rising ground. A goat or two, the chief goatherd, the chief goatherd's wife, and several of their babies came to anchorage in the verandah. All the rest of the available space was filled up with wet, bedraggled-looking hens and chickens; one never really knows how many fowls one possesses till the servants' quarters are flooded out. Of course, I had been through something of the sort in previous floods, but never before had I had a houseful of goats and babies and half-drowned hens, supplemented by a Bishop with whom I was hardly on speaking terms."

"It must have been a trying experience," commented Annabel.

"More embarrassments were to follow. I wasn't going to let a mere ordinary flood wash out the memory of that Crown Derby dessert service, and I intimated to the Bishop that his large bedroom, with a writing table in it, and his small bathroom, with a sufficiency of cold-water jars in it, was his share of the premises, and that space was rather congested under the existing circumstances. However, at about three o'clock in the afternoon, when he had awakened from his midday sleep, he made a sudden incursion into the room that was normally the drawing-room, but was now dining-room, storehouse, saddleroom, and half a dozen other temporary premises as well. From the condition of my guest's costume he seemed to think it might also serve as his dressing-room.

" 'I'm afraid there is nowhere for you to sit,' I said coldly; 'the verandah is full of goats.'

" 'There is a goat in my bedroom,' he observed with equal coldness, and more than a suspicion of sardonic reproach.

" 'Really,' I said, 'another survivor! I thought all the other goats were done for.'

" 'This particular goat is quite done for,' he said; 'it is being devoured by a leopard at the present moment. That is why I left the room; some animals resent being watched while they are eating.'

"The leopard, of course, was easily explained; it had been hanging round the goat-sheds when the flood came, and had clambered up by the outside staircase leading to the Bishop's bathroom, thoughtfully bringing a goat with it. Probably it found the bathroom too damp and shut-in for its taste, and transferred its banqueting operations to the bedroom while the

Bishop was having his nap."

"What a frightful situation!" exclaimed Annabel; "fancy having a ravening leopard in the house, with a flood all round you."

"Not in the least ravening," said Matilda; "it was full of goat, had any amount of water at its disposal if it felt thirsty, and probably had no more immediate wish than a desire for uninterrupted sleep. Still, I think any one will admit that it was an embarrassing predicament to have your only available guest-room occupied by a leopard, the verandah choked up with goats and babies and wet hens, and a Bishop with whom you were scarcely on speaking terms planted down in your only sitting-room. I really don't know how I got through those crawling hours, and of course meal-times only made matters worse. The emergency cook had every excuse for sending in watery soup and sloppy rice, and as neither the chief goatherd nor his wife were expert divers, the cellar could not be reached. Fortunately the Gwadlipichee subsides as rapidly as it rises, and just before dawn the syce came splashing back, with the ponies only fetlock deep in water. Then there arose some awkwardness from the fact that the Bishop wished to leave sooner than the leopard did, and as the latter was ensconced in the midst of the former's personal possessions there was an obvious difficulty in altering the order of departure. I pointed out to the Bishop that a leopard's habits and tastes are not those of an otter, and that it naturally preferred walking to wading, and that in any case a meal of an entire goat, washed down with tub-water, justified a certain amount of repose; if I had had guns fired to frighten the animal away, as the Bishop suggested, it would probably merely have left the bedroom to come into the already overcrowded drawing-room. Altogether it was rather a relief when they both left. Now, perhaps, you can understand my appreciation of a sleepy countryside where things don't happen."

THE PENANCE

OCTAVIAN RUTTLE was one of those lively, cheerful individuals on whom amiability had set its unmistakable stamp, and, like most of its kind, his soul's peace depended in large measure on the unstinted approval of his fellows. In hunting to death a small tabby cat he had done a thing of which he scarcely approved himself, and he was glad when the gardener had hidden the body in its hastily dug grave under a lonely oak tree in the meadow, the same tree that the hunted quarry had climbed as a last effort towards safety. It had been a distasteful and seemingly ruthless deed, but circumstances had demanded the doing of it. Octavian kept chickens; at least he kept some of them; others vanished from his keeping, leaving only a few bloodstained feathers to mark the manner of their going. The tabby cat from the large grey house that stood with its back to the meadow had been detected in many furtive visits to the hen-coops, and after due negotiation with those in authority at the grey house a sentence of death had been agreed on: "The children will mind, but they need not know," had been the last word on the matter.

The children in question were a standing puzzle to Octavian; in the course of a few months he considered that he should have known their names, ages, the dates of their birthdays, and have been introduced to their favourite toys. They remained, however, as non-committal as the long blank wall that shut them off from the meadow, a wall over which their three heads sometimes appeared at odd moments. They had parents in India—that much Octavian had learned in the neighbourhood; the children, beyond grouping themselves garment-wise into sexes, a girl and two boys, carried their life-story no further on his behoof. And now it seemed he was engaged in something which touched them closely, but must be hidden from their knowledge.

The poor helpless chickens had gone one by one to their doom, so it was meet that their destroyer should come to a violent end, yet Octavian felt some qualms when his share of the violence was ended. The little cat, headed off from its wonted tracks of safety, had raced unfriended from shelter to shelter, and its end had been rather piteous. Octavian walked through the long grass of the meadow with a step less jaunty than usual. And as he passed beneath the shadow of the high blank wall he glanced up and became aware that his hunting had had undesired witnesses. Three white faces were looking down at him, and if ever an artist wanted a threefold study of cold human hate, impotent yet unyielding, raging yet masked in stillness, he would have found it in the triple gaze that met Octavian's eye.

"I'm sorry, but it had to be done," said Octavian, with genuine apology in his voice.

"Beast!"

The answer came from three throats with startling intensity.

Octavian felt that the blank wall would not be more impervious to his explanations than the bunch of human hostility that peered over its coping; he wisely decided to withhold his peace overtures till a more hopeful occasion.

Two days later he ransacked the best sweet-shop in the neighbouring market town for a box of chocolates that by its size and contents should fitly atone for the dismal deed done under the oak tree in the meadow. The first two specimens that were shown to him he hastily rejected; one had a group of chickens pictured on its lid, the other bore the portrait of a tabby kitten. A third sample was more simply bedecked with a spray of painted poppies, and Octavian hailed the flowers of forgetfulness as a happy omen. He felt distinctly more at ease with his surroundings when the imposing package had been sent across to the grey house, and a message returned to say that it had been duly given to the children. The next morning he sauntered with purposeful steps past the long blank wall on his way to the chicken-run and piggery that stood at the bottom of the meadow. The three children were perched at their accustomed look-out, and their range of sight did not seem to concern itself with Octavian's presence. As he became depressingly aware of the aloofness of their gaze he also noted a strange variegation in the herbage at his feet; the greensward for a considerable space around was strewn and speckled with a chocolate-coloured hail, enlivened here and there with gay tinsel-like wrappings or the glistening mauve of crystallized violets. It was as though the fairy paradise of a greedy-minded child had taken shape and substance in the vegetation of the meadow. Octavian's blood-money had been flung back at him in scorn.

To increase his discomfiture the march of events tended to shift the blame of ravaged chicken-coops from the supposed culprit who had already paid full forfeit; the young chicks were still carried off, and it seemed highly probable that the cat had only haunted the chicken-run to prey on the rats which harboured there. Through the flowing channels of servant talk the children learned of this belated revision of verdict, and Octavian one day picked up a sheet of copy-book paper on which was painstakingly written: "Beast. Rats eated your chickens." More ardently than ever did he wish for an opportunity for sloughing off the disgrace that enwrapped him, and earning some happier nickname from his three unsparing judges.

And one day a chance inspiration came to him. Olivia, his two-year-old daughter, was accustomed to spend the hour from high noon till one o'clock with her father while the nurse-maid gobbled and digested her dinner and novelette. About the same time the blank wall was usually enlivened by the presence of its three small wardens. Octavian, with seeming carelessness of purpose, brought Olivia well within hail of the watchers and noted with hidden delight the growing interest that dawned in that hitherto sternly hostile quarter. His little Olivia, with her sleepy placid ways, was going to succeed where he, with his anxious well-meant overtures, had so signally failed. He brought her a large yellow dahlia, which she grasped tightly in one hand and regarded with a stare of benevolent boredom, such as one might bestow on amateur classical dancing performed in aid of a deserving charity. Then he turned shyly to the group perched on the wall and asked with affected carelessness, "Do you like flowers?" Three solemn nods rewarded his venture.

"Which sorts do you like best?" he asked, this time with a distinct betrayal of eagerness in his voice.

"Those with all the colours, over there." Three chubby arms pointed to a distant tangle of sweet-pea. Child-like, they had asked for what lay farthest from hand, but Octavian trotted off gleefully to obey their welcome behest. He pulled and plucked with unsparing hand, and brought every variety of tint that he could see into his bunch that was rapidly becoming a bundle. Then he turned to retrace his steps, and found the blank wall blanker and more deserted than ever, while the foreground was void of all trace of Olivia. Far down the meadow three children were pushing a go-cart at the utmost speed they could muster in the direction of the piggeries; it was Olivia's go-cart and Olivia sat in it, somewhat bumped and shaken by the pace at which she was being driven but apparently retaining her wonted composure of mind. Octavian stared for a moment at the rapidly moving group, and then started in hot pursuit, shedding as he ran sprays of blossom from the mass of sweet-pea that he still clutched in his hands. Fast as he ran the children had reached the piggery before he could overtake them, and he arrived just in time to see Olivia, wondering but unprotesting, hauled and pushed up to the roof of the nearest sty. They were old buildings in some need of repair, and the rickety roof would certainly not have borne Octavian's weight if he had attempted to follow his daughter and her captors to their new vantage ground.

"What are you going to do with her?" he panted. There was no mistaking the grim trend of mischief in those flushed but sternly composed young faces.

"Hang her in chains over a slow fire," said one of the boys. Evidently they had been reading English history.

"Frow her down and the pigs will d'vour her, every bit 'cept the palms of her hands," said the other boy. It was also evident that they had studied Biblical history.

The last proposal was the one which most alarmed Octavian, since it might be carried into effect at a moment's notice; there had been cases, he remembered, of pigs eating babies.

"You surely wouldn't treat my poor little Olivia in that way?" he pleaded.

"You killed our little cat," came in stern reminder from three throats.

"I'm very sorry I did," said Octavian, and if there is a standard of measurement in truths Octavian's statement was assuredly a large nine.

"We shall be very sorry when we've killed Olivia," said the girl, "but we can't be sorry till we've done it."

The inexorable child-logic rose like an unyielding rampart

before Octavian's scared pleadings. Before he could think of any fresh line of appeal his energies were called out in another direction. Olivia had slid off the roof and fallen with a soft, unctuous splash into a morass of muck and decaying straw. Octavian scrambled hastily over the pigsty wall to her rescue, and at once found himself in a quagmire that engulfed his feet. Olivia, after the first shock of surprise at her sudden drop through the air, had been mildly pleased at finding herself in close and unstinted contact with the sticky element that oozed around her, but as she began to sink gently into the bed of slime a feeling dawned on her that she was not after all very happy, and she began to cry in the tentative fashion of the normally good child. Octavian, battling with the quagmire, which seemed to have learned the rare art of giving way at all points without yielding an inch, saw his daughter slowly disappearing in the engulfing slush, her smeared face further distorted with the contortions of whimpering wonder, while from their perch on the pigsty roof the three children looked down with the cold unpitying detachment of the Parcæ Sisters.

"I can't reach her in time," gasped Octavian; "she'll be choked in the muck. Won't you help her?"

"No one helped our cat," came the inevitable reminder.

"I'll do anything to show you how sorry I am about that," cried Octavian, with a further desperate flounder, which carried him scarcely two inches forward.

"Will you stand in a white sheet by the grave?"

"Yes," screamed Octavian.

"Holding a candle?"

"An' saying, 'I'm a miserable Beast'?"

Octavian agreed to both suggestions.

"For a long, long time?"

"For half an hour," said Octavian. There was an anxious ring in his voice as he named the time-limit; was there not the precedent of a German king who did open-air penance for several days and nights at Christmas-time clad only in his shirt? Fortunately the children did not appear to have read German history, and half an hour seemed long and goodly in their eyes.

"All right," came with threefold solemnity from the roof, and a moment later a short ladder had been laboriously pushed across to Octavian, who lost no time in propping it against the low pigsty wall. Scrambling gingerly along its rungs he was able to lean across the morass that separated him from his slowly foundering offspring and extract her like an unwilling cork from its slushy embrace. A few minutes later he was listening to the shrill and repeated assurances of the nursemaid that her previous experience of filthy spectacles had been on a notably smaller scale.

That same evening when twilight was deepening into darkness Octavian took up his position as penitent under the lone oak tree, having first carefully undressed the part. Clad in a zephyr shirt, which on this occasion thoroughly merited its name, he held in one hand a lighted candle and in the other a watch, into which the soul of a dead plumber seemed to have passed. A box of matches lay at his feet and was resorted to on the fairly frequent occasions when the candle succumbed to the night breezes. The house loomed inscrutable in the middle distance, but as Octavian conscientiously repeated the formula of his penance he felt certain that three pairs of solemn eyes were watching his moth-shared vigil.

And the next morning his eyes were gladdened by a sheet of copy-book paper lying beside the blank wall, on which was written the message "Un-Beast."

QUAIL SEED

"THE outlook is not encouraging for us smaller businesses," said Mr. Scarrick to the artist and his sister, who had taken rooms over his suburban grocery store. "These big concerns are offering all sorts of attractions to the shopping public which we couldn't afford to imitate, even on a small scale— reading-rooms and play-rooms and gramophones and Heaven knows what. People don't care to buy half a pound of sugar nowadays unless they can listen to Harry Lauder and have the latest Australian cricket scores ticked off before their eyes. With the big Christmas stock we've got in we ought to keep half a dozen assistants hard at work, but as it is my nephew Jimmy and myself can pretty well attend to it ourselves. It's a nice stock of goods, too, if I could only run it off in a few weeks' time, but there's no chance of that—not unless the London line was to get snowed up for a fortnight before Christmas. I did have a sort of idea of engaging Miss Luffcombe to give recitations during afternoons; she made a great hit at the Post Office entertainments with her rendering of 'Little Beatrice's Resolve.' "

"Anything less likely to make your shop a fashionable shopping centre I can't imagine," said the artist, with a very genuine shudder; "if I were trying to decide between the merits of Carlsbad plums and confected figs as a winter dessert it would infuriate me to have my train of thought entangled with little Beatrice's resolve to be an Angel of Light or a girl scout. No," he continued, "the desire to get something thrown in for nothing is a ruling passion with the feminine shopper, but you can't afford to pander effectively to it. Why not appeal to another instinct, which dominates not only the woman shopper but the male shopper—in fact, the entire human race?"

"What is that instinct, sir?" said the grocer.

      *   *   *   *   *

Mrs. Greyes and Miss Fritten had missed the 2.18 to Town, and as there was not another train till 3.12 they thought that they might as well make their grocery purchases at Scarrick's. It would not be sensational, they agreed, but it would still be shopping.

For some minutes they had the shop almost to themselves, as far as customers were concerned, but while they were debating the respective virtues and blemishes of two competing brands of anchovy paste they were startled by an order, given across the counter, for six pomegranates and a packet of quail seed. Neither commodity was in general demand in that neighbourhood. Equally unusual was the style and appearance of the customer; about sixteen years old, with dark olive skin, large dusky eyes, and thick, low-growing, blue-black hair, he might have made his living as an artist's model. As a matter of fact he did. The bowl of beaten brass that he produced for the reception of his purchases was distinctly the most astonishing variation on the string bag or marketing basket of suburban civilization that his fellow-shoppers had ever seen. He threw a gold piece, apparently of some exotic currency, across the counter, and did not seem disposed to wait for any change that might be forthcoming.

"The wine and figs were not paid for yesterday," he said; "keep what is over of the money for our future purchases."

"A very strange-looking boy?" said Mrs. Greyes interrogatively to the grocer as soon as his customer had left.

"A foreigner, I believe," said Mr. Scarrick, with a shortness that was entirely out of keeping with his usually communicative manner.

"I wish for a pound and a half of the best coffee you have," said an authoritative voice a moment or two later. The speaker was a tall, authoritative-looking man of rather outlandish aspect, remarkable among other things for a full black beard, worn in a style more in vogue in early Assyria than in a London suburb of the present day.

"Has a dark-faced boy been here buying pomegranates?" he asked suddenly, as the coffee was being weighed out to him.

The two ladies almost jumped on hearing the grocer reply with an unblushing negative.

"We have a few pomegranates in stock," he continued, "but there has been no demand for them."

"My servant will fetch the coffee as usual," said the purchaser, producing a coin from a wonderful metal-work purse. As an apparent afterthought he fired out the question: "Have you, perhaps, any quail seed?"

"No," said the grocer, without hesitation, "we don't stock it."

"What will he deny next?" asked Mrs. Greyes under her breath. What made it seem so much worse was the fact that Mr. Scarrick had quite recently presided at a lecture on Savonarola.

Turning up the deep astrakhan collar of his long coat, the stranger swept out of the shop, with the air, as Miss Fritten afterwards described it, of a Satrap proroguing a Sanhedrin. Whether such a pleasant function ever fell to a Satrap's lot she was not quite certain, but the simile faithfully conveyed her meaning to a large circle of acquaintances.

"Don't let's bother about the 3.12," said Mrs. Greyes; "let's go and talk this over at Laura Lipping's. It's her day."

When the dark-faced boy arrived at the shop next day with his brass marketing bowl there was quite a fair gathering of customers, most of whom seemed to be spinning out their purchasing operations with the air of people who had very little to do with their time. In a voice that was heard all over the shop, perhaps because everybody was intently listening, he asked for a pound of honey and a packet of quail seed.

"More quail seed!" said Miss Fritten. "Those quails must be voracious, or else it isn't quail seed at all."

"I believe it's opium, and the bearded man is a detective," said Mrs. Greyes brilliantly.

"I don't," said Laura Lipping; "I'm sure it's something to do with the Portuguese Throne."

"More likely to be a Persian intrigue on behalf of the ex-Shah," said Miss Fritten; "the bearded man belongs to the Government Party. The quail seed is a countersign, of course; Persia is almost next door to Palestine, and quails come into the Old Testament, you know."

"Only as a miracle." said her well-informed younger sister; "I've thought all along it was part of a love intrigue."

The boy who had so much interest and speculation centred on him was on the point of departing with his purchases when he was waylaid by Jimmy, the nephew-apprentice, who, from his post at the cheese and bacon counter, commanded a good view of the street.

"We have some very fine Jaffa oranges," he said hurriedly, pointing to a corner where they were stored, behind a high rampart of biscuit tins. There was evidently more in the remark than met the ear. The boy flew at the oranges with the enthusiasm of a ferret finding a rabbit family at home after a long day of fruitless subterranean research. Almost at the same moment the bearded stranger stalked into the shop, and flung an order for a pound of dates and a tin of the best Smyrna halva across the counter. The most adventurous housewife in the locality had never heard of halva, but Mr. Scarrick was apparently able to produce the best Smyrna variety of it without a moment's hesitation.

"We might be living in the Arabian Nights," said Miss Fritten excitedly.

"Hush! Listen," beseeched Mrs. Greyes.

"Has the dark-faced boy, of whom I spoke yesterday, been here today?" asked the stranger.

"We've had rather more people than usual in the shop today," said Mr. Scarrick, "but I can't recall a boy such as you describe."

Mrs. Greyes and Miss Fritten looked round triumphantly at their friends. It was, of course, deplorable that any one should treat the truth as an article temporarily and excusably out of stock, but they felt gratified that the vivid accounts they had given of Mr. Scarrick's traffic in falsehoods should receive confirmation at first hand.

"I shall never again be able to believe what he tells me about the absence of colouring matter in the jam," whispered an aunt of Mrs. Greyes tragically.

The mysterious stranger took his departure; Laura Lipping distinctly saw a snarl of baffled rage reveal itself behind his heavy moustache and upturned astrakhan collar. After a cautious interval the seeker after oranges emerged from behind the biscuit tins, having apparently failed to find any individual orange that satisfied his requirements. He, too, took his departure, and the shop was slowly emptied of its parcel and gossip-laden customers. It was Emily Yorling's "day," and most of the shoppers made their way to her drawing-room. To go direct from a shopping expedition to a tea-party was what was known locally as "living in a whirl."

Two extra assistants had been engaged for the following afternoon, and their services were in brisk demand; the shop was crowded. People bought and bought, and never seemed to get to the end of their lists. Mr. Scarrick had never had so little difficulty in persuading customers to embark on new experiences in grocery wares. Even those women whose purchases were of modest proportions dawdled over them as though they had brutal drunken husbands to go home to. The afternoon had dragged uneventfully on, and there was a distinct buzz of unpent excitement when a dark-eyed boy carrying a brass bowl entered the shop. The excitement seemed to have communicated itself to Mr. Scarrick; abruptly deserting a lady who was making insincere inquiries about the home life of the Bombay duck, he intercepted the newcomer on his way to the accustomed counter and informed him, amid a death-like hush, that he had run out of quail seed.

The boy looked nervously round the shop, and turned hesitatingly to go. He was again intercepted, this time by the nephew, who darted out from behind his counter and said something about a better line of oranges. The boy's hesitation vanished; he almost scuttled into the obscurity of the orange corner. There was an expectant turn of public attention towards the door, and the tall bearded stranger made a really effective entrance. The aunt of Mrs. Greyes declared afterwards that she found herself subconsciously repeating "The Assyrian came down like a wolf on the fold" under her breath, and she was generally believed.

The newcomer, too, was stopped before he reached the counter, but not by Mr. Scarrick or his assistant. A heavily veiled lady, whom no one had hitherto noticed, rose languidly from a seat and greeted him in a clear, penetrating voice.

"Your Excellency does his shopping himself?" she said.

"I order the things myself," he explained; "I find it difficult to make my servants understand."

In a lower, but still perfectly audible, voice the veiled lady gave him a piece of casual information.

"They have some excellent Jaffa oranges here." Then with a tingling laugh she passed out of the shop.

The man glared all round the shop, and then, fixing his eyes instinctively on the barrier of biscuit tins, demanded loudly of the grocer: "You have, perhaps, some good Jaffa oranges?"

Every one expected an instant denial on the part of Mr. Scarrick of any such possession. Before he could answer, however, the boy had broken forth from his sanctuary. Holding his empty brass bowl before him he passed out into the street. His face was variously described afterwards as masked with studied indifference, overspread with ghastly pallor, and blazing with defiance. Some said that his teeth chattered, others that he went out whistling the Persian National Hymn. There was no mistaking, however, the effect produced by the encounter on the man who had seemed to force it. If a rabid dog or a rattlesnake had suddenly thrust its companionship on him he could scarcely have displayed a greater access of terror. His air of authority and assertiveness had gone, his masterful stride had given way to a furtive pacing to and fro, as of an animal seeking an outlet for escape. In a dazed, perfunctory manner, always with his eyes turning to watch the shop entrance, he gave a few random orders, which the grocer made a show of entering in his book. Now and then he walked out into the street, looked anxiously in all directions, and hurried back to keep up his pretence of shopping. From one of these sorties he did not return; he had dashed away into the dusk, and neither he nor the dark-faced boy nor the veiled lady were seen again by the expectant crowds that continued to throng the Scarrick establishment for days to come.

*   *   *   *   *

"I can never thank you and your sister sufficiently," said the grocer.

"We enjoyed the fun of it," said the artist modestly, "and as for the model, it was a welcome variation on posing for hours for 'The Lost Hylas.' "

"At any rate," said the grocer, "I insist on paying for the hire of the black beard."

THE SEVEN CREAM JUGS

"I SUPPOSE we shall never see Wilfrid Pigeoncote here now that he has become heir to the baronetcy and to a lot of money," observed Mrs. Peter Pigeoncote regretfully to her husband.

"Well, we can hardly expect to," he replied, "seeing that we always choked him off from coming to see us when he was a prospective nobody. I don't think I've set eyes on him since he was a boy of twelve."

"There was a reason for not wanting to encourage his acquaintanceship," said Mrs. Peter. "With the notorious failing of his he was not the sort of person one wanted in one's house."

"Well, the failing still exists, doesn't it?" said her husband; "or do you suppose a reform of character is entailed along with the estate?"

"Oh, of course, there is still that drawback," admitted the wife, "but one would like to make the acquaintance of the future head of the family, if only out of mere curiosity. Besides, cynicism apart, his being rich *will* make a difference in the way people will look at his failing. When a man is absolutely wealthy, not merely well-to-do, all suspicion of sordid motive naturally disappears; the thing becomes merely a tiresome malady."

Wilfrid Pigeoncote had suddenly become heir to his uncle, Sir Wilfrid Pigeoncote, on the death of his cousin, Major Wilfrid Pigeoncote, who had succumbed to the after-effects of a polo accident. (A Wilfrid Pigeoncote had covered himself with honours in the course of Marlborough's campaigns, and the name Wilfrid had been a baptismal weakness in the family ever since.) The new heir to the family dignity and estates was a young man of about five-and-twenty, who was known more by reputation than by person to a wide circle of cousins and kinsfolk. And the reputation was an unpleasant one. The numerous other Wilfrids in the family were distinguished one from another chiefly by the names of their residences or professions, as Wilfrid of Hubbledown, and young Wilfrid the Gunner, but this particular scion was known by the ignominious and expressive label of Wilfrid the Snatcher. From his late schooldays onward he had been possessed by an acute and obstinate form of kleptomania: he had the acquisitive instinct of the collector without any of the collector's discrimination. Anything that was smaller and more portable than a sideboard and above the value of ninepence had an irresistible attraction for him, provided that it fulfilled the necessary condition of belonging to some one else. On the rare occasions when he was included in a country-house party, it was usual and almost necessary for his host, or some member of the family, to make a friendly inquisition through his baggage on the eve of his departure, to see if he had packed up "by mistake" any one else's property. The search usually produced a large and varied yield.

"This is funny," said Peter Pigeoncote to his wife, some half-hour after their conversation; "here's a telegram from Wilfrid, saying he's passing through here in his motor, and would like to stop and pay us his respects. Can stay for the night if it doesn't inconvenience us. Signed 'Wilfrid Pigeoncote.' Must be the Snatcher; none of the others have a motor. I suppose he's bringing us a present for the silver wedding."

"Good gracious!" said Mrs. Peter, as a thought struck her;

"this is rather an awkward time to have a person with his failing in the house. All those silver presents set out in the drawing-room, and others coming by every post; I hardly know what we've got and what are still to come. We can't lock them all up; he's sure to want to see them."

"We must keep a sharp look-out, that's all," said Peter reassuringly.

"But these practised kleptomaniacs are so clever," said his wife apprehensively, "and it will be so awkward if he suspects that we are watching him."

Awkwardness was indeed the prevailing note that evening when the passing traveller was being entertained. The talk flitted nervously and hurriedly from one impersonal topic to another. The guest had none of the furtive, half-apologetic air that his cousins had rather expected to find; his was polite, well-assured, and, perhaps, just a little inclined to "put on side." His hosts, on the other hand, wore an uneasy manner that might have been the hallmark of conscious depravity. In the drawing-room, after dinner, their nervousness and awkwardness increased.

"Oh, we haven't shown you the silver-wedding presents," said Mrs. Peter suddenly, as though struck by a brilliant idea for entertaining the guest; "here they all are. Such nice, useful gifts. A few duplicates, of course."

"Seven cream jugs," put in Peter.

"Yes, isn't it annoying," went on Mrs. Peter; "seven of them. We feel that we must live on cream for the rest of our lives. Of course, some of them can be changed."

Wilfrid occupied himself chiefly with such of the gifts as were of antique interest, carrying one or two of them over to the lamp to examine their marks. The anxiety of his hosts at these moments resembled the solicitude of a cat whose newly born kittens are being handed round for inspection.

"Let me see; did you give me back the mustard-pot? This is its place here," piped Mrs. Peter.

"Sorry. I put it down by the claret-jug," said Wilfrid, busy with another object.

"Oh, just let me have that sugar-sifter again," asked Mrs. Peter, dogged determination showing through her nervousness. "I must label it who it comes from before I forget."

Vigilance was not completely crowned with a sense of victory. After they had said "Good night" to their visitor, Mrs. Peter expressed her conviction that he had taken something.

"I fancy, by his manner, that there was something up," corroborated her husband. "Do you miss anything?"

Mrs. Peter hastily counted the array of gifts.

"I can only make it thirty-four, and I think it should be thirty-five," she announced. "I can't remember if thirty-five includes the Archdeacon's cruet-stand that hasn't arrived yet."

"How on earth are we to know?" said Peter. "The mean pig hasn't brought us a present, and I'm hanged if he shall carry one off."

"Tomorrow, when he's having his bath," said Mrs. Peter excitedly, "he's sure to leave his keys somewhere, and we can go through his portmanteau. It's the only thing to do."

On the morrow an alert watch was kept by the conspirators behind half-closed doors, and when Wilfrid, clad in a gorgeous bath-robe, had made his way to the bath-room, there was a swift and furtive rush by two excited individuals towards the principal guest-chamber. Mrs. Peter kept guard outside, while her husband first made a hurried and successful search for the keys, and then plunged at the portmanteau with the air of a disagreeably conscientious Customs official. The quest was a brief one; a silver cream jug lay embedded in the folds of some zephyr shirts.

"The cunning brute," said Mrs. Peter; "he took a cream jug because there were so many; he thought one wouldn't be missed. Quick, fly down with it and put it back among the others."

Wilfrid was late in coming down to breakfast, and his manner showed plainly that something was amiss.

"It's an unpleasant thing to have to say," he blurted out presently, "but I'm afraid you must have a thief among your servants. Something's been taken out of my portmanteau. It was a little present from my mother and myself for your silver wedding. I should have given it to you last night after dinner, only it happened to be a cream jug, and you seemed annoyed at having so many duplicates, so I felt rather awkward about giving you another. I thought I'd get it changed for something else. and now it's gone."

"Did you say it was from your *mother* and yourself?" asked

Mr. and Mrs. Peter almost in unison. The Snatcher had been an orphan these many years.

"Yes, my mother's at Cairo just now, and she wrote to me at Dresden to try and get you something quaint and pretty in the old silver line, and I pitched on this cream jug."

Both the Pigeoncotes had turned deadly pale. The mention of Dresden had thrown a sudden light on the situation. It was Wilfrid the Attaché, a very superior young man, who rarely came within their social horizon, whom they had been entertaining unawares in the supposed character of Wilfrid the Snatcher. Lady Ernestine Pigeoncote, his mother, moved in circles which were entirely beyond their compass or ambitions, and the son would probably one day be an Ambassador. And they had rifled and despoiled his portmanteau! Husband and wife looked blankly and desperately at one another. It was Mrs. Peter who arrived first at an inspiration.

"How dreadful to think there are thieves in the house! We keep the drawing-room locked up at night, of course, but anything might be carried off while we are at breakfast."

She rose and went out hurriedly, as though to assure herself that the drawing-room was not being stripped of its silverware, and returned a moment later, bearing a cream jug in her hands.

"There are eight cream jugs now, instead of seven," she cried; "this one wasn't there before. What a curious trick of memory, Mr. Wilfrid! You must have slipped downstairs with it last night and put it there before we locked up, and forgotten all about having done it in the morning."

"One's mind often plays one little tricks like that," said Mr. Peter, with desperate heartiness. "Only the other day I went into the town to pay a bill, and went in again next day, having clean forgotten that I'd——"

"It is certainly the jug that I brought for you," said Wilfrid, looking closely at it; "it was in my portmanteau when I got my bath-robe out this morning, before going to my bath, and it was not there when I unlocked the portmanteau on my return. Some one had taken it while I was away from the room."

The Pigeoncotes had turned paler than ever. Mrs. Peter had a final inspiration.

"Get me my smelling-salts, dear," she said to her husband; "I think they're in the dressing-room."

Peter dashed out of the room with glad relief; he had lived so long during the last few minutes that a golden wedding seemed within measurable distance.

Mrs. Peter turned to her guest with confidential coyness.

"A diplomat like you will know how to treat this as if it hadn't happened. Peter's little weakness; it runs in the family."

"Good Lord! Do you mean to say he's a kleptomaniac, like Cousin Snatcher?"

"Oh, not exactly," said Mrs. Peter, anxious to whitewash her husband a little greyer than she was painting him. "He would never touch anything he found lying about, but he can't resist making a raid on things that are locked up. The doctors have a special name for it. He must have pounced on your portmanteau the moment you went to your bath, and taken the first thing he came across. Of course, he had no motive for taking a cream jug; we've already got *seven*, as you know—not, of course, that we don't value the kind gift you and your mother—— Hush, here's Peter coming."

Mrs. Peter broke off in some confusion, and tripped out to meet her husband in the hall.

"It's all right," she whispered to him; "I've explained everything. Don't say anything more about it."

"Brave little woman," said Peter, with a gasp of relief; "I could never have done it."

*   *   *   *   *

Diplomatic reticence does not necessarily extend to family affairs. Peter Pigeoncote was never able to understand why Mrs. Consuelo van Bullyon, who stayed with them in the spring, always carried two very obvious jewel-cases with her to the bath-room, explaining them to any one she chanced to meet in the corridor as her manicure and face-massage set.

HYACINTH

"THE new fashion of introducing the candidate's children into an election contest is a pretty one," said Mrs. Panstreppon; "it takes away something from the acerbity of party warfare, and it makes an interesting experience for the children to look back on in after years. Still, if you will listen to my advice, Matilda, you will not take Hyacinth with you down to Luffbridge on election day."

"Not take Hyacinth!" exclaimed his mother; "but why not? Jutterly is bringing his three children, and they are going to drive a pair of Nubian donkeys about the town, to emphasize the fact that their father has been appointed Colonial Secretary. We are making the demand for a strong Navy a special feature in *our* campaign, and it will be particularly appropriate to have Hyacinth dressed in his sailor suit. He'll look heavenly."

"The question is, not how he'll look, but how he'll behave. He's a delightful child, of course, but there is a strain of unbridled pugnacity in him that breaks out at times in a really alarming fashion. You may have forgotten the affair of the little Gaffin children; I haven't."

"I was in India at the time, and I've only a vague recollection of what happened; he was very naughty, I know."

"He was in his goat-carriage, and met the Gaffins in their perambulator, and he drove the goat full tilt at them and sent the perambulator spinning. Little Jacky Gaffin was pinned down under the wreckage, and while the nurse had her hands full with the goat, Hyacinth was laying into Jacky's legs with his belt like a small fury."

"I'm not defending him," said Maltilda, "but they must have done something to annoy him."

"Nothing intentionally, but some one had unfortunately told him that they were half French—their mother was a Duboc, you know—and he had been having a history lesson that morning, and had just heard of the final loss of Calais by the English, and was furious about it. He said he'd teach the little toads to go snatching towns from us, but we didn't know at the time that he was referring to the Gaffins. I told him afterwards that all bad feeling between the two nations had died out long ago, and that anyhow the Gaffins were only half French, and he said that it was only the French half of Jacky that he had been hitting; the rest had been buried under the perambulator. If the loss of Calais unloosed such fury in him, I tremble to think what the possible loss of the election might entail."

"All that happened when he was eight; he's older now and knows better."

"Children with Hyacinth's temperament don't know better as they grow older; they merely know more."

"Nonsense. He will enjoy the fun of the election, and in any case he'll be tired out by the time the poll is declared, and the new sailor suit that I've had made for him is just in the right shade of blue for our election colours, and it will exactly match the blue of his eyes. He will be a perfectly charming note of colour."

"There is such a thing as letting one's æsthetic sense over-ride one's moral sense," said Mrs. Panstreppon. "I believe you would have condoned the South Sea Bubble and the persecution of the Albigenses if they had been carried out in effective colour schemes. However, if anything unfortunate should happen down at Luffbridge, don't say it wasn't foreseen by one member of the family."

The election was keenly but decorously contested. The newly appointed Colonial Secretary was personally popular, while the Government to which he adhered was distinctly unpopular, and there was some expectancy that the majority of four hundred, obtained at the last election, would be altogether wiped out. Both sides were hopeful, but neither could feel confident. The children were a great success; the little Jutterlys drove their chubby donkeys solemnly up and down the main streets, displaying posters which advocated the claims of their father on the broad general grounds that he was their father, while as for Hyacinth, his conduct might have served as a model for any seraph-child that had strayed unwittingly on to the scene of an electoral contest. Of his own accord, and under the delighted eyes of half a dozen camera operators, he had gone up to the Jutterly children and presented them with a packet of butterscotch; "we needn't be enemies because we're wearing the opposite colours," he said with engaging friendliness, and the occupants of the donkey-cart accepted his offering with polite solemnity. The grown-up members of both political camps were delighted at the incident—with the exception of Mrs. Panstreppon, who shuddered.

"Never was Clytemnestra's kiss sweeter than on the night she slew me," she quoted, but made the quotation to herself.

The last hour of the poll was a period of unremitting labour for both parties; it was generally estimated that not more than a dozen votes separated the candidates, and every effort was made to bring up obstinately wavering electors. It was with a feeling of relaxation and relief that every one heard the clocks strike the hour for the close of the poll. Exclamations broke out from the tired workers, and corks flew out from bottles.

"Well, if we haven't won, we've done our level best." "It has been a clean, straight fight, with no rancour." "The children were quite a charming feature, weren't they?"

The children? It suddenly occurred to everybody that they had seen nothing of the children for the last hour. What had become of the three little Jutterlys and their donkey-cart, and, for the matter of that, what had become of Hyacinth? Hurried, anxious embassies went backwards and forwards between the respective party headquarters and the various committee-rooms, but there was blank ignorance everywhere as to the whereabouts of the children. Every one had been too busy in the closing moments of the poll to bestow a thought on them. Then there came a telephone call at the Unionist Women's Committee-rooms, and the voice of Hyacinth was heard demanding when the poll would be declared.

"Where are you, and where are the Jutterly children?" asked his mother.

"I've just finished having high-tea at a pastry-cook's," came the answer; "and they let me telephone. I've had a poached egg and a sausage roll and four meringues."

"You'll be ill. Are the little Jutterlys with you?"

"Rather not. They're in a pigsty."

"A pigsty? Why? What pigsty?"

"Near the Crawleigh Road. I met them driving about a back road, and told them they were to have tea with me, and put their donkeys in a yard that I knew of. Then I took them to see an old sow that had got ten little pigs. I got the sow into the outer sty by giving her bits of bread, while the Jutterlys went in to look at the litter, then I bolted the door and left them there."

"You wicked boy, do you mean to say you've left those poor children there alone in the pigsty?"

"They're not alone, they've got ten little pigs in with them; they're jolly well crowded. They were pretty mad at being shut in, but not half as mad as the old sow is at being shut out from her young ones. If she gets in while they're there she'll bite them into mincemeat. I can get them out by letting a short ladder down through the top window, and that's what I'm going to do *if we win*. If their blighted father gets in, I'm just going to open the door for the sow, and let her do what she dashed well likes to them. That's why I want to know when the poll will be declared."

Here the narrator rang off. A wild stampede and a frantic sending-off of messengers took place at the other end of the telephone. Nearly all the workers on either side had disappeared to their various club-rooms and public-house bars to await the declaration of the poll, but enough local information could be secured to determine the scene of Hyacinth's exploit. Mr. John Ball had a stable yard down near the Crawleigh Road, up a short lane, and his sow was known to have a litter of ten young ones. Thither went in headlong haste both the candidates, Hyacinth's mother, his aunt (Mrs. Panstreppon), and two or three hurriedly summoned friends. The two Nubian donkeys, contentedly munching at bundles of hay, met their gaze as they entered the yard. The hoarse savage grunting of an enraged animal and the shriller note of thirteen young voices, three of them human, guided them to the sty, in the outer yard of which a huge Yorkshire sow kept up a ceaseless raging patrol before a closed door. Reclining on the broad ledge of an open window, from which point of vantage he could reach down and shoot the bolt of the door, was Hyacinth, his blue sailor-suit somewhat the worse for wear, and his angel smile exchanged for a look of demoniacal determination.

"If any of you come a step nearer," he shouted, "the sow will be inside in half a jiffy."

A storm of threatening, arguing, entreating expostulation broke from the baffled rescue party, but it made no more impression on Hyacinth than the squealing tempest that raged within the sty.

"If Jutterly heads the poll I'm going to let the sow in. I'll teach the blighters to win elections from us."

"He means it," said Mrs. Panstreppon; "I feared the worst when I saw that butterscotch incident."

"It's all right, my little man," said Jutterly, with the duplicity to which even a Colonial Secretary can sometimes stoop, "your father has been elected by a large majority."

"Liar!" retorted Hyacinth, with the directness of speech that is not merely excusable, but almost obligatory, in the political profession; "the votes aren't counted yet. You won't gammon me as to the result, either. A boy that I've palled with is going to fire a gun when the poll is declared; two shots if we've won, one shot if we haven't."

The situation began to look critical. "Drug the sow," whispered Hyacinth's father.

Some one went off in the motor to the nearest chemist's shop and returned presently with two large pieces of bread liberally dosed with narcotic. The bread was thrown defty and unostentatiously into the sty, but Hyacinth saw through the manœuvre. He set up a piercing imitation of a small pig in purgatory, and the infuriated mother ramped round and round the sty; the pieces of bread were trampled into slush.

At any moment now the poll might be declared. Jutterly flew back to the Town Hall, where the votes were being counted. His agent met him with a smile of hope.

"You're eleven ahead at present, and only about eighty more to be counted; you're just going to squeak through."

"I mustn't squeak through," exclaimed Jutterly hoarsely. "You must object to every doubtful vote on our side that can possibly be disallowed. I must *not* have the majority."

Then was seen the unprecedented sight of a party agent challenging the votes on his own side with a captiousness that his opponents would have hesitated to display. One or two votes that would have certainly passed muster under ordinary circumstances were disallowed, but even so Jutterly was six ahead with only thirty more to be counted.

To the watchers by the sty the moments seemed intolerable. As a last resort some one had been sent for a gun with which to shoot the sow, though Hyacinth would probably draw the bolt the moment such a weapon was brought into the yard. Nearly all the men were away from their homes, however, on election night, and the messenger had evidently gone far afield in his search. It must be a matter of minutes now to the declaration of the poll.

A sudden roar of shouting and cheering was heard from the direction of the Town Hall. Hyacinth's father clutched a pitchfork and prepared to dash into the sty in the forlorn hope of being in time.

A shot rang out in the evening air. Hyacinth stooped down from his perch and put his finger on the bolt. The sow pressed furiously against the door.

"Bang!" came another shot.

Hyacinth wriggled back, and sent a short ladder down through the window of the inner sty.

"Now you can come up, you unclean little blighters," he sang out; "my daddy's got in, not yours. Hurry up, I can't keep the sow waiting much longer. And don't you jolly well come butting into any election again where I'm on the job."

In the reaction that set in after the deliverance furious recriminations were indulged in by the lately opposed candidates, their women folk, agents, and party helpers. A recount was demanded, but failed to establish the fact that the Colonial Secretary had obtained a majority. Altogether the election left a legacy of soreness behind it, apart from any that was experienced by Hyacinth in person.

"It is the last time I shall let him go to an election," exclaimed his mother.

"There I think you are going to extremes," said Mrs. Panstreppon; "if there should be a general election in Mexico I think you might safely let him go there, but I doubt whether our English politics are suited to the rough and tumble of an angel-child."

THE END